# The Lost Woman

## KAREN MULVAHILL

Published by BardOwl Arts LLC



ISBN(eBook): 979-8-9943051-0-2
ISBN(Paperback): 979-8-9943051-1-9
ISBN(Hardcover): 979-8-9943051-2-6

Cover Design: JD Smith

Title Production: The BookWhisperer

For how will humanity ever be healed unless all its
rottenness is exposed? How will the world be cleansed
unless it is made to understand the full extent of the
evil it is doing?

— HÉLÈNE BERR

BORN MARCH 27, 1921 IN PARIS, FRANCE
DIED APRIL 10, 1945 IN BERGEN-BELSEN, GERMANY

# 1

# ROBERT

"My father was arrested when I was eighteen and I never saw him again."

That's pretty much how Nicky Kincaid started the conversation, after a perfunctory greeting and invitation to sit down. Although I hadn't met her before, I'd seen her often enough in the society pages, head of this or that charity fundraiser. I saw a lot of my clients in those pages. Surrounded by skinny blondes wearing angular strapless dresses—what had Tom Wolfe called them, X-rays?—Nicky Kincaid stood out. Her dark, gray-streaked hair was always pulled back and she dressed in cable knit sweaters and tweed skirts, like my old English teacher. I'd worked with Mrs. Kincaid's husband, Walt, a few years ago on the restoration of some paintings at the New York Club, when he'd been its president. So when I got the call from Mrs. Kincaid, I was prepared for a similar request.

She lived in a magnificent old brownstone on the Upper West Side. The furnishings were classic except for an oversized chandelier of colored glass that looked like someone had shot a piñata. But even that couldn't prevent my eyes from devouring the paintings on the south wall of the room. Iconic artists of the twentieth century—Jasper Johns, Lichtenstein, Basquiat, Rothko. An eclectic selection that smelled more of money than oil paint. Her opening remark hung there like the remnants of a dissonant piano chord.

"It was Paris, you see, 1941," she continued. "My friend Nadia's father had already been arrested, but for a time my life as a Sorbonne student went on as before. We discussed literature, argued philosophy, compared notes on the idiosyncrasies of our professors. Until the day my father was arrested, my chief worry had been that a boy I liked wouldn't notice me." She plucked at a velvet pillow with long-fingered, blue-veined hands that had the grace of Stieglitz's photographs of O'Keeffe's. I waited as she stood and went to the window. She was still as marble; I thought of a statue of Artemis, the Greek goddess of the hunt. As if on cue, a large English setter trotted in and posed beside her. All that was missing was the quiver of arrows. She turned to scratch the dog's head. Her face was finely lined, as if she hadn't used it much.

When she finally turned back to me, I wasn't sure how to respond. Maybe she had me mixed up with a long-lost nephew. I cleared my throat. "Is there some way I can help you?" I asked.

"Yes," she said. "I received a letter. From someone whose path crossed mine briefly in Paris. A British parachutist. You know those alarms that say, In Case of Fire, Break Glass? That letter was the fire. And the glass behind which I'd trapped the past began to shatter."

She paced the room as her story tumbled out. She'd grown up in her family's art gallery in Paris, their friends and clients a who's who of the art scene of the 1930s. Picasso, Matisse, Dalí. I'd been to Paris many times and could easily picture the storefronts on the narrow streets she described. As catastrophic as the 1940s had been, the old parts of the city had not changed much. Hypnotized by her story, envying her connection to the artists I idolized, I nearly jumped when she stopped short and said bluntly, "My family's paintings were stolen during the war. I want you to find them."

My mouth must've dropped open, because she quickly reached into the pocket of her sweater, pulled out a piece of paper and walked over to me. "This is a list of the ones that my parents owned at the beginning of the war. I've included the name of the artist and the title or description of the painting. This first one, that was my favorite." Her smile was tight, controlled, emotionless. Like something she had practiced. "Perhaps you can at least get that one back for me."

The list was carefully written in a hand that still contained a hint of the European. The first item read Picasso, Portrait of a Woman. Five more followed—masterpieces, paintings I could only imagine seeing in a museum, by painters even my wealthiest clients couldn't afford. Corot, Cézanne, de La Tour, Cranach, Rembrandt. Her family had owned these paintings? Once, when I was a kid, my friend Jack showed me a baseball signed by every member of the 1978 Yankees World Series team. I was envious. But more than that, I was afraid to touch it. I had that same feeling now.

"My mother modeled for the Picasso," Mrs. Kincaid was saying. "The La Tour hung above my bed for many years. The first thing I'd see when I opened the door to our apartment was the Cézanne. The blues and greens made me feel like I was diving into a pool."

I swallowed hard. I'd expected to be asked to oversee a restoration, a sale, an appraisal—but this? I had no idea how to do something like this. "It's been so long," I said slowly, trying to recover my businesslike composure. "I know some paintings surface now and then and make the headlines, but overall, it's rare. Unless these have been publicly sold, I just don't know how likely finding them would be."

But what if—just what if—I could find one of these, hold it in my hands for even a minute?

"Look," she said quietly. "I'm not asking for any guarantees. I'm just asking you to try. Will you, please? Try?"

Like a ventriloquist's dummy, I said something I had no control over. "Yes, Mrs. Kincaid, I'll try."

Nicky Kincaid stood and held out her hand, probably anxious to get rid of me before I wised up. "Please, call me Nicole. Just send me bills as you need to. Do you want an advance?" I shook my head and took her small hand in mine, inwardly squirming as I pictured Don Quixote waving his sword at a windmill. Nicole's face softened into a smile that changed her entire visage. For the first time, I caught a glimpse of the girl who had lived above an art gallery in Paris.

She turned toward the door; then, almost as an afterthought, turned back to face me, her hands knotted in front of her. "There's something else." She hesitated, as if trying to decide whether to go on or not. She looked down. "You see, in the midst of the carnage of the war, while my parents were missing and most likely dead, with an empty stomach and only the most hazy of futures, I fell deeply in love." Her voice trailed off. "My first love," she murmured, as if to herself. "His name was Sam Popinski, an American soldier. He made me want to live. I've always wondered what happened to him." She looked up at me again, then slid her eyes sideways. I waited.

"I last saw him in 1944. He was part of the invasion force that liberated the city. We only had six weeks together before his unit was assigned to push further north, into Germany I think. We had talked of marriage, of my moving to America. But I heard nothing, not even after Germany's surrender, and then Japan's. He wasn't listed among the dead, but I couldn't get any information about him from the army. And then, well, I figured it was just another wartime romance that meant more to me than to him."

Her eyes were fixed firmly on mine now, as if she thought I should know what she was asking. I feared that I did.

"I just want to know what happened to him. Apparently, memory is not self-selective. The glass broke and now all the memories are pouring out." She pulled the collar of her sweater up around her neck and gave a little shiver. "Oh, I know this must all sound hopeless and crazy. But while you're looking for the paintings, you'll probably run across information about people from that time. Maybe it wouldn't be all that much more trouble? I mean, of course, I will pay you whatever it costs."

I shrugged uncomfortably. "It's not the money, it's just that I never looked for a person before. I mean, I don't think..." I was stammering, at a loss.

"Please," she said, her gray eyes displaying a vulnerability I guessed not many people had ever seen in Nicky Kincaid. "Please. Just try."

# 2

## NICOLE

Sometimes an artist, unhappy with an earlier work, paints over it. As time passes, the surface wears away, exposing the older image. My father said the Italians call it a pentimento, meaning repentance. But is it repentance for flaws in the original picture or repentance for having painted over it? I spent decades growing the thick shell that I molded into Nicky Kincaid, New York wife and philanthropist. Now, as my skin thins to parchment, Nicole Cassin, the girl I left for dead in Paris so many years ago, is breaking through the surface.

---

Darwin got it wrong, at least where humans are concerned. Survival is not of the fittest but of the luckiest. The accident of birthplace, era, gender, race, parents, culture—each brings a blessing or a curse. In occupied France, being a Jew was the original set from which many subsets of the unlucky sprouted.

Were you home the day of the July round-up or were you standing in line, waiting for potatoes? Did a German officer in a bad temper cross your path and take you in for a bit of torture? Was the ambush of a German soldier in the morning responsible for your random execution in the afternoon?

During the war, I became an automaton with one goal: to survive until I could see my parents again. As millions of people were sifted through the sieve of war, I, for some unknown reason, landed in the 'survive' pile, my armor intact. People have always admired my strength. In a crisis, I'm the one stanching the wounds, calmly driving to the hospital, comforting a friend whose husband has died, finding a new job for someone who's been fired. The truth of the matter is I keep my emotions bottled because my rage is like the land mine you don't notice until you're missing a leg. That's the choice: affectless or berserk. I've always been that way. So when I stood before a Nazi for the very first time, it was pretty clear how it would go.

It was early August 1939. My father and I were working on the accounts in the back of the gallery when the door opened and two men entered. The first wore a double-breasted charcoal gray suit of fine worsted wool, with knife-sharp trouser creases, and a black homburg that raised his already tall stature by several inches. The other man, in a brown rumpled suit and fedora, shadowed him. They spoke German. I had learned a bit of German in school and began to stand. Except for our regular clients and his friends, Papa usually let me approach gallery visitors. On this occasion he put a hand on my shoulder and held me down, shaking his head.

The first man, ramrod straight, stood surveying the gallery with a smirk. Then he noticed a portrait by Lucas Cranach. It was of a young German boy, with shoulder-length blond curls and deep-blue eyes. The boy wore a red damask robe and a crown of flowers. The two men approached it, leaned in to examine it, then stood back. "Quite nice," said the man in the brown suit, continuing to gaze at it. "An excellent example of his work."

The tall man removed his homburg and tipped his head to one side. "It is just the kind of work the Reichsmarschall wants for his country house."

"Cranach's also one of the Fuhrer's favorites," said the brown-suited man, looking toward us and raising his finger.

"Stay here," Papa hissed as he stood, swung his jacket from the back of the chair and slipped into it. He walked over to the men and spoke in German. "May I help you?"

I couldn't believe it. A Nazi! In our gallery. Just last year they'd smashed the businesses and homes of countless Jews in Germany. For no reason. My breathing began to speed up, as did my heart rate. How dare they show their faces here! And how dare Papa treat them as if they were normal customers! I watched Papa begin to answer their questions about the painting. The pencil I held broke in two as I pressed it harder and harder against the desk. I wanted to kill them. I sprang from my chair and strode out to where they stood speaking in normal tones, as if they gave a damn about art. To me art was sacred. But just as they defined what type of people deserved to live, so the Nazis defined what type of art deserved to exist—and they destroyed works of genius. Papa was all too familiar with my rage. He stepped toward me, putting his hand on my forearm. "Nicole," he said, his voice firm but containing a note of pleading. "Please, let me handle this." I shook him off.

I was young; I had absolute faith in right and wrong. I've always had a passion for justice; thanks to the war, I just don't expect it any more. Back then, though, I don't remember feeling any fear, only pure unstoppable rage. I raised my chin and looked the tall Nazi in the eye. "Get out! We don't sell to murderers!" I said, my voice loud and confident. He stared back, unflinching, a tiny smile tickling the corner of his lips, as if I were a misbehaving child. This just fueled my anger. "Did you hear me?" I screeched. "Papa," I demanded, "make them leave now."

Papa took my arm and pulled me away from the men. He began to say something. If he had apologized, I think I would never have forgiven him. As it was, he said, "You heard my daughter. We don't sell to Nazis."

Donning his homburg, the man stared at Papa. His eyes narrowed. "Perhaps another time, then," he said softly, turning on his heel. The brown-suited man trotted after him.

I looked around at the other customers, who quickly looked away, pretending nothing had happened, the way so many would in the years that followed.

# 3
# ROBERT

I gripped the wheel as if this gentle hill were Mt. Everest itself. The whine of the old Volvo echoed my own sense of a steep challenge. The two-lane Vermont highway had more curves than straightaways, its yellow centerline vanishing behind banks of pines and cedars and reappearing up a hill in the distance. Family farms still existed here. Houses with wide porches, weathered barns, orchards of twisted apples, the occasional horse or cow—the visual charm no doubt belying the difficulty of making a living this way.

I took a deep breath and thought about my meeting with Nicole. What was making me so anxious? Sure, this assignment was about as familiar to me as bowling. But I did possess some of the requisite skills: art expertise, knowledge of the market, contacts in the art world, familiarity with the best research sources. I couldn't possibly be as bad as I had been the one time I went bowling and heaved my ball into the adjacent alley. I'd been honest with Nicole. She knew I might not find anything.

I rounded a corner and passed a weathered gray house, windows broken, weeds growing through the porch slats, a collapsed barn in the distance. City people were starting to buy these places up and put their stamps upon them. An infinity of infinity pools. Multiple-car garages, some with their own elevators or turntable thingies, like the ones streetcars in San Francisco turn around on. A new barn to store the boat or jet plane.

I had a bad case of the jitters, which is why the car was pointed toward my grandparents' farm. Maybe talking to my old friend Jack would help. I hoped for a decent signal as I wound through the hills and called him. He picked up. "Hey, Robert. What's up?"

"Wow. Where to begin. I've just had one of the more interesting conversations of my life," I began, relaying all that had transpired during my visit with Nicole.

"Man, sounds like you've got your work cut out for you this time. I mean, interesting and all that, but what are the possibilities of you actually finding anything? I hope she's paying you by the hour!" Jack laughed and I could picture him shaking his head, as he often did when listening to one of my stories about art forgeries or multi-million-dollar valuations of paintings. Jack always said he couldn't understand why anyone would pay that much when you could go to the Sunday painters' sale at the farmers market and get something bigger for less than $100. Maybe even on velvet.

"I know, I know. The minute I agreed to help her, I wanted to take the words back. But still, to maybe find a missing Rembrandt? Plus, I just remembered something about my grandfather. He didn't talk about it, but he had something to do with recovering paintings during the war."

Jack's voice came back garbled, as I dipped into a valley. "Seems to be the norm for guys who served in any war. They come back scarred and just want to bury it all."

The sun lit up the leafy maples as the road twisted in front of me. My spirits always lifted as I approached the farm but now I was curious, too. About Grandpa's war experiences. He'd moved to the farm right after.

"Hey, Jack, you might be able to help me out with this. Can you run the name Sam Popinski through your databases and see what you can find? Serviceman during the war, should be on some government list. Would be ninety-something if still alive."

Jack had always wanted to be a policeman when we were growing up together. "Cops and robbers" was his unfailing answer when I'd ask, "What do you want to play?" And, of course, I always had to be the robber, because Jack wanted to be the cop—and Jack was bigger. After studying pre-law at NYU he went on to get a Master's in Criminal Justice, then joined the FBI's New York Bureau.

"Sure, I'll give it a go. Don't hold your breath, though."

My grandparents had been in their sixties when I first moved in with them, after my father died. My mother had taken a job as an executive secretary in New York and had little time for—or interest in, truth be told—a ten-year-old boy. After she remarried, her weekend visits became more and more infrequent. She died when I was in grad school. I hadn't seen her for three years and felt no obligation to attend the funeral.

The farmhouse walls were covered with paintings and prints; small sculptures were crammed in here and there—on tables or between stacks of books on the shelves. Grandpa had worked at the Met in New York before they moved out to the farm after World War II. He taught art history at the local community college. Most of the art in the house had been purchased from friends or local galleries. "Even Rembrandt was a beginner once," he told me. "The fact is, art is about the process of responding to the world, to life, paying homage to it, or drawing attention to its wrongs." He really believed, even as a teacher, that the end result was less important than commitment to the process. It was nearly a religion with him. He believed that if everyone could express themselves through art we'd all understand each other better. "To be human would also be to be humane," he'd say. Once he followed it up with, "War would be unthinkable."

I can't remember a single time that Grandpa mentioned his own war experience. But this meeting with Nicole jarred a distant memory. Grandma was showing me a photo in which Grandpa stood, young and bareheaded, in a rumpled uniform, next to a stack of paintings in a brightly lit field. The front painting was a Rembrandt, she'd told me.

And that was it. The only time I'd ever heard anything about Grandpa's involvement in the war. Why hadn't I questioned him more about his past when he was still alive? I must have been around twelve at the time and, to me, Grandpa wasn't a man with his own life, he was just Grandpa. By the time I was grown, I was busy with my own life. I thought I knew everything about him, and yet I really knew nothing. Like when you drive the same five miles to work every day, past the same unspooling filmstrip of shopping centers, gas stations, restaurant chains, car dealerships and perhaps, depending on the neighborhood, rent-by-the-hour motels with names like The Palms or The Flamingo. One day you notice a bulldozer and a crane and there's a gaping hole in the middle of a strip of shops and you can't for the life of you remember what was there just yesterday. All you can see is the rough shape of something that had become so familiar as to be invisible. My grandparents died when I was in my twenties and left a gaping hole and the farm I still think of as theirs.

Set on thirty acres of hilly Vermont countryside, it was half-covered by second-growth forest and most of the rest was reclaimed pasture, dotted with scrubby low evergreens, volunteer apple trees and waist-high grasses. A former pine plantation, an outpost of order in the haphazard landscape, occupied the northwest corner. Its regal spires, rough and red-barked, towered over a thick carpet of pine needles where, as a boy, I read books and consumed the lunches Grandma packed for me.

That first time I went to the farm after they were gone—but no, they weren't "gone," as if they'd packed up an RV and taken to the road on some sort of final bucket-list trip. They were dead. And, no, I don't see them traveling on some sort of Stairway to Heaven either. They didn't exist anymore except as memories, and the memories brought great pain. Anyway, that first time, I stood on the porch readying myself. I'd never been there when one of them wasn't lurking about somewhere.

How does a house express emptiness? Where once the smell of spices and roasted meat and tangy apples suffused the air, now the house smelled of dust, with the barest hint of stale tobacco. Air moves when people are in it, and now it was noticeably stagnant. I was caught off-guard multiple times a day —seeing a jacket hanging from a coat stand, turning and expecting to see my grandfather. A clatter from the kitchen— when my cat Felix knocked over a saltshaker—and I saw my grandmother tossing salt over her shoulder to ward off evil spirits.

I can't say I was suicidal—I'm not big on commitment and that seems the ultimate form of it—but I had a bad case of what I called "what's-the-point?" You go through the motions, you love or don't, you work or don't, you travel or don't... In the end, if you don't go first, you just keep losing people. I considered selling the farm. But over time, I found comfort there. There's this thing called muscle memory—like how you can ride a bike years after having last been on one. So no matter how much you avoid actual memories, the brain—or maybe it's your heart—

exercises muscle memory. And then, when you return to a place where you once spent a lot of time, you feel the way you once did. In my case, safe and content and most truly myself.

---

I sat at Grandpa's desk, where I usually set up my laptop when I'm at the farm. The desk was old, oak and unadorned except for heavy metal drawer pulls that had aged to a deep, flat brown. The wood had mellowed to gold, and the desktop was so deep I could barely reach the other side. It reminded me of those two-person desks I've seen on TV shows, where each person works on one side of the desk—simultaneously. I can't even work in the same room with someone else; and frankly, if a temporary neutron bomb could be dropped on my building while I'm working, that would suit me just fine.

There was plenty of room for my printer, which was currently informing me that it was out of ink. I thought I remembered throwing some spare cartridges in the drawer a couple months back. Or was I remembering that I had intended to? The center drawer was surprisingly shallow but stretched way back to the far edge of the desk. A plastic organizer held the usual stuff: paper clips, rubber bands, a letter opener with an insurance company logo, a stapler and a small compartment of mystery keys. I have my own container of these, as I suspect most people do, and I'm terrified to throw any out. It's like my techie box, where I throw mystery cords and plugs. One never knows.

I reached all the way to the back of the drawer and swept my arm forward, exposing those things that had slid farther back with each opening of the drawer. A checkbook, some dull pencils, an eyeglass fixing kit, more tape and some business cards for local service providers. Still no ink cartridges. But I hadn't been able to reach all the way back, so I stood and retrieved the yardstick I keep on a bookshelf and pushed it into the back of the drawer. Feeling something back there, I took heart and swept the yardstick forward. A small, leather-bound notebook I'd never seen before appeared. It was brown and stained, the corners worn. When I opened it, I recognized my grandfather's handwriting. He had written his name on the first page, "Kenneth Ames."

# 4
## KENNETH



I could understand an avalanche. Earthquake. Hurricane. Any of the unpredictable natural disasters that are part of the bargain of living on Earth. But this devastation was by the hand of man, against mankind. This ruined village, full of dead bodies and vacant-eyed survivors, the stench of smoke and blood and flesh—this was all so unnecessary. I'm not ashamed to admit it. I, Kenneth Ames, a 38-year-old captain in the U.S. Army, cried. It was my first assignment as a Monuments Man.

I walked on. Masonry that had once made up the foundations of a town, had become mere chunks of rock. Homes, furnishings and people had become ruins, broken mementos and gore. Streets were now buried beneath an undifferentiated plain of rubble, including pieces of tanks and hunks of metal, abandoned military gear of all sorts. No, this was no act of Nature. The silence was eerie. The troops had moved on, after ensuring that there remained no more serious German resistance. No one wanted this village anymore. It had always been as meaningless as a domino to be toppled in a deadly game. The civilians I saw did not weep, did not even lift their eyes.

Just as a spoiled child with a stolen toy will crush it rather than return it, in the wake of their retreat the Germans destroyed infrastructure and accelerated deportations and executions. After four dark years, the French had greeted us as liberators. American flags had been sewn from bits of fabric and hung from buildings. Children had run out to give us what little they had—a biscuit, a flower. But now, in German territory, I tasted victory as a bitter combination of smoke, grit and blood.

The terms of the war had been laid out by Hitler, and civilians were not to be spared. Nor the German boys who were conscripted at younger and younger ages. A boy rushed out from a half-standing house yesterday, as the last of the American combat troops passed by. There was a glint of gun, a hail of bullets, and the boy lay dead, his helmet fallen away, exposing a shock of silky hair above a face like that of a Raphael cherub.

When I signed on to the MFAA, I knew I would be close to the front. But nothing could've prepared me for the sights I've witnessed. Last week, I toured Buchenwald. It occupies my thoughts like the residue of a terrifying nightmare. The stacks of corpses, the living skeletons who could not even eat what we soldiers so eagerly gave them, their bodies having shut down all normal functioning to preserve the small flame of life that remained. How could anyone, even the Nazis, be so lacking in empathy, pity and compassion? Even for children.

# 5
## NICOLE

People these days may wonder why the Jews didn't just leave. In hindsight it's easy to see that flight was the right decision. But there was only a small window of time between being able to leave France and being forbidden to emigrate. An infinitesimal gap, in the grand scheme of things, during which nothing was certain. It was like a game of roulette on which you had to bet every chip you had—your home, your friends, your country, your livelihood—against your life. You were forced to play, and yet the odds were fluctuating, uncertain from day to day.

One day we did talk about leaving. It was an unseasonably warm day in the fall of 1939. We were in the car, driving out of the city for a picnic at the Bois de Vincennes. Papa said his parents had taken him and his brother there frequently on Sundays, when the gallery was closed.

"I'm so glad they're not alive to see what's happening. And you—" His eyes sought mine in the rearview mirror. "To think that you have to see this. You should go and stay with my brother Frederick in New York."

"I'm not leaving," I said vehemently. What was Papa saying? I couldn't imagine leaving him, leaving the gallery, leaving Paris. As far as I was concerned, no damn German was going to walk across the border and steal our property.

"I'm not going anywhere," I repeated firmly. "In the fall I start at the Sorbonne. Where else am I going to find a school like that? And all my friends are here! Everyone at school says if the Germans invade, it'll only be long enough to sign a treaty with us and England. Then things will go back to normal."

"You're right, love," said my mother, comfortingly. "I'm not going anywhere either." She reached over and placed a hand on Papa's shoulder, pulling his earlobe. "Come on now, this is a family picnic. We haven't been here in so long." The subject was clearly closed. Papa kissed Maman's hand.

"There it is!" he exclaimed, turning at a small sign for the Bois de Vincennes into a parking area beyond the trees that lined the road. From there, several paths were visible along a small lake and into the woods. By the time I got out of the car, Papa was already running and shouting, "Over here, come on! I have something to show you!"

"You two go ahead," Maman called. "I'll arrange the picnic."

Papa trotted along the lake path, then veered to the right into the woods, with me at his heels. Ahead, I could see the path as it skirted a hill. Suddenly Papa stopped and stood still, panting, his eyes searching for something. Then he began to move again, approaching a rocky slope. "Stay behind me and be careful," he admonished, disappearing into a thicket of shrubbery. His voice came to me, sounding far off. "Here! I found it!"

I pushed my way through the thicket, thin branches whipping my face, tangled roots grasping my ankles. After a few feet of this struggle, I found a dark, narrow slit, barely visible, that entered the rock. "Papa?"

"In here!"

Flattening myself against one side of the rock, I slipped through the niche. The confinement made me think of a tomb. But I could see a light from Papa's flashlight. The narrow niche opened into a small cave where Papa stood triumphantly, playing the light across the rocky walls. "It's been years since I was in this cave. But once I discovered it on one of our family picnics, I came here every time. It was my own private fort. I still don't know if anyone else knows about it."

I touched the cool stone, imagining Papa as a boy. "Didn't you ever bring any of your friends here?"

"No, never. I didn't even tell my parents. I had some candles and would smuggle matches out of the house, and while my parents napped on the quilt, I'd come in here and imagine all sorts of worlds. I wanted to keep it all to myself. So you, my darling, are possibly the only other human ever to step into this cave!"

I shivered and wondered if that could be true. Perhaps. There were no signs of other inhabitants, human or animal. It was dry and pleasant, though. A good place to while away an afternoon dreaming of a handsome prince. When we returned to the picnic area, Maman was sitting on a blanket, her legs folded under her. Her father had been a French Jew, her mother Swedish. Maman had inherited her mother's thick blonde hair and wore it now in a braid coiled on the back of her head. I ran ahead of Papa and settled in next to her, hugging her around the shoulders.

"You look just like a little peasant girl, sitting there like that!"

Maman laughed. "Thank you, my love. Did you find the cave?"

"We certainly did!" Papa replied as he joined us. "And worked up an appetite in the process."

Maman passed Papa a baguette and began pulling the chicken apart. "Don't worry, there's plenty of food."

I would think of that chicken many times in the dark years to come.

# 6

# ROBERT

Nobody painted when I was in art school. We made statements with a capital S. Conceptual art, performance art, installations. People like Rachel Whiteread were winning the Turner Prize—she for House, a concrete casting of the inside of a house that was slated for demolition in London. I remember seeing Damien Hirst's installation called Pharmacy, white shelves of pill bottles in a white room. It was a metaphor for the way people, like so many of my own clients, buy art the way they buy sundries at the drug store. Ironic that I would remember that work in particular. I majored in sculpture, creating pieces that I imbued with meaning known only to myself, unless you read the treatises that accompanied them. To the casual observer, however, my best piece probably looked like a pile of hangers left in a dusty corner after a widow emptied her dead husband's closet. Those few students who used any paint at all favored strong, statement-making paints: acrylics and oils. Now I painted with watercolor—and only when at the farm.

Watercolors are the most ephemeral of paints, dangerously

uncontrollable. They force me to let go, to accept accidents, to revel in all the spontaneity that I carefully excise from my life. But even this process has a certain ritual to it. First, I raise the palette and inhale the scent of paint. Each small compartment contains a sculpted mound of color. Cadmium red, burnt umber, verdigris, ultramarine. Ochre, cobalt, crimson and Payne's gray. I love the words nearly as much as the paints. In the center of the palette is an open space where vestiges of the past remain in washes of color that overlap.

I tape a thick piece of textured paper to a board that rests on an easel in the center of the room and run my hands over its rough surface before spraying it with water in even sweeps. Lifting the largest brush from the jar standing on the adjacent table, I stroke my palm and then my cheek with the red sable, soft like my mother's cool fingers grazing my face. My mother praised my drawing skills and was disappointed when I gave up fine art for an academic career. Of course, I now know that I did it partly to spite her. I dip the brush into a glass of water and then rub it savagely across the palette, merging colors into dirty dishwater. This I spread over the blank paper to destroy its intimidating purity.

Next, I use a medium-sized brush and mix greens and yellows to match the leaves of the potted orchid on the windowsill. I fight my urge to render it exactly, instead splashing on the green, watching paint sink into paper and find its own way, free of boundaries. Continuing to apply color, darker where the paper has dried a bit, lighter where the surface remains wet, I experience a sense of peace and timelessness that I imagine all the painters before me—great or amateur —have shared. Hours pass in this fashion, until I begin to think about food. I step back, look at the painting and am pleased. Orchid-like but not orchid, a memory trying to emerge, an uncaptured dream.

I wash the brushes, return the lid to the palette and untape the painting from the board. It's good but not great. If I cannot be a master, let me be a monk, making sand paintings. I cross the room and place it on the burning logs in the fireplace. Watching the paper curl and the colors char, I fight the instinct to hold on—I never want to forget Grandpa's lesson: art is expression, not product.

When Jack called, I was back in New York, propped against the pillows in bed, a Scotch on the bedside table, the page of my book yellowed by the light from the antique library lamp. Reaching for the phone, I disturbed Felix, my black and white cat, who shares—or, more accurately, rules—my loft. Stretching and favoring me with an affectionate scold, Felix was back on my lap before I even said hello.

"Robert?"

"Hey, Jack, what's up?"

"Yeah, sorry to call you so late, but if I know you, you'll appreciate the interruption. I mean assuming you haven't got company or anything." Jack was always razzing me about the women—or lack thereof—in my life.

"Wait. Let me show the models out of the bedroom first."

"Oh?" Jack paused. "Maybe I should come over and tell you in person. Oh, but wait, this is Robert we're talking about here. Not models. Maybe a roomful of librarians."

"Yes, but they've taken off their glasses and loosened their hair."

Jack snorted. "About that guy you wanted me to help you find? I checked the military records and found a Sam Popinski that meets your criteria: age would be about ninety-three, served in the army in France."

"Dead?" I guessed.

"Nope. Living in an old folks' home outside of Detroit."

"Got an address?"

"Just a sec." I could hear him shuffling through some papers. "It's Friendly Village, Pleasant Ridge, Michigan."

"Friendly Village, Pleasant Ridge? Who else lives there? The Seven Dwarfs?"

Jack snickered. "Well, you are embarking on a fantasy, after all. Let me know how it goes—with the librarians, I mean." I could hear Jack's children shouting in the background, the dog barking. What was Ellen doing? Sometimes I wondered if she'd been "the one" and I'd let her slip away. For which Jack periodically thanked me.

"Okay, bro. Really appreciate your help. Say hi to the family."

"You got it."

I replaced the phone on the table, careful not to jostle Felix, who merely opened one eye, then covered it with a front paw.

# 7
## NICOLE

For the first time, I spoke to another human being about the war.

Robert is a good, patient listener. His deep brown eyes evoke sympathy but not pity. I couldn't bear pity. Under his quiet prompts, I found myself narrating my story as if telling it to myself. Reminding myself of events that I'd tried to forget for so many years. He asked me questions about the gallery, people we knew, other things that might help him in his search. I like him; he's sincere. I know he's worried he'll disappoint me. I want to tell him what my children are always telling me: lighten up! I watched from the window as he left the building and walked down the street.

It's hard to explain how I feel. Yes, the memories are painful, but there's a sense of relief at finally letting them out. As if a balloon, overinflated and ready to burst has been relieved of some air. All these years I've lived with a fear I wasn't even conscious of, fear of what remembering would do to me.

And yet suppressing my memories may have been more

damaging. There's a feeling of wholeness beginning to emerge. I've even had some dreams of Maman and Papa, dreams of normal domestic life; and it's like being with them again after all these years.

And yet. There are days when I wake in the grip of horror. And fear the memory that will kill me.

My earliest memories of Papa are of the scratchy wool of his jacket, the sense of weightlessness as he swung me up from the ground, the tobacco smell of his breath, the pomade of his hair. And his laugh. As a child, I was a little afraid of this man who took such liberties with me, because he was a bit of a stranger. He was either in the gallery doing business, or off on a trip to visit an artist's studio, or at a café endlessly discussing art with his colleagues and friends.

When he was home—shirt sleeves turned up, tie loosened, a cigarette dangling from his lips—he was quick to laugh and affectionate with Maman and me. He was different among colleagues and clients in the gallery, where he was known for his intimidating brilliance and reverence for art. Papa was very sure of himself and his ability to judge the talent of new artists. Twentieth-century artists were his passion. He often exhibited them on the first level, hoping to snare the interest of gallery visitors before showing them to the mezzanine, where the more traditional pieces were displayed.

When France declared war on Germany after it invaded Poland, Papa immediately enlisted and went to the country for a few weeks of training. Everyone was saying that there would be an armistice, that Germany wouldn't want to take on France and England, and that it would settle for their acceptance of the Poland invasion, or some partition of Poland. I learned never to believe what "everyone" says.

When Papa came back on leave, I begged him to let me tag along to Les Deux Magots where he was to meet his friends Roger, Marcel and Jean. Papa looked strange in a uniform. His hair had been shorn, and his eyebrows looked especially dominant over eyes that had a tiredness about them I'd never seen before. Marcel was a beefy painter with black hair that stood up on his head like a platoon of drunken soldiers. Roger, an art critic, was tall, pencil-thin and always fastidiously dressed. And Jean was a banker whose most distinguishing feature was that he had none. It was the spring of 1940. All anyone could talk about was war.

Les Deux Magots was one of the cafés popular among artists and writers, a place I expected to frequent once I began my study of literature at the Sorbonne. The street was filled with honking cars and taxis, the after-work rush in full swing. Colorful umbrellas fought for space above trench-coated pedestrians. Heavy raindrops tapped upon the canvas awning, running back and forth like small animals. Huddled against the window in wicker chairs, we sipped Sancerre and watched the evening lights puddle in the street.

"It's weird to see so many uniforms around here," Jean noted, after we'd been seated. Brightly clad women contrasted with the drab hues of the soldiers. The raucous laughs issuing from those tables carried a whiff of desperation.

"What do you think of this so-called phony war?" Marcel asked. "Are we really in danger of an attack?"

I'd been devouring the newspapers daily, praying that Papa would not have to fight. I could not imagine him carrying a rifle.

Jean was nodding. "Oh yeah, it's coming all right. And the Allies, as they're being called, sure are bungling things so far."

"Why don't we just attack the pricks right now, then? To hell with this waiting for them." Marcel banged his glass down.

I agreed with Marcel, but in these sessions with Papa and his friends, I rarely spoke. The men were vociferous and aggressive in their opinions. I didn't want to say anything that might risk my future participation.

"That might've been a good idea a while back," Jean replied smoothly. "But they've been very busy producing armaments. I guess our best bet right now is to hope they'll be satisfied with what they've got." Jean paused to light a cigarette. "André, you're awfully quiet. What are you hearing?"

Papa brushed his hands back and forth across his bristly hair. "A lot of wishful thinking. Hitler's seen nothing but compromise and accommodation on our part. So why stop now?"

Marcel motioned to the waiter scurrying around wiping tables and the few empty chairs that were quickly taken up by more customers. He tucked his white towel into his cummerbund as he approached us. "Another bottle, monsieur?" Marcel nodded and handed him the empty.

An older woman in a fox stole at the table next to us reached down and offered her tiny white dog a piece of baguette larded with liver pâté. He snapped it up instantly. "I don't think that dog fully appreciated the famous Les Deux Magots pâté," Papa observed.

"In some places, that dog would be considered quite a morsel himself!" Jean laughed, blissfully unaware of the prescience of his remark.

---

Although everyday life went on, a cloud of uncertainty hung over the city. One evening in March, or maybe April, the Huets announced they were leaving. They owned a gallery two blocks down Rue de Seine from ours and were good friends of my parents. I'd spent the afternoon typing provenances for the paintings in our new exhibition and was sleepy. The bells startled me as Josephine and Laurent Huet entered the gallery.

"Bonsoir, ma chérie," Josephine called out as she glided through the gallery in a gabardine trenchcoat, a black cloche pulled low over her forehead. Laurent closed the door and followed her in his soft, double-breasted, gray jacket. They were expected for dinner. I greeted each of them with a kiss to both cheeks.

"Please go on up. I have one more provenance to type and then I'll join you."

Josephine's glamour always made me feel a bit dull, but I never did have much interest in clothing. Most of the money I earned from working in the gallery went into the bank. My parents had promised to pay my tuition at the Sorbonne but expected me to contribute to the other expenses that would be required. I finished typing the last provenance, then went upstairs.

The Huets and my parents were standing in the dining room drinking wine and picking at the hors d'oeuvres on the buffet. "What was it like posing for Picasso?" Josephine was asking Maman, as they gazed at the portrait above the fireplace. The men moved off and began to talk about the gallery business. I joined Maman and Josephine.

"No one believes me," Maman said, "but it was pretty boring. At first I was really self-conscious. He'd stare at me for awhile, then step back and stare some more. After awhile, I became sleepy and struggled to keep my eyes from closing."

"You know, Frida," Josephine laughed, "your nose is in the wrong place."

"True. But that's Picasso. Always experimenting. That's what André loves about the modernists. Look at that color. Doesn't it just make you smile?"

"And André doesn't care about having that weird painting of you above his fireplace?"

Maman laughed. "Are you joking? He loves it and was so flattered that Picasso wanted to paint a portrait of me, he insisted on buying it."

"I don't think Laurent would approve," Josephine said. Obviously, the glamorous Josephine had not been asked to pose. I looked at Maman's un-blemished skin and cornflower blue eyes. Just now her cheeks were flushed. It was clear to me why an artist would find her inspiring.

The conversation died down as our maid served the main dish and we busied ourselves with our cutlery. Seated on one side of the table next to Papa, I could see our images in the mirror across the room. It struck me then for the first time how alike we were. We had the same dark eyebrows and curly hair. I was thankful to have been spared Papa's jutting chin, but I had his full, wide lips.

Papa began to recount the story of the Nazis who had visited our gallery the previous summer, a story which had now entered our family folklore and which he liked to give an airing to when I was around. "Yes, my little girl threw them out," he said, laughing and tugging on one of my curls. "'We don't sell to murderers!' she shouted! 'Get out!' Oh, she was terrifying. If I'd been a Nazi, I'd have run all the way back to Germany!" I looked down, embarrassed at being teased.

"Good for you!" Laurent exclaimed with a gesture that almost upset his goblet. "Why should we be civil to them?"

Josephine spoke up. "I understand your sentiment, but is there really any point in provoking them? Lots of people say that, given half an excuse, they'll invade all of Europe."

"But what about what they're already doing—to the Jews?" I burst out. "We may not be religious, but we're Jews, nevertheless! How can we stand by and let that happen? I think France should attack Germany right now!"

Papa covered my hand with his. "Look," he said, "you have to understand that for many of us, the Great War wasn't all that long ago." He looked somewhere into space, then went on. "I cannot convey the horror. The carnage. The destruction of so many lives. The grief of the entire country. The thought of having to live through such a thing again... It's unbearable."

Laurent raised his wine glass. "Enough of that," he said. "I want to propose a toast. To the Cassin Gallery. Congratulations on a spectacular exhibition!"

The others raised their glasses and sipped their wine. I stared down, remembering those horrid men. "Actually," Papa was saying, "our current show was inspired by the so-called 'degenerate art' exhibition the Nazis organized a couple years ago. They had intended to make a mockery of modern art but it attracted more viewers than any other recent exhibition in the country. And not because it wasn't liked!"

Laurent shook his head. "It's amazing how many fantastic pieces have come on the market since then. The German dealers are selling or trading modern works that they've pulled out of their own museums. They want nothing but traditional art—the stuff that Hitler thinks glorifies Germany."

"Actually, I think one of the two men who visited our gallery in August was Karl Haberstock, Göring's main dealer."

Josephine interjected. "We've also decided not to do business with them. In fact—" Josephine nudged Laurent with her elbow.

He cleared his throat. "We have something to tell you."

We looked at him expectantly.

"We're going to America for a while."

There was a moment of stunned silence before Maman said quietly, "What?"

"We don't like the situation here. Look, everybody said Germany wouldn't invade Poland and everybody was wrong. Now everybody's saying they wouldn't dare invade France. But we're officially at war with them now. What does that mean? I just don't like the odds."

Not a single fork moved. Laurent looked defiant. "I shipped some paintings to a friend of mine in New York a couple months ago, and we're going to do business over there for a while. Just until we see how things play out here." He hesitated, then added firmly, "You should come with us."

Papa's lips were set in a firm line. Maman's eyes were welling up. Would we all move to New York? When I contemplated leaving the gallery and our home, dread enveloped me like a cold vapor.

"When will you leave?" Maman asked.

"Next week," Josephine responded, eyebrows raised, as if to say, what could I do?

Maman got up and walked around the table to embrace her friend. "So soon?" she whispered.

After their announcement, the room felt like the air had been sucked out of it. The Huets said no to dessert and left shortly afterwards, leaving my parents and me to linger at the table, drinking tea.

Papa was firm in his determination to stay in Paris. He'd witnessed what his parents had gone through to establish and grow the business he now ran. Walking away from that would be a betrayal. "Besides," he said, "I fought for France in the last war and I'm not going to abandon her now."

Maman looked at me, then back at Papa. "But what about doing something like the Huets are doing? Just go to New York for a little while. Just to see what happens."

"I won't," Papa replied. "But you could. In fact, maybe you should. You and Nicole. I've actually been thinking about this a lot lately."

"No," said Maman, shaking her head slowly.

"Just listen. You take Nicole to New York. I'll keep an eye on things here. If I see it's really going wrong, I'll join you. Otherwise, you come back." As he spoke, he seemed to get more invested in the idea. "You could even go with the Huets. It would only be for a little while."

Anger surged in my throat. They were talking about me as if I wasn't there. "I thought we'd settled that," I said. "I'm not going anywhere." Maman leaned over and took my hand. Papa began to speak but Maman interrupted him. "It's as you say, André. We will wait here with you until things get bad. Then we'll go. Together."

I replayed that conversation in my head so many times after the war. What had made me so certain we should stay? Was it youthful bravado? My selfish reluctance to part with my dream of attending the Sorbonne? If only I had been smarter, quicker to see what was developing, maybe we all could've been saved. I remember with embarrassment that, when the Huets said they were leaving, I thought they were being cowardly. I remind myself that I was only seventeen, a mere girl. Can't I finally forgive myself?

---

I don't believe in God. I think the world operates more like a giant kaleidoscope. Some mechanism in the universe turns a tiny bit and everything changes. I dream of turning it back, back to when my parents were still alive.

In May of 1940, on the brink of the unknown, we all developed a desperate appreciation for the familiar, the predictable.

If I close my eyes, I can smell the lemon scent of my mother's hair when she hugged me before breakfast. I see the flowered teapot, a ray of light falling across my blue china cup, a tiny vase of violets next to the cracked white sink. I feel butter squeezing into my mouth from a warm baguette, followed by the crunch of crust. I see my parents holding hands across the table, hear the peaceful silence when a flock of crows squawking outside the window suddenly flies off. It was one of our last normal mornings.

To my parents and all the others who had lived through the Great War, utter incredulity attended memories of a lost generation of young men. What sadistic god would put them through it again? For my friends and I, futures that had looked solid as stone began to crumble like sandcastles.

It was June when we first heard the sounds of distant artillery. Rumors flew the way a flock of swallows will point in one direction, then suddenly dive and swirl the opposite way. Hunker down, some said, wars last for years. It'll be over quickly, others swore. The Germans will be stopped at the Maginot Line. The Germans will stop at nothing to get even for the last war.

Everything had happened so quickly. Papa had still not been deployed. Only six weeks earlier the Germans had crossed the border and now they were just outside Paris. As for running, it made little sense. We had no relatives in the country. What awaited us but sleeping outdoors and scrounging for food? How safe would we be in the mass of hopeless and angry refugees? How long would it take Germany to sweep south? For these reasons and, not least of all, because we were reluctant to abandon everything we had to looters, we stuck by our decision to stay. We watched the city empty southward, a torrent of automobiles half-buried under mattresses and luggage; carts and bicycles loaded with lampshades and rocking chairs; people drowning under backpacks and duffels. It was a Dalí landscape come to life. Sounds, like broken instruments, banged off-key, off-tempo, accompanied by a whimpering choir. Observing this flow of desperate humanity, I was relieved, come what may, not to be a part of it. But I had no idea what would come. Nor how bad it would be.

I didn't turn over the Open sign that hung on the gallery door downstairs. No one would be in. Not with the fighting so close and rumors that the Germans could be in Paris even by the week's end. I had developed a habit of twisting the fingers of my right hand in my left and did this as I rose from the table and paced the living room. "Quick, Maman, Papa, look! Soldiers!" I stood transfixed at the window. Papa and Maman rushed over and gazed down at the street. Bedraggled, slump-shouldered, some using sticks for crutches, some carrying others on stretchers, all listless and yet hurrying. French.

"They are retreating," Papa muttered. "They are abandoning us to the Germans." He turned away in disgust and walked over to the fireplace, where he lit his pipe and stared into the dark grate.

---

We heard the German bombs falling upon the Renault factory. Papa and I moved as much art as we could from the gallery to the tiny cellar, leaving room for the three of us to sit. The bitter scent of burning wafted through the air and ash settled on the streets. The French government was burning files and blowing up munitions and fuel depots in preparation for their abandonment of Paris. On June 10 the military commander of France declared Paris an open city. I asked Papa what that meant.

"It means we will give up without a fight," he replied contemptuously. "In return for the Germans not destroying anything, we'll let them have Paris. We will mount no defense of the city."

"Does that mean they've won the war?"

"Not exactly yet, but for all intents and purposes, yes. Most of our soldiers that were deployed along the Maginot Line have been captured. It's doubtful we could withstand an attack elsewhere in the country, but it is humiliating to just let them walk in without a shot."

Everyone had said that the Germans wouldn't be able to get through the Maginot Line. But they had driven straight through Belgium, leaving the French forces suddenly behind enemy lines. They called it Blitzkrieg—lightning war.

"What will happen now?" I was terrified but trusted that Papa would know what to do.

"Look," he said, "maybe this is for the best. If we sign a peace treaty with them, life could go on pretty much as usual. We'll just have to accept their annexation of Poland and agree not to join forces with England. But we'll still be France, we'll still have a government. And certainly, a lot of lives will be saved. The POWs might even be released as part of the terms of an armistice."

I'd never heard Papa speak in such a resigned, flat tone. I had only to look into his eyes to know that he did not believe a word of what he was saying.

A few days later, a black truck crawled down our street like a large rat. A loudspeaker mounted on top blared, "You have been completely betrayed. There is no longer any efficacious resistance you can mount against German-Italian military superiority. It is useless to continue the struggle. Think of your children, of your unfortunate wives. Demand that your government end this struggle that has no hope of success."

That night, lured from my bedroom by the strangeness of the scene outside my window, I slipped out and moved like a cat, slinking along the edges of the buildings. Paris gleamed softly in the moonlight that blued the old stone walls, like a stage set after the show. The City of Light—darkened. I saw no one. Three quarters of the citizens had fled south, and the other quarter were closed up inside their homes, waiting for what would come when the light returned. I stood with my back pressed against a cold column of the Eglise de la Madeleine and listened to sounds that had never been audible beneath the usual cacophony that was my Paris. A crumpled paper bag slid along the street intermittently, like a brush sweeping a cymbal. A lamp hanging from a chain swayed with a deep-throated croak. My own breathing was like the wheeze of a concertina. A car's engine whined, then geared down as it slowly passed. Its headlamps, covered with blue fabric, cast a faint, short light. The air was cool and I pulled my cardigan around me. I could smell flowers in air now emptied of the competing smells of exhaust, damp wool, cigarettes.

The ancient Egyptian obelisk in the center of the Place de la Concorde pointed skyward like a cautionary finger raised to stop time.

Papa slammed the newspaper down on the table. "I would never have believed it. Never."

We were drinking our Sunday morning coffee in the apartment's spacious kitchen. I looked at Maman, who raised an eyebrow.

"After everything we soldiers did just—what?—twenty years ago? To save France? To protect the world from Germany? Now this monster piles insult on top of carnage."

"What are you talking about, Papa?"

Papa poured himself a cup of coffee and sat at the table. He flattened the paper and stabbed a photograph with his index finger. "This."

It was a railroad car sitting in the middle of a forest.

"Hitler. He got the same railway carriage and took it to the same spot where Germany signed the armistice with us after the last war. And made France sign this armistice. He's laughing at us all, at everything we sacrificed back then. He's humiliating us as much as possible." Papa dropped his forehead into his hands.

Maman walked over and placed her hands on his shoulders and kissed the top of his head. "Look, my dear, we must keep up some sort of hope. And now it's time that you explain to us exactly what is going to happen, so that we can be as prepared as possible."

Papa lifted his head and nodded. Maman took her seat. Glancing at the paper now and then, Papa explained that under the terms of the armistice, certain areas of northern France, including Paris, would be occupied by the German army. The Southern Zone would be unoccupied and run by the French government which had moved to Vichy.

"Here's another slap," Papa growled. "France is to pay for the costs of the German occupation." He shook his head. "And Marshal Petain signed this. The supposed hero of the last war gives in without a fight." He paused and looked at us. "I'm sorry, I really can't tell you what this means for us."

---

My parents forbade me to leave the apartment alone, but I was young, I felt invulnerable and I couldn't stand being cooped up. So I slipped out to watch the Germans' victory parade down the center of the Champs-Elysées. After so many days of quiet streets, the crowd was overwhelming. Many people had emerged from their self-imposed imprisonment to view the high-stepping horses, gleaming tanks and rows and rows of soldiers. Some in the crowd cheered but most stood silently. The soldiers did not look menacing, as I'd expected, but like tired and curious young men. Although some maintained a strict, face-forward military bearing, others looked out along the streets and up at the buildings. One particularly handsome young man smiled at me. It pains me to recall the thrill of excitement I felt watching this display of discipline and power. I started to smile at the young man; then, ashamed of myself, turned and ran home.

At first, there weren't a lot of changes, other than the curfew. The Germans that one met in the streets were polite to a fault, tipping their heads and often smiling. We still believed that the occupation would be short-lived and there would soon be an armistice between Germany and Britain that would end the war. Of course, most people didn't stop to consider what might have to be given up in return for the Germans leaving France.

But slowly and steadily, Paris became a foreign country. It reminded me of a trip we'd made to Holland a few years earlier. Then, all the daily tasks of living that I'd taken for granted had to be considered anew. The most banal of tasks—riding a bus, ordering a coffee, even flushing a toilet—were done just differently enough that they required focus. It had been exhausting. Now, too, the comfort of routine was gone. Even though the language itself was still French, every thought had to be translated before spoken, translated into the language of innuendo. Many things couldn't be said at all for fear of reprisal. The country was foreign in a different way every day, as the curfew would change, Métro stops close, or the electricity shut off without notice. Making a mistake would cost more than a tourist's mild embarrassment; it could cost one's life. People stayed in their neighborhoods, kept to themselves, trusted no one. The only ones comfortable on the streets were the Germans on leave, who relished Paris like exuberant tourists.

# 8

## ROBERT

The bar was a man's man's place and dark—the better to hide the dirt, I always thought. But it was one of Jack's favorites. Water-stained, glued-on paneling bedecked with beer logos, a dark-green carpet mottled like a turtle's back where rivulets of spilt beer darkened it in patches. Cheap chicken wings on Friday afternoons. Jack was at the bar, casually leaning back on his elbow and chatting with a good-looking brunette. I took the stool on the other side of him and lifted a finger toward the bartender.

"What can I get ya?" The guy was pot-bellied and red-faced, with all the friendliness of an airport security agent discovering a bottle of water in your carry-on.

"Bourbon." I preferred my bars a little more upscale, where I could sample higher quality bourbons, but here bourbon was bourbon and real men drank beer. Preferably Budweiser. There were a few other people at the bar. One of them could've played an extra in any show involving a down-and-out bar in a gritty neighborhood. His rotund head sported a baggy brown knit beanie from which sprouted twisted gray hair, frayed like the bottoms of his over-sized jeans. He was accompanied by a woman, equally rotund, with hair that resembled a pyramid of steel wool.

Jack turned away from the brunette long enough to give me a friendly slap on the back, then introduced me to her. "Pamela's a real estate agent," he announced, the equivalent of being a MacArthur genius grant winner in this joint. "She could probably help you with that move you're contemplating." He turned and winked at me, then said, "Maybe we should switch seats."

I rolled my eyes up to the ceiling and downed the bourbon. Jack was always trying to fix me up. He either wanted to share his marital bliss by finding me a bride, or live vicariously through me, figuring he'd be owed some stories if he set me up. Either way, no matter how many times I told him to bugger off, Jack persisted.

"I'm sorry," I said, "but the move's on hold since I lost my job and my wife got pregnant." Pamela's face fell and Jack glared at me.

A pony-tailed young man in an iridescent green parka slid between Jack and the brunette and leaned toward the bartender. "Do you have a beer menu?"

Jack elbowed me and nodded toward the guy. Obviously out of place.

The bartender looked the young man up and down. "No." He resumed rearranging bottles on the back wall.

"What kind of beer do you have?" the young man persisted.

Without turning, the bartender responded, "What kind you want?"

Jack looked up at the young man. "Hey, just order a Bud, man. Make it easier on yourself."

The young man looked confused for a minute then nodded. "Got it. I'll have a Bud."

I motioned for another bourbon. Behind the bar hung a painting of a reclining nude, not badly done but not particularly good, either. There were all sorts of stories about that painting, where it had come from, who the model was. Some said she was the wife of a wealthy magnate who lost all his money during the Depression. Others swore she was the moll of one of the alcohol smugglers during Prohibition. At some point in time, she'd been christened Daphne, an unintentionally fitting name. In Greek mythology Daphne was a nymph associated with fountains and springs, and this was a watering hole after all.

Jack elbowed me. "Hey, so spill. Find any priceless paintings yet?"

I filled Jack in on my plans to go to Detroit and track down Sam Popinski. "Plus, I've been searching some online databases of lost art, but nothing's come up yet. And I'm trying to track down some of the primary dealers of the time to see if I can find out what they did after the war. Did they continue to trade art? And where might works that they had at the time have gone?"

"Sounds like looking for a snowball in hell."

"Thanks for your encouragement." I nodded to the bartender and pointed to my glass. He refilled it. "I've yet to nail down their exact locations, but most of these dealers got off lightly and continued their careers. Some were even considered model citizens and awarded the proverbial keys to their cities."

"That's fucked up. So, you just gonna go marchin' into somebody's gallery and ask if they've got any stolen paintings?"

I whirled the ice in my glass, looking down. "I don't know. I really don't know what I'm going to do. You're FBI, I thought you might have some ideas."

Jack stood up. "I get it. You're gonna make me work. Then you're paying the tab. Let's go to a table where we can speak more privately."

"Okay, Yuppie," Jack said as soon as he entered my loft. "Get out the good bourbon." It was about a week after our discussion at the bar. Through a combination of his size—big shoulders from his college football days—and his personality, Jack occupied a room the way a tsunami occupied a beach. He roared in, turned everything upside down and left a mess in his wake. I assumed the reason Ellen could live with him was that she was so mild-mannered. She was like an unsinkable tugboat, chugging above the fray.

"Oh, sure," I said. "You're always telling me the cheap stuff is good enough when I'm over at your place, but when you're round here, you suddenly appreciate quality."

Jack laughed. "Just wait till you see what I've got for you. You'll not only want to give me free booze, you might even want to kiss me!"

"Only if you've brought me the Picasso, and even then, I'd have to give it some thought." I opened a cabinet below the counter and pulled out a nearly full bottle of Black Maple Hill and two glasses and headed for the sofa.

"No, we need to sit at your desk," Jack said, pulling out the desk chair and sliding one of the barstools over.

I poured the bourbon and returned the bottle to the counter, then looked at Jack expectantly. "Now what?"

"Okay, you sit on the stool behind me and I'm gonna show you something that is right up your alley. Something sure to impress any librarian you manage to lure over here." Jack started to type, then looked back at me. "Password?"

"Felix3."

"Yeah, that would've been hard to crack. Might've taken me three tries!" Jack laughed and continued typing.

"Okay, see this here? This is the entry screen to the

National Archives database. I'm gonna put in my password and don't look because I wouldn't want to get into any trouble giving you a password to a database you're going to kiss me for. You ready? Got a pencil and paper in case you accidentally look?"

I reached for the scratch pad on the desk and pulled a pen out of my shirt pocket. As Jack typed in his password—a confusing mix of letters, numbers and symbols—I copied it. Jack pressed Enter. Another page loaded that said National Archives, Authorized Users Only. In the search section, Jack typed "Holocaust collection." Up came a grid with different titles across the screen.

"Now," Jack said, "I don't want you to think I'm betraying our country just on account of our friendship. In fact, this database is in beta testing and will be public as soon as the kinks get worked out. Most of the material in here was declassified in the mid-Seventies, but it would've taken a pretty talented researcher to get through all the microfiches and find anything. My understanding is that there are about twenty million pages of documents in here."

I whistled, gazing over Jack's shoulder, my fingers itching to get at the keyboard and see what the database held.

"Yeah, I know you," Jack said. "No way." He stood up and pushed me toward the living area. "We'll sip a little bourbon, smoke a cigar and have our man talk. After I leave, you can spend the night with your favorite companion—that computer!" He stopped a moment and pulled a folded paper out of the front of his sweatshirt. "By the way, here's a list of those dealers you wanted and where they or their evil spawn are now located." He shoved me again. "No peeking till I'm gone."

As soon as Jack left, I went over to the computer and clicked on "Holocaust collection." Late as it was, I wasn't sleepy. I had rationed my bourbon, knowing I'd want to look around a bit in the database before I went to bed. I scrolled down through the choices:

```
Munich Property Cards
ERR Card File and Photos
OMGUS-Monuments, Fine Arts, and
Archives
WWII OSS Art Looting Investigation
Reports.
```

There were nearly a dozen headings, and these were just the ones relating to cultural property. Others were more chilling:

```
Dachau Entry Registers
Mauthausen Death Books
Nuremberg Interrogation Records.
```

I clicked on "Munich Property Cards." I clicked on the first. A photo of an index card popped up. The card was divided into boxes for recording data about the artwork. Information was typed within the sections in old-fashioned typescript, slanted upward, as if a soldier had fed the card into the typewriter roller hurriedly. I began to read:

```
Classification: Paintings.
Author: Nicolaes Berchem.
Subject: Landscape with cattle.
Material: Oil on canvas.
Measurements: 32 x 75.
```

```
Arrival condition: good—slightly
damaged.
```

The next box caused my skin to prickle.

```
Depot possessor: ERR—Hitler.
```

The dealers. I was convinced that the answer, if there was one, was to be found by tracking the dealers. The paintings had been looted and most likely held in the Jeu de Paume in Paris until they were claimed by Hitler or Göring or their representatives. I returned to the main category, "Holocaust Files," and scrolled down. "WWII OSS Art Looting Investigation Reports."

Lohse and Hofer were two of Göring's most important art dealers. Nicole had told me that they were the primary dealers accessing the Jeu de Paume inventory, along with Hans Wendland, a dealer in Switzerland who had been a partner of Hofer. I scrolled down, looking for Wendland.

The documents were small and of such poor quality I had my face eight inches away from the screen. Wendland. I had to see if there was anything on Wendland. Lots of von this and von that. No Wendland. I clicked on Hofer.

The summary on Hofer included specific examples of confiscations and purchases at rock bottom prices. Then, on page five, appeared the name "Hans WENDLAND."

```
WENDLAND had a strong influence on
HOFER... He was HOFER's chief contact and
agent in Switzerland.
```

The report went on to specify various transactions between Hofer and Wendland, including lists of paintings, to whom they were sold and for how much. The dull throbbing in my head had become more insistent, but still I couldn't stop. I pored over the list of paintings obtained in this manner, but none had belonged to the Cassins. Following the summary report was a list of Hofer's clients and the paintings sold to them. I examined the list, then sank back in my chair. None of the Cassin paintings were listed. I clicked through to the next page. "List of Dealers from whom HOFER made Purchases."

And there they were. From "LAPIERRE, ROLAND, Picasso, Pablo, Portrait of a Woman." From "WENDLAND, HANS," the Cranach and the La Tour.

# 9
## NICOLE

Any cooperation with the Germans was collaboration. That's what Papa's friend Jean believed. Young as I was, with no experience of insecurity or privation, in those early days I agreed with Jean, the most radical of the group. As the war went on, I found myself facing situations that put such an inflexible stance to the test. Did working for the Germans matter if, at the same time, it gave one an opportunity to work for the Résistance? Was cozying up to the occupiers worse than watching your children starve? Was taking a principled stance that could result in your execution necessary, or could you stay alive, vowing to get revenge later?

Visiting the Alhambra brought such debates to the forefront. Because, except for the preponderance of German uniforms in the audience, it might have been any night before the German troops marched down the Champs-Elysées, any night before the curfews and arrests and round-ups of Jews, any night when the international colony of artists who called Paris home had come out to play. Many had fled to the unoccupied zone immediately after the German victory. But lack of work and nostalgia for Paris, along with encouraging reports from friends who'd stayed, had persuaded a good number of them to return. The festive scene at the Alhambra was replicated in more than 100 nightclubs in Paris, where some of the most popular entertainers had resumed their careers a few short months after the occupation began. Maurice Chevalier, Charles Trenet and Edith Piaf were among those continuing to attract large crowds.

Jean's knuckles were white around the stem of his wine glass. "The performers act as if these Germans are just another group of tourists, even while outside this very door they've posted a list of the latest executed. Very few—Josephine Baker, for one—have refused to perform for them. She went to the Unoccupied Zone and has announced that she's part of the Free French forces." Jean was a Résistance leader masquerading as an art dealer. There were so many art dealers in Paris, he claimed, it was one of the most innocuous personas he could don. Adaptable as a chameleon, splotches on his cheeks were the only signs of his emotion. They were red now, but it could've been the wine.

"Oui, I heard that as well. But she's famous," Papa said thoughtfully, "and that gives her more freedom. What about your average chorus girl who can't afford to leave, who has no home in the South, and who needs to earn a living? What should she do? Quit and get a job as a waitress? Is serving them any different from entertaining them? It's a difficult question. I myself walk a fine line at the gallery. I'm selling art to them, but I have refused to accept consignments. I know where those works come from." He looked down and picked at a gash in the wooden table. "I'd like to refuse to do business with them altogether, but what good will it do my family if I'm arrested or shot?"

Marcel wore his emotions in his hair—the wilder the hair,

the more dangerous his mood, as he habitually raked his hands through it when upset. Just now there was barely a strand that lay flat. Twisting and tipping his wine glass as he spoke, he stared at the viscous liquid forming legs along the inside of the glass. "The fascists," he continued, "have been calling us decadent for years. Yet here we are, under the thumb of the worst of them, and isn't it funny how many of these black-jacketed potato-beetles scuttle through the clubs and brothels every night?"

Scantily clad dancers pranced and kicked and puckered their painted lips. Champagne flowed and the orchestra played a German song that the soldiers accompanied raucously with their husky voices. If some in the audience were ashamed to be there celebrating during the city's occupation, they shrugged the feeling aside and joined in the pretense that nothing had changed. To do otherwise was to have to commit to action of some sort, and it was clear what risks that would entail. With the regularity of the dancers' kicks, citizens were arrested and disappeared.

"Picasso has gone south; Matisse, too. Dali, Lévi-Strauss and Léger have gone to America," Papa reported.

"Some of them are beginning to return," Marcel observed. "I heard Picasso is back. Also the American, Stein."

"Well, you do have to wonder. Is living under Vichy so much better? And then, of course, Paris is Paris. Hard to leave for long." Roger had discovered Paris and his life as an art critic twenty years earlier and could not imagine returning to the provincialism of the countryside.

"Did you know, nearly all the publishers have signed a censorship agreement?" Jean asked disgustedly. "Now, that's collaboration."

"That's horrible," I interjected. "How could any writer agree to publish under censorship? It goes against the very grain of what a writer is!" I was passionate about writing, in no small measure because the writers I studied took risks, wrote about things that made one think about right and wrong.

"But what should they do? If they don't, they're out of business. And this way, some of our writers can continue to be heard," Roger argued.

"What are we hearing, though? Only what the Germans want us to hear!" Jean retorted.

"Oh, come on, not all art is political. Aren't there plenty of books that have nothing to do with Germany and this war?" Marcel asked. He was a painter and all he wanted was to paint. "There's not much interest in my painting these days. I hear the Germans have set up an entire bureaucracy just to steal art from the Jews. They raided some châteaux out in the Loire the other day. Now all anyone wants is a bargain basement masterpiece, not something from a regular living French artist—who happens to be pretty good, if I do say so myself." Marcel preened.

Jean shot a frigid look Marcel's way. "Some might say, myself included, that in this situation there is no art unless it speaks against this unspeakable horror. As Brecht said, you cannot write poems about trees when the woods are full of policemen! These Neanderthals are trying to impose their culture on us, to destroy our very souls. Check this out." Jean slipped a magazine onto the table. It was written in German and featured a photograph of the Eiffel Tower on the cover.

"What's that?" Marcel asked.

"It's a tourist magazine for German soldiers. Apparently, Hitler has promised every soldier a leave in Paris. We've become a playground for the conquerors!" Jean snorted. "Do you know, they've even approved certain brothels for visits by the soldiers? So our women, too, are becoming their playthings." His lips narrowed. "They will pay when this is over. I figure once the British sign an armistice, most of the Germans will leave town, and then what's due will be collected."

I looked into Jean's eyes and shivered.

---

Over the years, my memories often flooded in unbidden at night. I would get up and read a detective novel, something to take me into another world. Eventually, the tide of memories would slip back and lay dormant. But sometimes they would be triggered by the most unexpected things. Like when I first met Walt's sister. Her feisty, flighty nature reminded me of my best friend, Marie.

Papa hadn't approved of Marie. He saw only her frivolous side and found it difficult to believe she'd been accepted to the Sorbonne. I think we balanced each other out. She inspired me to loosen up and I reined in some of her more scatter-brained ideas. But mostly, we made each other laugh the way only young girls can.

One day, shortly after the Germans occupied the city, Marie entered the gallery as she always did, throwing the door open with a flourish of bells. Her dyed blonde bob swinging across kohl-rimmed eyes, she sashayed forth on high-heeled shoes as she trilled a singsong, "Bonjour, Nicole!" Papa gave me a look. I'd been reading as much as I could in my spare time to prove, in this my first semester, that I was worthy of the Sorbonne. Marie occasionally accompanied me to the library, but her motivation tended toward checking out boys.

"Bonjour, Marie! Let's go!" I grabbed a sweater and my book bag. "We're off, Papa. I'll be back before supper."

"Be careful," Papa admonished. "Remember what I told you."

We stepped out into brilliant sunshine. Vibrant red geraniums trailed from window boxes clinging to the iron balconies that studded the old stone buildings.

"What did your papa mean?" Marie asked.

"Oh, you know him. He's morphed from don't-talk-to-boys to don't-talk-to-soldiers." I harrumphed to show my disgust. "As if I would!"

"Hmm, I must say I've seen a few handsome ones!"

"Marie!" I shook her arm and she giggled.

"My papa says they're not going to be here very long, anyway. He says as soon as England signs a treaty with Germany, the war will be over and things will get back to normal."

"I don't know. They conquered us, after all. They're going to want something out of it."

"My papa says they just wanted to neutralize us. That all they really wanted was Austria and Poland, but they had to attack us because of that stupid alliance we had with Poland. That's why we gave up so fast. My papa says there was no point in having the shit bombed out of us!"

"But Marie. Look what they've done to Poland, Holland, Belgium. And what they're doing to the Jews. Is it really okay with us if that happens as long as they leave us alone?"

"Well, I don't know. Where do you draw the line? And my papa says they were so much better armed than us that we hadn't a chance in hell of winning anyway."

We walked up Rue de Seine, stopping now and then to admire something in one of the art galleries' windows, then cut over to Quai de Conti along the Seine. The river shuddered under a light breeze that churned the intermittent sunlight into the depths. The bridge to the Louvre, Pont des Arts, was deserted but for two black-clad soldiers. In the uncertainty of the occupation, fewer people were out on the streets. Suddenly I stopped.

"What's wrong?" Marie asked. She followed my gaze to the Bibliothèque Mazarine. Founded in the mid-1600s as one of the biggest libraries in Europe, it was my favorite place to study, partly because it was so close to home but also because of its history. In the long, narrow reading room, books were shelved to the ceiling between ornate wooden columns. Busts of famous thinkers stood on marble stands; precious volumes lay open under glass. The chairs were occupied by students of all ages, and I felt as one with a long line of historical scholars. Diffuse light from narrow windows gave the air itself a golden glow, half-illuminating all the people who had come here before me in search of knowledge.

Now, a red banner with a black swastika nearly covered the façade of the library's entrance.

***

These days I often find myself referred to as cute. Certainly not by anyone who knows me but by the multitude of young health aides who pop in daily, wearing their bunny-printed smocks. "Oh, you look so cute today, Mrs. K," they'll say. Or, if introducing me to a new one, "Isn't she just the cutest?" I can't be bothered to stop it. It's part of the life cycle. One goes from cute, as a child, to pretty, as a young woman, to attractive at middle age, and back to cute. I think what's cute is the fact that at my age I am still walking and talking like some sort of trick monkey. It's certainly not my hair of steel wool, gnarly hands and skin as baggy as a Shar Pei's.

But when I was young, I really was cute, with Papa's dark hair and Maman's fair skin. And in 1940, despite the ominous presence of the Germans, I was still trying to believe in my life as a pretty young woman and carefree student. After much prompting by Marie, I agreed to go to a jazz club with her. She came into my room as I finished dressing.

"No, don't wear that, you'll look fuddy duddy," she said, pushing me aside and rummaging through my closet. "Mon Dieu, mon amie, haven't you a single decent skirt? You should've told me; I'd have brought you something."

I looked sorrowfully at the dress Marie had ripped from my hands and cast down on the floor. It was my favorite, a simple black jersey gathered at one side. "But Marie," I pleaded, "I love that dress! What if I wear it with some jewelry and high heels? I'll even borrow your lipstick—but not until we leave here. Papa would suspect something."

Marie ignored me and continued making her way through the closet. Finally, she sighed. "Let me see that again," she commanded, reaching for the dress. She held it up and eyed me thoughtfully. "Well, at least it's tight. Let's jazz it up with some jewelry, for sure."

I donned the dress while Marie dug through my jewelry box. She selected a rather garish rhinestone necklace given to me by Madame Huet. Having long admired how Madame Huet looked, I supposed this was fashionable. High-heeled black pumps finished off the look. Marie reached over and fluffed up my chin-length curls. "I am so glad you got that haircut. These bangs are perfect for you. They frame those big brown eyes." She paused and stepped back. "Oui, now you look hot."

Gazing into the full-length mirror on the door of my closet, I was surprised to see that the plain and studious teenager who usually gazed back at me was now a young woman—and rather attractive at that. "I'm still not sure this is such a good idea," I demurred.

"Oh, don't flip your wig. Serge and Albert are going to meet us there. Besides, you have to take advantage of the swing dance lessons I gave you. You're not going to believe what a blast it is. And the Germans hate it, so in a way, we're practically heroes for going!"

Marie wore a short, black-and-white checked skirt, white sweater, black and white striped stockings and clunky shoes. Her neck was wrapped with colorful scarves that flowed down her sweater like a fountain of colored water. She had explained that this was the look favored by the Zazous, the jazz-crazy young people who hung out primarily in the Latin Quarter. She looked at me critically again. "Wait a minute," she said, rolling down her stockings. "You wear the stockings. And take off that necklace. You can have a couple of my scarves instead."

I did as I was told and finally Marie was satisfied. "We just need to get you a skirt and some different shoes for next time."

I'd told my parents that Marie and I were going to Albert's house to play records, something we often did on a Saturday night. They were in the dining room finishing a bottle of wine they had opened for supper. My new look would raise suspicion. "Let's try to sneak out," I whispered to Marie. We left my room and quickly passed the door to the dining room. "We're off!" I called as we approached the back stairs. A murmured assent came back, then Papa's voice.

"Be sure you're back before curfew!"

We tumbled down the stairs, suppressing laughter and shoving each other, and strode up the alley toward the Latin Quarter. Marie paused, pulled a pair of large sunglasses out of her bag and put them on. "I forgot to tell you to bring sunglasses," she said, frowning. "Do you have any with you?"

I shook my head. Marie dug further down into her bag and came up with a lipstick and a compact that she handed me. Carefully I applied the red lipstick and blotted it on the handkerchief Marie handed over. The club we were going to was near the Sorbonne and frequented mostly by students. We walked with our heads up, defiantly returning the stare of a German soldier on the Boul' Mich.

A narrow stone stairway led down the side of a building to a small landing and a door into the club. Marie grabbed my hand and pulled me past the crowd lingering near the door to the edge of a dance floor jammed with young people. Loud music reverberated in my chest as Marie was swallowed by the crowd. It was Cab Calloway's Minnie the Moocher, one of the favorites among the group that listened to records at Albert's. I caught sight of Serge on the dance floor with a blonde. Marie was already out there with a long-haired young man. Just then someone tapped me on the shoulder. "Want to dance?" He was wearing a jacket that fell down to his knees, a narrow tie and thick-soled shoes. His long black hair rose to a pouf in front and gleamed from some sort of pomade.

Without waiting for an answer, he pulled me into the center of the dance floor and began to swing. The crowd was ecstatic and shouting "Hi-De-Ho" along with the music as they shook their fingers and spun around. I caught Marie's eye. She gave me a broad wink and twirled away. I found myself grinning at my dance partner as we swung to the beat. My hair began to dampen at my temples. Suddenly, my partner put his hands around my waist and lifted me high before setting me down again. I laughed and began moving to the music in my own way. Marie's lessons had given me a foundation, but this sort of dancing called for creative abandon!

When the song ended, my partner introduced himself. "I'm Philipe," he said in English. "Want to get something to drink?" When I nodded, he took my hand and led me to a crowded bar at the back of the room. Most of the men were wearing clothes similar to Philipe's. Their jackets had extra pockets sewn onto them and multiple half-belts on the back. Philipe slithered through the wide-shouldered coats of those at the bar and came back with two Cokes. He handed them both to me, then pulled a flask out of one of his pockets, opened it and poured a golden liquid into each glass. Screwing the top back on and replacing the flask, he took one of the glasses back from me and lifted it. "To swing!" he said, again in English.

"To swing!" Although I drank wine frequently with meals, I'd rarely tasted whiskey. It was not particularly to my liking, but I liked the warmth that traveled from my throat through my entire bloodstream. That first drink made my head lighten. Or was it the music? Or the handsome, if odd-looking, boy I was standing with. "Why are we speaking English?" I asked him.

"Aren't you Zazou?" he said, looking down and flipping one of Marie's scarves.

I was embarrassed, caught impersonating something I was not. I took another big gulp of the drink. "I love swing and came here with my friend, but this is my first time here. I mean... Well, I guess I don't even really know what Zazou is."

Philipe smiled. "It's okay. You shouldn't dye that beautiful hair of yours anyway. But perhaps your friend will convert you."

He took a drink and looked over my head toward the dance floor. I was sure that he was looking for someone else to dance with, someone hotter. Another Zazou. He returned his gaze to me. "So, we speak English to show we identify with the English and the Americans over the Germans and the French fascists. We wear these long coats as a protest to the fabric rationing. Of course, we have to go to thrift shops and make our own, but it's our way of saying we do not accept these values they are trying to force on us. Country, family, work." He made a spitting motion but did not actually spit. "We are young! We want freedom, experimentation, swing! When people see us in these clothes, they know where we stand." He drained his drink and motioned to me to do the same. I did and he grabbed our glasses and shoved them through the crowd back onto the bar. "Basically," he said loudly as he pulled me back to the dance floor, "I love SWING!"

---

By late 1940 the Champs-Elysées had become the literal stomping ground of the German army. They paraded; their marching bands performed. But on Armistice Day that year, the scene along this famous boulevard could not have been more different. It was the day when France traditionally celebrated the end of the Great War. The Germans had prohibited its commemoration, afraid it might stir up any latent militance on the part of our cowed population. But while ex-soldiers and government officials, teachers and librarians, bankers and bakers, grandparents and parents abided by the proclamation against public gatherings, 20,000 students occupied the Champs-Elysées. I was one of them.

It was a chilly day, devoid of sunlight, but I was warmed by the crowd, exuberant and darkly thrilled by our demonstration of defiance. I'd learned about the planned protest in leaflets that high-school students had passed around at the Sorbonne. My friends Albert, Serge, François and Jaqueline were there, too. I'd asked Marie, but Marie said her papa would kill her if the Germans didn't kill her first. Although I was sure my parents would've prohibited my attendance had they known of my plans, I believed they would be proud.

Serge pulled out a flask and passed it around. The event had aspects of a street party, except for the undercurrent of danger. German army personnel and French police were highly visible but stood aside. We had begun beneath the Arc de Triomphe at the Tomb of the Unknown Soldier, where we laid wreaths and flags. Then we marched to the statue of

Georges Clemenceau, the prime minister during the Great War. A few students made speeches, after which the crowd began to drift away. "Let's go to my place and listen to records," Albert suggested. Jaqueline and I quickly assented, filled with pride and a desire to celebrate our bravery.

The next morning, as I approached the breakfast table, Papa slapped the open paper with the palm of his hand, then jabbed his finger at a headline. "Stupid, reckless youth!" he exclaimed. "Probably even some of your friends!"

"What are you talking about, Papa?" I asked, with a pang of trepidation.

"Protests! Students protesting the German occupation. It's amazing no one was killed. Believe me, Nicole, that's what will happen next time. Don't you go getting any ideas from your crazy friends. The time for heroics may, God help us, come, but it's not now. Anyway, it looks as if you have the day off. They've closed the Sorbonne."

Papa slid the paper over to me as I sat down. After my friends and I had left the protest, several thousand other students had stayed on past nightfall, chanting and scuffling with fascist youth groups. The Germans had charged the group, fired shots into the air and arrested more than 100. I stifled a gasp. Photos showed soldiers dragging students toward waiting cars. Blood dripping from his forehead, his face frozen in a grimace of pain, François stared up from the kitchen table.

# 10

## ROBERT

Fidgeting with the radio of the Ford Fiesta I'd rented at the airport, I looked for a jazz station. Or classical. Or maybe some of the soul music that had put Detroit on the world map musically. Smokey Robinson or Marvin Gaye, perhaps. Lacking success on the commercial airwaves, I plugged in my phone and called up a soul compilation I'd made. "I heard it through the grapevine," I sang, nodding my head and going for my falsetto. " ... And I'm just about to lose my mind. Honey, honey."

Since I'd never been to Detroit before, I followed the freeway east then exited downtown and drove around, noting some new developments around the sports arenas and a number of gorgeous, classic pre-war skyscrapers. Detroit had once been called the Paris of the Midwest. North of downtown, boarded-up windows and graffitied walls lined the fabled Woodward Avenue. Quite a contrast between the slick new edifices downtown and these tattered blocks with missing buildings. Abandoned factories sprawled over multiple blocks, festooned with razor-wire fences that hadn't managed to keep the graffiti artists at bay. It was hard to imagine this city during its heyday just following World War II. Humming and vibrant, the state-of-the-art machine for the country's war effort.

As I continued north, the buildings began to show signs of occupancy. Crumpled papers and drink cartons no longer surged like surf up and down the curbs. Flowers sprouted from window boxes; parking lots were frosted black with fresh asphalt. "Welcome to Pleasant Ridge." Pleasant Ridge was a leafy suburb, filled with vintage homes dating mostly from the early twentieth century. West of Woodward the homes were mansions, lining boulevards divided by lushly landscaped islands. East of Woodward the homes were equally picturesque but smaller. Friendly Village suited the neighborhood. From the outside, it looked like one of the big old mansions, creepily similar to the ones that often get converted to funeral homes.

The lobby of Friendly Village was spacious and featured groupings of furniture and large plants that looked real. I touched one. It was real. A woman sat behind a reception desk, high and wooden like that of a hotel check-in counter, flanked on either side by double doors. She smiled broadly and called out, "May I help you?" before I even reached the desk.

"Hi." I smiled back winningly, giving her the full force of my gaze over the top of my glasses. I didn't know if there were rules about who could visit the patients but figured my friendliest persona wouldn't hurt. Abetted by a little white lie. "I'm here to see Sam Popinski."

"And you are?"

"Robert Ames, his nephew from New York."

"Oh, how nice," she said, still smiling while handing me a pen and indicating a sign-in clipboard. She turned her attention to the computer, then said, "14B."

After signing in, I favored her with another smile, then pushed open one of the doors on the left. It led into a large atrium filled with round tables and chairs. There were a few people seated at a table playing cards. A hallway veered off to the left. I passed rooms 1 to 10 to the end of the hall, which then opened up into a small lounge with a TV and some chairs. A woman sat in a wheelchair watching a game show. Another hall led off to the right and I followed it to room 14. Slowly, I approached and peered into the room.

A bedside table with a large styrofoam cup on top of it stood adjacent to an empty bed with rumpled covers. It had all the promise of one of those movie scenes where the protagonist finds his loved one has just died. But usually, in those scenes, the bed is stripped or neatly made. Beyond the bed was a partially drawn curtain, past which the bottom half of another bed was visible. Stepping around the curtain, I saw a very old man sitting in a wheelchair beside the bed. Although the television was on, the man was staring out the window at the parking lot.

"Mr Popinski?" I called hesitatingly. This whole outing was weird. First of all, this man might not even be the man I was looking for, and in that case I was just bothering some poor old guy. Secondly, what if he was the guy? What was I supposed to say? Your old girlfriend from 1944 wants to say hi? What kind of fool's errand was this anyway? This strange romantic tale and mystery of the lost paintings. Sounded like something out of a book. One that I wouldn't read. I'd half a mind to turn around, call Nicole and tell her I'd been wrong. I couldn't help her.

The man in the chair turned. "Oh, hello," he said, as if expecting me.

"Hello. May I join you for a few minutes?"

"Is it four o'clock already?"

"No, it's about 3:15."

"I thought my appointment wasn't until 4:00. Are you the

new PT? I really don't see how exercise is going to help me all that much at this point."

"I'm sorry," I replied. "I'm not the PT, just someone who wanted to visit you."

"Oh! In that case, please do sit down. I don't get many visitors. Who are you?"

"Just a friend of a friend."

"I thought all my friends were dead by now!"

I wished I'd choreographed this a little better. Weather—talking about the weather was always a good icebreaker.

"It's so lovely out this time of year. I saw lots of flowers blooming on the way in from the airport."

"Oh? Where are you from?"

"New York."

"New York," the man repeated, frowning. "Yes, I was there once, long ago. Just after I came back from the war."

My pulse ticked upward. This man was not only not dead but had his wits about him.

"The war? Would that have been World War II?"

"Mm-hmm."

"Where did you serve?" I asked.

"What time is it?" he responded.

"About 3:15."

"My appointment isn't till 4:00," he said querulously.

"It's okay," I reassured him. "I'm just here to visit you. We were talking about your service in the war."

"Who are you?"

"I'm a visitor. From New York." I hoped the repetition of New York would get him back on track.

"New York," the man repeated. "Never been there. See it a lot on TV, though." He turned away from me to the television mounted on the wall in front of him.

I thought I'd try a different tack. "Ever been to France?"

The man continued to focus on the television and began to laugh as Lucille Ball's toe got stuck in a bathtub drain.

"Sam." I tried to get his attention. "Sam, what about France? Paris?"

His eyes remained focused on the TV set. I picked up the remote and shut it off. Sam glared at me.

"You don't know me!" He began to shout. "You don't know me!"

I panicked and quickly put the TV back on. I patted Sam's forearm. "I know, but I know someone you know and—"

I couldn't finish my sentence because Sam was really shouting now. "You don't know me! Nobody knows me!" He was struggling to stand up from his chair. I began to back out of the room when someone in a smock printed with hearts came in.

"You'd better leave now," she said. "He gets like this some-times." Seeing the look on my face, she added, "Don't worry. It's not your fault. We'll sedate him and he'll be fine in a few hours."

---

The chicken in my Caesar salad was a little less than spry, but it would do. It was my usual fare when out of town and gener-ally dependably dull. The Hilton, too, was my regular choice—not so much for the points I earned but for the consistency of its facilities and service. I sometimes felt I should be more adven-turesome and stay at a place known for its local color, but travel had a tendency to make me anxious. The unimaginative routine proved a comforting counterpoint to being in a new place. I stabbed a piece of romaine. Crisp.

The next morning, I dressed and checked my appearance. I've been told I look professorial: tall and lanky, with fine sandy hair going silver. I cultivated the look with tortoise-shell glasses and a wardrobe of corduroy blazers, black turtlenecks and charcoal wool pants. Early on I'd realized this appearance gave my clients confidence in me; the additional benefit was that I never had to think about what to wear.

Downstairs, I elbowed aside the extended families who were there for a hockey tournament and had apparently never seen food before. Disdaining the dried-up scrambled eggs and make-your-own waffle stand, I grabbed a dry muffin, planning to swing by Friendly Village again. Given Popinski's comment about the war, I suspected I'd found Nicole's former love, but I hoped for more confirmation than an off-hand comment about the war immediately followed by disavowal of ever having been to New York.

Inside Friendly Village's lobby, the receptionist from the day before was perched behind the high counter like a judge. Unlike yesterday, she did not greet me warmly but looked somewhat dismayed. Had she found out I wasn't a nephew? I approached the desk.

"Good morning!" I flashed an innocent smile.

"Oh," she said, flushing. "You're here to see Mr Popinski again?"

"Yes," I replied, beginning to sign the visitors' log.

"Well, ... well," she stammered and pulled at the log. "Please have a seat for a minute."

I looked up over my glasses.

"It'll be just a minute."

I walked over toward a group of chairs and spotted a coffee stand next to the door. I'd just tossed my coffee stirrer into the trash and turned around when a woman wearing a Friendly Village name badge around her neck approached me.

"Dr. Amy Wexford," she said, extending her hand.

She had a cool, firm grip. She was tall, with shoulder-length dark, curly hair, and was dressed simply in a blue, cable-knit sweater and black pants.

"Robert Ames," I said, checking her name badge quickly, as I had been distracted by her appearance and hadn't paid attention to her name.

"I understand you're here to visit Sam Popinski?"

"Yes." I paused. "Is there something wrong?" I hoped I hadn't been reported for upsetting Popinski yesterday.

"Please. Let's talk in my office." Dr. Wexford turned. I followed her through the double doors and across the dining room where the residents were finishing their breakfasts. The smell of bacon mingled with the musty scent of an over-heated room full of people. Dr. Wexford's office was just beyond the dining room. I could still smell the bacon.

"Please sit down," she said, motioning to a chair across from her desk. "May I ask what your relationship to Mr. Popinski was?"

I stared at her. Was? I straightened in my chair and crossed one leg over the other. I thought I'd better be frank at this point. "A friend of Mr. Popinski's asked me to come and see how he was doing."

Dr. Wexford was tapping a pencil against her desk blotter. "I am very sorry to have to tell you that Mr. Popinski passed away last night. Please accept my condolences."

Damn it! I just barely stopped myself from saying it aloud. I said nothing for a minute while Dr. Wexford's brown eyes searched mine. "Well, I only met Mr. Popinski for the first time yesterday, but my friend is going to be very sorry to hear this news. What happened? He was okay yesterday—I mean, except for the mental confusion."

"I know," Dr. Wexford replied. "But he was ninety-three, after all. He had a stroke in the middle of the night. There was nothing we could do."

I sipped my coffee and let my eyes rove around the office. There were the usual framed diplomas—psychiatry, I noted—and stacks of books behind her that looked to be clinical treatises. Lining the walls were photographs of sailboats, some in sunny, calm seas, some in wild, green waters that threatened to swallow the boat.

"Is there anything I can do for you?" Dr. Wexford asked. "I know this must come as a shock. Have you come far?"

"I live in New York." I pulled out a business card holder, fingered one out of the case and handed it to her. Robert Ames, PhD, Art Historian. "I came here yesterday, expressly to speak to Mr. Popinski, but he got very confused and, frankly, based on that conversation, I can't even be sure he's the man my friend wanted me to check on."

Affecting an anxious, disturbed look—which is how I really felt, but I usually take care not to show it—I raked a hand through my hair and blinked rapidly. I knew psychologists had the same client privacy standards as did lawyers and priests but was hoping I could disarm her enough to learn something—anything—about Sam Popinski.

"Did his family come to visit much?"

Dr. Wexford hesitated. "You know, I can't really give you much information. Perhaps you should contact one of his family members."

Her phone buzzed. "Excuse me a minute," she said, picking it up. "Yes, yes, yes... I'll be there in a minute." She hung up the phone and looked at me apologetically. "I'm sorry, but I have to do my patient rounds now."

I took off my glasses, pulled out a handkerchief and began polishing the lenses, stalling for time. Now what? I couldn't go back to New York without some sort of confirmation of Popinski being the person Nicole was looking for. I was just too close.

Talking rapidly and as sincerely as I could, I tried again. "I'm sorry, I know you must be very busy, but this is all, well, all very upsetting. I'm only in town until tomorrow. This is probably an imposition, but do you think you could spare just a little time later today? I know you can't tell me anything confidential, but maybe there are just a few things—how Sam spent his time, was he happy—that would comfort my friend. She's also in her nineties."

The phone buzzed again. Dr. Wexford ignored it but looked harried and bent down to make a quick note in pencil. "I'm not sure how much help I can be, but I can meet you at 5:30 at Neptune's. It's just north of here on Woodward."

"Thanks so much, Dr. Wexford, I really do appreciate it. See you then." I shook her hand and headed for the lobby, hoping the invitation to meet outside the office might mean she'd be off-guard—and also, truth be told, maybe she found me as attractive as I found her.

I opened the door to Neptune's and a mélange of heat, savory smells, music and conversation poured out into the chilly spring night. The walls were painted in brilliant hues and hung with oversized paintings of cartoony-looking people dancing, picnicking and playing instruments. The table linens and dinnerware were similarly festive. Strings of colored lights looped haphazardly from the ceiling, creating prisms of the wine glasses and champagne flutes arrayed on the tables. Even though the voices in the crowded room overpowered it, I recognized the music: Miles Davis's classic, Kind of Blue. The bar was crowded so I asked for a table where Dr. Wexford and I would be able to talk more comfortably. I was seated on the upper level, from where I could view the diners below. It was much quieter there, with only two other tables occupied. I was nervous about this meeting. Would it look bad to be drinking wine already when she got there? I checked my watch: 5:35. Just then, I spotted her making her way to the stairs. She wore a lightweight trench coat over her sweater and pants and a black beret tipped over her dark curls.

As she approached the table, I began to rise to greet her. "No, please, sit down," she said, draping her handbag over the back of the chair and removing her coat. Once she had settled herself, we each ordered a glass of wine. I'd already decided not to approach the subject of Sam Popinski right away. I hoped to get her to shed some of her professionalism first, maybe warm up to me, trust me a little. I'd found that people always thought I was smartest and nicest when I barely talked but steadily listened, so I began the conversation by asking her what had made her choose psychology as a profession.

"Actually, as an undergrad, I studied art history," she began. "I wanted to be a museum curator. Picture this. Me, twenty-two years old, armed with a BA in art history from a little-known Michigan college. Off to New York I go. To the Met, no less. The man at the Reception desk is probably a decade older than I, looking all arty, and I pity him that he has such a lowly position. I explain that I am there to apply for a job in the curator division and he laughs. I mean just laughs in my face. 'Really,' he says, more like a sarcastic statement than a question. He points down the hall toward the employment office, then adds, 'By the way, everyone you meet here, including the janitor, has a PhD in art history and is waiting to get onto the curatorial staff. Best of luck.' Deflated, I slunk down the corridor, put in my application and never heard another word."

Dr. Wexford laughed and took a sip of wine.

"What then?" I prodded.

"I went back home, applied to grad school and got my PhD

in psychology. Initially, I thought I would do something like art therapy but, as it happened, I needed to support myself. I did a stint in corporate America until I realized that HR departments' goals actually have nothing to do with the welfare of the employees. So I do a little consulting, work at the Village a few days a week and have some private clients." She shifted in her chair and tossed her curls as the waiter laid a menu at her elbow. "But enough about me. What does an art historian do exactly?"

I removed my glasses and massaged the bridge of my nose. "Yes, well, I did the crazy thing and went on to get a PhD in art history from Syracuse. Followed by a series of low-paying, little-appreciated museum jobs and a stint at Sotheby's. But I'd always been interested in the subject of forgery and loved stories about fakes being unmasked. Probably all related to my obsession with film noir in my teens. I think The Maltese Falcon bears an inordinate responsibility for my career choices. Anyway, I apprenticed myself in my spare time to one of the best authenticators around and now that's my primary business. Researching provenances and authenticating artworks, primarily for auction houses. Also advising clients on restorations."

An hour later, I still hadn't broached the subject that lingered in the back of my mind like a felon in the shadows. I wasn't doing anything criminal, I reminded myself. Just trying to get a little information. So far, I'd discovered that Dr. Wexford—Amy, she asked me to call her—had a vibrant sense of humor, liked jazz and sailing, had bicycled through various places in Europe and the US and read voraciously—many of the same books I enjoyed, even an obscure Italian sci-fi novel.

"Oh my God," she laughed. "I think you, me and his mother are probably the only ones who read that!"

Once we finished dinner, I leaned back in my chair,

affecting a sense of ease I didn't feel. The waiter delivered two crèmes brûlées, and, as Amy stabbed the brittle crust of hers, I began.

"Now that I know you a little better, I think you might find my current case interesting. It's not my usual thing, but I'm trying to track down various artworks that belonged to a family living in Paris just before the Germans marched in."

Amy's head came up, her eyes wide.

"Really?"

"Did you know that the Nazis confiscated art belonging to Jews and sold it, or sent it on to German museums, or often kept it for their own collections? I mean, I'm talking about Rembrandts, Renoirs, priceless masterpieces."

"I've read about that, especially every now and then when one is discovered somewhere and there's a fight about giving it back."

"Yes, well, as you can imagine, it's very difficult to locate such pieces so many years later, especially given the chaos that reigned during the last years of the war. I mean, there were Germans, French, Red Army, Brits, Americans—and in addition to the Nazi confiscations, some of the soldiers themselves believed they deserved a little souvenir after watching their buddies get massacred. Just about the last thing on anyone's mind was preserving art. Thousands of pieces were lost. Within a few years after the war, pretty much all official efforts to recover them ground to a halt."

"But why? Why give up so quickly?"

"People were tired of it all. They just wanted to get on with their lives. The American military wanted to wrap things up and get the hell home. You can hardly blame them. But they left a ton of loose ends. Not just art-related. Even the hunt for war criminals waned."

I noted that Amy's spoon was still embedded in the dessert. I continued.

"There was one group whose official purpose was to go into areas where cultural treasures existed, as soon as possible after the territory was secured by the Allies, and try to preserve them. These guys were known as Monuments Men. My grandfather belonged to this unit. He worked at the Met prior to the war."

"Is that what sparked your interest in art?" Amy asked.

"Uh-huh. I spent a lot of time at my grandparents' house in Vermont. Their walls were covered in paintings. My father's form of filial rebellion was to become a CPA, but I couldn't resist the romance of art."

I took a spoonful of custard and savored the crunchy crust before continuing.

"In fact, speaking of romance, the friend I told you about— the one who was my connection to Sam Popinski? She's actually my client in this case. Nicole Cassin was her name back then, during the war, in Paris, where she met and fell in love with Sam Popinski."

"Really? He never mentioned her—" Amy stopped herself.

I shook my head. "No, because he left Paris in 1944 and she never heard from him again."

"Ah, one of those wartime romances. Sam always did have an air of mystery about him." Amy's eyes bored into mine.

I tipped my chin down and looked over the top of my glasses. "I had really hoped to deliver a message to him from my client."

Amy was quiet for a minute. "I sense that you want something from me. Information. Information about Sam. And I told you before, I really can't help you. I'm truly sorry you've gone through all this trouble, Robert. I don't think I'm breaching Sam's privacy to tell you that whatever message your client wanted to send, I am not sure he would have understood it. You saw him yesterday."

I swirled my teaspoon in my coffee and looked into the cup as I replied, "All she wanted, some seventy years after she'd last seen him, was to tell the love of her life that she hoped he'd been happy."

"It's too bad you couldn't have gotten here sooner," Amy said quietly. "Maybe he would have understood."

I looked up. Were those tears in her eyes?

"At this point," I said, "I just hope I can confirm for her that this was her Sam and maybe find out a little more about his life. Yesterday, he said something about having served in World War II. Can you at least confirm that?"

"Sam was a very sweet man," Amy said. "His obituary will be available on our website, and you'll be able to learn a little about his life and also about his next of kin there."

# 11

## NICOLE

Whenever I see a long, black car on the city street, I freeze. My breath stops for an instant until I remind myself: New York, twenty-first century; not Paris, 1941.

I was returning to the gallery from the Sorbonne when I saw Papa being shoved into a dark car, Maman slumped on the sidewalk weeping. I dropped my books and began to run, screaming, "Stop! Stop!" But by the time I reached the gallery, the car had pulled away. I slid to the ground and lifted Maman's shoulders. Between wracking gasps, she said the men had demanded that Papa accompany them for questioning, then had beaten him when he protested. I stood and pulled Maman up by the hand and led her through the gallery and upstairs to our apartment.

We had been afraid of such a possibility. Since the German occupation began, numerous laws had been enacted of the sort that were already in place in Germany and other occupied countries: curfews for Jews; prohibitions against working in various professions; confiscation of the property of any Jew who

left the country; and, of late, a practice referred to as Aryaniza-
tion. Jewish-owned businesses would be confiscated and sold at
rock-bottom prices to Aryan buyers. The trouble was, there was
no way of knowing which businesses would be targeted next.

Before they'd left, the Huets had transferred title to their
gallery to their non-Jewish manager, with the agreement that
he would transfer it back at some future date. Papa had begun
to talk of making such an arrangement but had not yet identified an appropriate "buyer." I still wonder, if I had pushed him
to do so, would things have been different? Maman sat on the
sofa, shaking. I'd never seen her look so helpless. In that
moment, I grew up. "Maman," I said, sitting next to her and
smoothing back her hair, "he's just been taken for questioning.
That's what they said, no?"

She nodded.

"So he will be back. I'll find out where he is and make sure
he's all right. I'll get Papa back. Don't worry."

I went downstairs, picked up the shards from the floor and
swept up the remaining slivers. The pieces were unsalvageable.
But it didn't matter, because they would soon belong to
someone else. I looked around at the gilt-framed paintings,
antique clocks and statuary and, for a fleeting moment, considered setting it on fire. But no, I would not give up hope that
quickly.

People are capable of darkness one might never suspect in a
casual meeting. Papa's arrest was only the first in a long list of
events that taught me there is no fairness in the world. That's
why I didn't develop many friendships later in life. I doubted
everyone's motives. I wondered, why are they being nice to me?

What do they want? I always looked out for the knife ready to be plunged into my back.

Following Papa's arrest, Maman and I went about the apartment in shock. We didn't open the gallery. I rose early and made coffee for Maman, as Papa had done every day. We talked in barely audible monosyllables. Friends came by and brought meals, but I couldn't eat and felt Maman's eyes on me as I pushed my food away. I'd gone to the Prefecture of Police the day after the arrest and been told not to come back, that we would be informed of the charges against Papa and his location "in due time." It was most likely that he'd been taken to Fresnes Prison. Several other friends and colleagues had ended up there after being arrested. Gisèle Lefebvre came almost every day, bringing whatever little treat she could scrounge. Her husband was now a POW.

"See? Fresnes!" Gisèle exclaimed. "I know people who have had postcards from prisoners at Fresnes. And you can visit there, too, I'm told. You'll see André soon. I know it!"

She hugged me and kissed my cheek, seeing that Maman could do little to comfort me, being in a state of shock herself. One day, Gisèle was taking her daughters to the country for a picnic and insisted that we accompany her. Neither of us wanted to. But Maman joined Gisèle in prodding me to go.

"I need to stay here, in case there's any word," she said. "But Nicole, please go. Gisèle has been so kind, and she could probably use help with the girls."

"Yes, it's so hard to manage both of them if they get it into their heads to act up," Gisèle quickly agreed. "You'd be doing me a huge favor, Nicole."

"I'll get my things," I mumbled.

It was a splendid, unseasonably warm day. The trees were budding and, as our train left the city, the sun illuminated the greening grass. Puffy clouds lined up just above the horizon.

Cows lolled about in the fields. At the park, Gisèle set up a large cloth near the lake and unpacked the basket she had brought. The girls, Lisle and Monique, took off their shoes and dipped their toes into the water, shrieking.

"Be careful!" Gisèle called over to them. "Just your feet! We don't have any dry clothes for you."

I sat down on the grass and looked up. The trees waved lazily back and forth. Their twisted trunks attested to more violent weather, but today all was peaceful. A tiny sparrow hopped around, hoping for crumbs. The burble of a creek that emptied into the lake slowed the chaotic thoughts that caromed inside my head. I shut my eyes; the heat of the spring sun coaxed a long shuddering breath from deep within me. It was so beautiful and yet so indifferent. This scene had been here long before my birth and would be here long after I was gone. Of what importance was my life? Any life? Once, I'd felt an intimacy with nature, but now I realized how little it cared. Once, I'd believed in art, in literature. Now, I knew that all the poetry in the world couldn't compensate for what was happening.

Sitting upon a large boulder, I contemplated a pebble in the shallows of the lake. A wave covered it and I remained focused upon the spot until the pebble reappeared. It required faith. Larger waves obliterated the pebble for longer periods of time. And sometimes, a powerful wave moved it, so I had to adjust my gaze in order to stay focused upon it. Like something harder to believe in. Like the life I'd once had.

---

I was angry all the time. Angry at myself mainly. How could I have let this happen? Why hadn't I insisted that Papa sign the gallery over to someone else? I should've tried to persuade him to leave, at least temporarily. And now he was in prison. Why had I been so stupid and selfish and ignored the Huets' entreaties to leave? In high school, I'd walked through the Sorbonne's campus and seen all the young men and women as they sat on the grass or walked, deep in conversation, sometimes laughing, sometimes arguing intently. I'd wanted to learn things, to be able to debate philosophy, art, history and literature with intelligent people.

Now, I mocked my dream of studying there. I'd been so intent on it that I'd shut my eyes to the reality of what was happening. I'd continued to live in my little-girl dream-world despite all the evidence to the contrary. Things had piled on gradually. Each restriction of liberty was awful at the time, but one got used to it. Then the next one came, and people thought, well, we'll get used to that, too, and after all, it won't be for much longer. And now, here I was at the gates of the Sorbonne, no longer allowed to take classes, because I was a Jew.

For a while after Papa's arrest, I continued to go to the Sorbonne every day. I was loath to give up the dream, and perhaps the talk of the Allies' imminent invasion was true. Maybe I'd wake up from this nightmare and everything would go back to the way it was. Even after the prohibition against Jews, the professors allowed me to sit in on the classes I would've been taking. I lingered afterwards in the halls to plan study times and discuss the day's lectures with my friends. No one talked about what was really going on. There was an occasional pitying smile, a hand on the forearm, as future careers were discussed.

I alternately envied and hated my fellow students. My girlfriends suddenly seemed incredibly shallow. How could they chat about lipstick and boys when my father was in prison and people were being executed daily for speaking their minds—just what the university was supposed to encourage? Some of the best professors had been imprisoned or deported. Jews were not allowed to teach there anymore. And yet, there were no protests. The heat was being turned up and the community closed its eyes drowsily. Eventually, I couldn't bear to go there. It was not real. What was the point of having friends if you couldn't talk to them about the most important things in your life?

Isolated and lonely, I rarely left the gallery. I had recurring nightmares in which I left to do something frivolous—see a movie or a concert or hang out in a café—and returned to find either Maman or Papa or both missing, the gallery door wide open, the contents smashed. I'd try to run inside but couldn't move.

Maman attempted to convince me to continue my education. "You'll see," she argued. "It won't be wasted. When this is over, you'll be on track with your classmates and can finish your degree."

"Maman," I retorted, "how can I go to this beautiful leafy fairyland and talk about literature and art when Papa is in prison and could be killed any day? When you and I may find the Gestapo outside waiting for us at any moment? I've changed. I don't belong there anymore. I used to think literature was as essential as breath. Now I know breath is more important."

Maman sighed. "I would do anything to give you back your girlhood."

"It's not up to you, though, is it Maman?"

"I should've listened when your father said we should leave."

"It's not your fault. We both decided we wouldn't leave him. And he wouldn't go."

"And now, he is gone and we are left."

Impenetrable as a tomb, a brick behemoth punctuated by rows of dark, barred windows, Fresnes rose up before me. A line of women snaked down the block, many holding small children and baskets covered with tea towels. I clutched my basket and lifted my chin, pointedly not seeing the uniformed Germans, ominous as gargoyles, lining the prison wall. As I walked along the row of women toward the back of the line, an eerie silence accompanied me. Occasionally, a child's wail was heard, quickly suppressed. The women did not speak. They dared not say anything about whom they were visiting or why. They stood. They waited. And I joined them.

For every woman let through the door, three or four were turned away. Would they let me see Papa? I prayed inwardly and shuffled along with the others. Finally, I was at the front and a guard asked for my papers. Handing the papers to him, I was angry at myself for the way my hand shook. I straightened my spine and willed myself to be strong, no matter what. The guard consulted an open portfolio on the table in front of him, then thrust my papers back and gave a slight jerk of his head toward the door. "Vorgehen."

I entered a courtyard surrounded on three sides by the prison's walls and was immediately accosted by a woman wearing a black uniform. "Halt," she commanded, grabbing my basket, ripping off the tea towel and rummaging through the cheese, bread and jam packets, spilling some to the ground. I bent to pick them up as the guard shoved the basket back. Indicating that I was to follow, she strode across the courtyard and entered a door that led to a narrow, dark hallway lined with doors. Opening the nearest one, she pushed me into a small room. "Off!" she barked in heavily accented French. "Clothes off!"

For a moment I imagined I was to be imprisoned, that this plan to visit Papa had been a grave mistake. I hesitated, then began to undress. I'd never stood naked in front of a stranger before and reddened with shame. The guard searched my clothing thoroughly, then threw it back at me. I dressed and followed her back to the courtyard, up a few steps and through another doorway. Here, the hall was wider and, after a short distance, opened into another courtyard dwarfed by looming walls, four stories high, lined with cell after cell barred by heavy wooden doors. Metal stairways at either end of the courtyard provided access to the cells. Our steps echoed on the concrete as I followed the guard to one of the stairways.

On the third tier, the guard turned right and led me along the cells. I dared not slow but turned to look at the impassive doors I passed, each with a small opening covered by a sliding wooden panel. The guard unlocked one of the doors and pushed me inside.

"Nicole!" Papa stumbled forward from the back of the cell. I sidled through the other four men in the cell to embrace him. Stepping back to offer the basket, I was shocked by the welts on Papa's face. But he merely smiled and peered inside the basket. "Gentlemen!" he intoned. "We'll feast tonight!"

Weak smiles appeared on the faces of the other prisoners, some of whom also had visible welts and bruises. The smell of body odor and urine was pervasive. I willed myself not to fall apart, taking my cue from Papa, who was acting as if this were a normal social visit. Papa introduced me to the other prisoners, who crowded against the front wall of the cell to provide us with a little privacy.

"Papa, what have they done to you? Are you all right?" As I lifted a hand to Papa's face, he took it and kissed my palm.

"Ah, chérie, just a little roughing up, that's all. Nothing

compared to what some of these fellows go through. They did not unleash the Gestapo on me, just a regular German."

"But what for? What do they want? Why are they keeping you?"

"My dear, these people are more like barbarians than soldiers. They want everything. Our home, our possessions, our gallery, everything. They want me to sign bills of sale for everything and, of course, the price is a tiny fraction of what these things are really worth."

"But Papa, why are you resisting? They'll just go ahead and take it anyway! Why risk your life?"

"Nicole, they want to make this look right, legal, and as long as I don't sign this and they are forced to just confiscate everything, it will be clear what thugs they are."

"Clear to whom? We all know this already. They'll never admit it to themselves anyway. You might as well sign those papers and get out of here!"

"And then what? Where will we go? My father came here for a better life and worked himself into an early grave starting his business. I, too, have worked very hard, Nicole, to make a good life for you and your mother. Am I meant to just hand everything over to a band of thieves?"

I knew how stubborn my father could be, but I also knew he would do anything to protect me and Maman. I would use that.

"Papa," I began. "I didn't want to tell you this, but they have threatened Maman and me, too. They've said that if you don't sign, they'll throw us into prison as well, and never let us out until you do. I could handle it, but you know how Maman is. I don't think she could survive a place like this."

Papa grasped my hands and dropped his head, shaking it back and forth. "No, no, no."

"Papa, you must not allow Maman to go to prison. You must sign the papers."

The men at the front of the cell moved back as the guard threw open the door. "You, come!"

I embraced Papa tightly and whispered in his ear. "You must sign, Papa. For Maman's sake."

He gripped my shoulders. "Wait!" He leaned over to whisper in my ear. "I've hidden a painting. If I don't get out, you may need it—"

His words were cut short as the guard roughly grabbed my arm and yanked me toward the door. I glanced back to see Papa standing there, looking as I had never seen him look before: helpless.

I've always admired Papa for his integrity and courage. But when I think back on that day and what happened afterward, I am angry. How could he have been so stubborn as to risk everything? Couldn't he have just signed the damn papers? Would he still be alive? Would Maman?

---

It didn't happen the way it had happened so many nights in my dreams. It was broad daylight. I was at the gallery when a large moving van pulled up outside followed by a black car. Two men in German uniforms entered, followed by three men in white coveralls. The Germans gestured to the other men who began to remove paintings from the walls.

I ran up to them and pulled at the sleeve of one of the workmen carrying out a Renoir. "Stop! Put that down!" I shouted, grabbing the painting and trying to wrestle it from his grip. Suddenly, my hair was pulled violently back. I lost my grip on the painting and fell to the floor. One of the Germans bent down and slapped me hard across the face. Maman ran over to me, pulled me up and dragged me back to the rear of the gallery.

"It's happening," she said. "They're taking over. Look, go out the back door, over to Gisèle's, and wait for me there."

"No!" I shouted.

The Germans looked over at us. Maman grabbed my shoulder.

"Yes," she hissed. "They are just here to steal everything. If they were here to arrest us, we'd be in the car already."

"Fine, then you come, too."

"Nicole, listen to your mother. If you slip out the back, they're unlikely to notice. If we both go at once, they'll think we're guilty of something and then they will arrest us. Besides, even if they are here to arrest us, what good will it do for both of us to go to prison? I'll need to know that you'll be out here trying to free your father and me."

I tried but couldn't stop the tears.

"You know what I'm saying is best. Go. Go quickly and quietly."

The Germans were busy directing the movers to the largest paintings and sculptures. I hugged Maman and slipped out the back door. Maman did not show up at Gisèle's that day; and that evening, when I walked over to the gallery, there was a board across the door and no sign of her.

My family makes fun of me. Sometimes they call me a "depression baby." I just laugh, because I don't want to explain. What seems like an obsession with using all our leftovers has nothing to do with deprivation during the Depression in the

United States and everything to do with living in Paris under the German occupation. I will never forget being hungry and not knowing where the next meal was coming from.

By 1941, much of the food that our French farmers produced was being shipped to Germany. Rationing permitted barely enough food for the citizens of Paris to survive—that is, after waiting in line for hours. Suddenly, shop owners were more powerful than the upper classes who had once lorded it over them. They weren't shy about playing favorites when it came time to dole out their meager inventories. Watching their children's thinning bodies, many parents cajoled relatives or acquaintances in the countryside to take them for periods of time. Food was still more plentiful on the farms and the children would return with their cheeks a bit more plump and rosy.

When Gisèle Lefebvre heard about the seizure of the gallery and my mother's arrest, she immediately offered me a home. The Lefebvres lived in a two-bedroom flat not far from the gallery. The second bedroom was usually occupied by their two daughters, but Monique, the youngest, had been sent to the country for a month. Gisèle planned to send the older girl, Lisle, as soon as Monique returned, so I was able to occupy the spare bed in the girls' room. Gisèle had a job at the Post Office, sorting mail. I helped her prepare the evening meals, during which we would discuss our strategy for the following day. Much depended on neighborhood rumor—which shopkeeper was said to be getting butter the next day, or bread or meat. Bread was never sold fresh anymore; it had to be at least a day old, because the authorities believed people would be inclined to eat less that way. Still, when it was thought to be available, the queue would start early and last for hours. Gisèle and I took turns standing in lines.

"You know, she belongs to that POW wives' association,"

Gisèle cautioned me one day about the building's concierge, Madame Vaillaud. "It's really nothing more than a collaborationist front. Some of the women believe joining it and cooperating with the Germans will bring their husbands back sooner, but they're fools. And their magazine!" Here Gisèle rolled her eyes heavenward and shook her head. "It's all about how to be the proper wife and mother and care for the home until your husband's return. While eating what, I ask? Between working and standing in lines for meager rations, we are supposed to be home sewing and cleaning? Unbelievable.

"Anyway," she went on, "you watch out for her. She would denounce you for a Jew as soon as look at you. Avoid her. I've told her you're my niece, your mother is dead and your father a POW. But we should probably make a hiding place somewhere in the apartment, just in case." She paused, noting what was probably my horrified expression. "I mean, I'm sure we won't need it, but we should still be prepared."

My shoulders stiffened. Even this welcoming flat was not entirely safe. The Germans had announced financial incentives for denouncing those thought to be enemies: foreign Jews, unregistered Jews, anyone harboring a Jew, anyone thought to be in the Résistance, black marketeers, those trying to avoid being sent to work in Germany, communists, people who listened to the BBC, escaped POWs... The list just got longer and longer. People would use denunciation as a threat against those they merely disliked and as a weapon against those toward whom they bore a more severe grudge. It was as if the storm clouds brought by the Germans watered long-germinating distrust among various French factions.

Whenever I began to worry for myself, I'd think of my parents. Papa was possibly still in Fresnes, or perhaps deported to a German camp. Maman had been taken to who knows where. Was Maman in Fresnes, too? I tried to console myself with the thought that perhaps my parents had been reunited, even if in prison. Fear for myself—that was a luxury I had no right to.

It was an incongruously gorgeous day as I walked to work. I marveled at the way the pansies sprawled from window boxes, blithe as pretty girls oblivious of the goings-on below. The stone streets traversed by Black Marias taking Jews to trains bound for Auschwitz had known the bump of wagons carting Royalist prisoners to the guillotine. The late summer sun hung just above the buildings, causing me to shade my eyes with one hand as I hurried along toward the gallery, now called Galerie Patriotique. The outline of the name Cassin was still visible where the letters had protected the stone from street grime before their removal. But only someone looking for it would notice the shapes beneath the new letters. I gritted my teeth, turned abruptly down a narrow alley and beat my fists against the stone wall until I was gasping for breath. I could not let Roland see my anger.

Shortly after the gallery had re-opened under the owner-ship of Roland LaPierre, I'd mustered up the most confident air I could and waltzed into the place that I still considered mine. There was an air of dishevelment about it that had never been in evidence under Papa's care. Paintings leaned here and there and, as I approached the rear of the shop, I could see stacks of papers strewn across the desk. Roland came out to greet me, smiling as if at a potential customer, but his brow was furrowed and his glasses askew. I introduced myself as Nicole Lefebvre. Turning on all the charm I could muster, I explained to Roland that I wanted to offer my services as a gallery assistant. He looked doubtful, and I explained that, although I looked young,

I had previous experience at a gallery but could not provide references. The owners, I explained vaguely, had left the country. I could tidy up his office, file and type invoices, I said, pointedly looking at the office mess. He could try me out for a week first and not pay me if he wasn't satisfied.

Just then the bells jangled and a man in a gray suit entered the gallery. Roland rushed out to greet him, obsequious as he bowed and shook the man's hand vigorously. "Welcome, welcome, Herr Wendland." I would later discover that Wendland was one of Göring's chief dealers and often on the prowl for something for his boss's collection. He went over to one side of the gallery where several stacks of paintings leaned against the wall and began flipping through them. Suddenly he paused and pulled out a small landscape, a Böcklin. He held it up and gazed at it for a few moments, then turned to Roland.

"What can you tell me about this Böcklin?"

"Yes, that just came in, but we haven't catalogued it yet. I think it's one of the ones from the Jeu de Paume. It's a... uh..." Roland raked his hand through his hair.

Carrying an easel, I walked up to the man and smiled. "Oh, monsieur, I see you have excellent taste. That's a wonderful example of Arnold Böcklin's later works. Here, let's put it on an easel so you can take a better look." Wendland set the painting on the easel, and I pulled a small wooden pointer from my pocket and directed it toward the painting. "It's called The Honeymoon. Although better known for his Isle of the Dead paintings, here Böcklin has created a sweet sunny composition of youth in love. He's Swiss, you know."

Wendland's nodded. "Of course. I lived in Switzerland for a number of years."

"Then you will especially appreciate the beauty of this landscape," I said reverently, although the setting was probably in Italy where Böcklin spent most of his time. "And the simplicity of the message of love and country." I paused. "There's been quite a demand for Böcklin's work lately, as he is said to be favored by Herr Hitler." In fact, I knew that Hitler owned several Böcklins. "So this one will not be available for long."

Roland saw the hook go in and stepped forward to set it. "True. I've had several clients ask me to let them know if a Böcklin came in, but as you see, I've just been too busy to get to this stack yet." In a matter of minutes, a deal was struck and Wendland walked out with the painting. "Can you start tomorrow?" Roland asked as he jotted a note on his copy of the bill of sale.

The worst part of working for Roland—who wasn't really evil, just a crook and an opportunist—was waiting on war criminals. And the worst of them was Hermann Göring. "Ah, Miss Lefebvre," he would say as I came out from the office. From his smug look of power, he clearly assumed I was in awe of him, and, much as I wanted to grab his walking stick and beat him with it, I'd tip my head politely, reminding myself that I had a longer-term purpose, even though I wasn't yet sure what it was. While Göring made occasional visits, more often he sent Wendland and Hofer, who had a gallery in Munich, to buy and trade art for him. There were plenty of non-German buyers who wanted to believe they were not doing business with the occupiers; so if Hofer brought in confiscated paintings to sell, Roland would happily serve as the intermediary. Of course, provenance was not mentioned. It wasn't as if the buyers didn't really know who was behind the transactions.

Gulping down the bile that rose in my throat each time I entered the gallery, I reminded myself that I was shepherding the business until my parents' return. I took copious notes regarding sales and purchases, which I hid in my bedroom at Gisèle's. Occasionally, while tracing the history of a piece, or explaining its importance in the canon, I forgot that it was not my gallery anymore, that my parents were in prison, that I had not been allowed to visit Papa in weeks, that I was not even sure he was still in Fresnes, and that I had been unable to find out where Maman had been taken. For a few moments, it was just me sharing my knowledge and love of art.

# 12

## ROBERT

I'd been crafting semi-plausible excuses to get in touch with Dr Wexford again. Then I got an email from her, saying she'd be in New York on business the following week, and did I want to meet for coffee. Before I could change my mind, I emailed her back and invited her to dinner at my loft. I hoped I wasn't coming across as too forward, offering to cook for her at home instead of going out; but, truth be told, I was feeling like taking the risk. I wanted to get to know her better, and shouting at one another over the din of a Manhattan coffee shop wouldn't have been a good way to do that. I was encouraged by the fact that she replied within an hour that she'd love to come. Once the chicken tagine started bubbling in the oven, though, I began to get nervous. What if she was a vegetarian? Or hated spicy food? What if I wanted to get rid of her at 9:30 and she showed no sign of leaving? What if she got bored and left at 8:30?

"I've always thought of art as driven from some sort of sublime inner spirit—transmitted directly from the human soul to the canvas, or sculpture or whatever." Amy shook her head slowly, then sipped her wine before continuing. "That sublimity is then experienced by the person standing in front of the work, who shares the emotion, the attempt to capture something of the glory—and, in many cases, pain—of life, always trying to interpret, to respond, to understand, to transcend. But what you're describing are some of the most evil men in history, obsessed with collecting art."

She was now sitting on my sofa with her shoes off, her feet tucked under her. One hand held a glass of wine and the other was idly petting Felix, who had insinuated himself along the length of her thigh. Pleasantly warm and relaxed, I shook my head slowly before responding.

"I don't think any of those guys experienced art in the way you're describing. I think they loved a painting the way someone else would love a perfect diamond. For the surface of it, for the value of it, for what others would think of their owning it. What it really represented was their proclamation that they were the new elite. Princes, kings, czars—they all had extensive art collections and patronized artists. And the just plain wealthy, too, have always amassed art collections. So when Hitler and his henchmen came to power, displaying magnificent art collections at their mansions and estates was about showing power, quantifying it and competing on the basis of it. That's why suddenly all of Hitler's guys were after the same masterpieces."

"That makes sense." Amy paused. "Because how could you have an emotional connection with, say, a Rubens Madonna and Child, and then go out and order the murder of women and children?"

I walked over to the fireplace, above which hung a luminous abstract painting suggestive of water and sky. I stared at it, trying to get my bearings. It had been a while since I had so enjoyed a woman's company. Amy was not only very attractive but great fun to talk to. I turned back to her.

"You would know better than I that humanity contains a base evil. History's full of examples. And art is neither proof of purity nor a cure. Wagner's a prime example. Everyone is in general agreement about his talent, but he was an anti-Semitic jerk."

Felix jumped down, strolled over to me and pawed my leg. I picked him up and held him over one shoulder while stroking his back.

Amy smiled. "I see he's got you trained. Just like mine."

"Oh yeah. No doubt about who's boss in this household."

Amy stretched her legs out in front of her. "Okay, so these guys may have actually liked some of the stuff they bought, but mainly the paintings were status symbols, just as today people might own flashy cars, mansions, jewelry and—still—art. It's classic materialism, believing that things will make you happy, using things to boost self-esteem. I saw plenty of that during my stint in corporate America. Only that which can be quantified is important. Bigger profits, higher salaries, more expensive suits, houses and cars. Employees become human 'resources.' As if humans were veins of copper being mined for corporate profits."

"Exactly. Like the commodification of art. And, of course, in Hitler's case, you get the psychological baggage of an aspiring artist who'd been refused entry to the art school he wanted to go to. So he labels the sort of modern art that was finding favor over his traditional landscapes 'degenerate.' According to him, the purpose of art was to celebrate country, work and family. Which to him included only families of the Aryan race. The Nazi leadership were generally paunchy middle-aged men. They had to exhibit their power through symbols." Nothing like trying to bore her. "I'm sorry. I'm sounding a bit like a professor in a lecture hall. I get like that sometimes."

Amy protested. "No, no. I think this is fascinating. I'm embarrassed I didn't learn more about it in my history classes. I was just thinking about what you said about the, um, glorification of the working class. Because here they were extolling the peasantry and then ruling over them as despots, just like the royalty and gentry before them. Napoleon, Stalin, Hitler. Forgive the cliché, but doesn't it all just boil down to the old saying: power corrupts, absolute power corrupts absolutely?"

I bent down and released Felix. "Well, to quote another cliché, which came first, the chicken or the egg? Do you think that people who are attracted to powerful positions already have some tendency toward corruption?"

I felt intoxicated. By the wine, by the conversation, by the sight of Amy's bare legs.

"May I get you another glass of wine?" I asked, crossing the room and reaching for her glass.

Amy stood. "Oh, I can get it myself," she said moving toward the kitchen. Blocking her path, I took the wine glass from her hand and set it down on the end table. She looked up at me. I ran my hands through her hair, then tilted her head up and bent down to kiss her.

We were lounging on my bed when the conversation turned once again to art. "Would you sacrifice a life for a painting?" Amy, her hair rumpled, lay back on a pillow looking vulnerable and kissable. I leaned in and kissed her.

"Whose life?" I asked.

"Does it matter?"

"Well, what if it was the life of a man on death row for raping and killing a child? And what if the painting was a portrait of Elvis on velvet?"

Amy laughed, then paused. "You know, I don't know if this question really allows for gray areas."

"Are you saying human life trumps everything when deciding what to save, what to sacrifice?"

"I don't know. I'm thinking..."

I continued. "Let's say we're not talking paintings. Is there nothing you would sacrifice a human for? What if a herd of elephants were stampeding toward a guy, and you could shoot at them and they would all veer off the narrow path of the gorge that they're on and tumble to their death, but the man will live. And, by the way, these are the last elephants on earth. And the guy is a murderer."

"That's not fair. I'll bet you got an A in philosophy."

"Maybe, but I can see you're now thinking perhaps there is some set of human/other thing equations where the other thing is more worth saving." I took her hand, kissing her fingers. "I know, I know—what you were really asking. Whether I—art lover, art historian—would sacrifice a random human being for a painting. Never."

"Not even a Rembrandt?"

"Nope. Nor a Mondrian, Monet or Manet. What's a painting? A bit of canvas or wood covered with pigments created by a person. And what is a person? It is beyond my ability to know or say." I pulled a tendril of her hair straight and watched it bounce back up. "All I know is, I'd order all the museums in the world burned down, just to save you."

Amy reached up and cupped my face, guiding my lips toward hers. "I don't believe that for a minute," she murmured. "But thanks."

I made Amy coffee and warmed up a couple of the croissants I had picked up yesterday—just in case. My desk was brightly lit by the late morning sun streaming in from the wall of windows. These had once provided light for the women who'd worked exhausting hours in this former garment factory. They'd been immigrants mainly, and when I'd first seen the place I wondered at the irony that, now, that same tedious, poorly paid work was still being done in poor conditions, but the workers stayed home to do it. The US didn't have to face up to the social costs of such grinding poverty and exhausting work but could still have its material goods cheap. These old buildings had been turned into lofts, the sales literature touting the wide expanses of glass that "artists would love." Few working artists would ever be able to afford such a place, but plenty of other people fell in love with the buildings and plunked down their money. I had been one of them.

Across from my desk, at the other end of the open space, was a seating area. A wood stove from the 60s, orange and pyramidal, faced a modular sofa, low-slung and cream-colored, dotted with pillows in vibrant reds and purples. The old brick walls were covered with paintings, and colorful rugs lay haphazardly on the distressed wood floor. Adjacent to my work area was the gleaming kitchen. The countertops were of a beautiful green granite that had streaks of dull red running through it.

"It's called Riverbottom," I told Amy when she admired it. "I didn't know one could fall in love with granite, but this was love at first sight." The master bedroom suite was behind the living area and separated from it by a plaster wall. Much as I liked open floorplans, I drew the line at an exposed bedroom and bathroom. Now I sat at the computer and printed out a document. I smoothed the pages down on the glass desktop.

"Everything I've found out about Sam Popinski so far. Born: 1920, Green River, Iowa. Parents: farmers. Father died 1942, on a merchant ship in the Pacific. Sam shipped out to France as an infantryman, 1941. Look! I found an article from the Green River paper, with his picture. Sure looks like a good old apple-cheeked farm boy, doesn't he?"

Amy reached for the picture and examined it closely. "Poor Sam. So young. I wouldn't have recognized him." I continued, while Amy stared at the young face looking out toward the future with such innocence.

"Returned to Iowa, 1946. Continued to farm, with his mother and uncle. Married, 1954. Two children, Peter and Katherine. Inherited the farm when his mother died in 1965, sold it to Monsanto in 1968, and then ran a little antique shop. The Monsanto deal must've netted him a fair amount of cash, as the kids went to good schools. When his son took a job in Detroit, Sam moved there. Now Peter works as an investment banker in New York, and Katherine is a struggling actress in Hollywood—occasional bit parts, commercials. Popinski sold the antique shop before moving to Detroit and lived the life of a comfortably well-off retiree. Traveled a bit with his wife: Europe, South America, Russia. They both moved to Friendly Village about five years ago. His wife died two years ago. I guess that was before you started there."

Amy nodded. "To think one's life can be wrapped up so succinctly, that in a single paragraph you've summed up Sam Popinski. And now he's gone. All of his hopes and dreams and secret thoughts and loves and fears and everything that was so important to him at the time is just over and done with and forgotten, and what's remembered are these markers of where he lived when. None of the dreams remain."

We were both silent for a moment. I was thinking about the opening newsreel in the film *Citizen Kane*, how his life was reduced to his business interests, his marriages, his political ambition. But then one of the editors says something like, "There's got to be more, who was he really?" And all the reporters go searching for the answer, for the meaning of his final word, "Rosebud," but never find it. And how Kane died alone, friendless.

What would Sam Spade do? I asked myself. I called Sam Popinski's son, Peter, at his office. "I'm a busy man," he said abruptly, in response to my queries about his father. "I know little to nothing of my father's activities in France. I doubt that I can be of any assistance to your client." I felt as if I were painting a picture, and my initial rough concept was too abstract for Peter. As I layered on more detail, the picture became compelling. I could feel it in the sudden silence on the other end of the phone. But as if not wanting to contradict his initial declaration of uninterest, he cleared his throat and spoke tightly.

"You oversaw the Turner restoration at the New York Club, didn't you?" It sounded more like an accusation than a question. I confessed. "Yes, well, nicely done," he said in a tone like an English aristocrat. "I suppose I could spare you a few moments. I'll transfer you back to my secretary to make an appointment." Peter's secretary asked if I could come to see him Saturday, at his home.

I was amused at the avid interest Amy had developed in the case. She told me it was probably all the Agatha Christie books she'd read as a girl, not to mention her curiosity about Sam. When I phoned her about my appointment to meet Sam's son, she practically begged to come along, like Felix doing figure eights in front of the treat cupboard. (If sheer determination counted for anything in this world, he'd grow a thumb and open it himself.) I could foresee no harm in taking her along—besides, she had known Peter's father. It might make the meeting a little easier. I invited her to come for the weekend; we'd visit Peter together on Saturday.

In the taxi on the way to Peter Popinski's, Amy sat craning her head up to admire the beautiful brownstones beribboned with wrought iron. We drove slowly past a cluster of designer shops—Ralph Lauren, Prada, Gucci, Fendi.

"Oh my God!" Amy exclaimed, tugging my arm. "Armani Junior? Really? What do you think a kid's tee shirt costs in there?"

"A lot." I could see the cabbie looking back at us through the mirror with a knowing smile.

"Where you from?"

I was offended at having been taken for a tourist and answered with a slight edge to my voice. "New York." After a pause, I added, "My friend is from Michigan." The cabbie nodded and quickly swerved to cut around a bus.

We exited the cab in front of a high-rise apartment building on the Upper East Side. The doorman was expecting us and tipped his head politely when I gave my name. Nodding toward the elevators, he said, "Go right on up. Mr. Popinski is on 39." The apartment occupied an entire floor, so when the elevator doors opened, we found ourselves in a large, lavishly decorated entryway.

Amy whispered, "This is about the time the butler comes out to take our coats and walking sticks." Just then a middle-aged man came through the door at the other end of the vestibule. Short and slightly balding, he wore a white Oxford shirt, open at the neck, gray flannel slacks and burgundy penny loafers that looked soft as velvet. After introducing himself as Peter Popinski and accepting our condolences, Peter led us into a large drawing room. Or that's how I thought of it. Not just a living room, or front room, as they called it when I was growing up. This was an enormous room with furniture and paintings and plants and pillows and knick-knacks—or more appropriately, collectibles. There was a silver tea tray on a low table surrounded by silk-covered chairs. I wondered where the servants were. Because, clearly, there were servants. I looked around for a long velvet tasseled rope hanging somewhere to summon them. Probably these days it was an app—Beckon-a-Butler.

Peter was pouring tea for himself, coffee for Amy. "Mr Ames?" he inquired.

"Coffee, please." I thought Amy was looking a little nervous. Maybe it was the sumptuous surroundings. They used to make me nervous, too, but at this point in my career, I'd dealt with lots of clients whose money outpaced their taste. As we settled back into our chairs, holding our cups, Peter crossed one leg over the other and I noted that he was sock-less, an affectation of the wealthy of certain Brooks Brothers enclaves. I imagined it was supposed to look like you had just come in off the yacht or something. The penny loafers contained no pennies. Nor gold doubloons.

"Well, Mr. Ames," Peter Popinski interrupted my shoe speculation, "perhaps you can give me some idea of why you are here."

"Please, call me Robert. As you know, I'm an art historian. In addition to work such as the restoration I did for your club, I occasionally take on assignments that involve searching for a particular piece of art. As I mentioned on the phone, my client also asked me to find out what had happened to a man she had known in Paris in 1944. Your father."

"Why?" Peter asked bluntly. "Forgive me, but knowing of my wealth, people often come out of the woodwork thinking I owe them something."

I put down my coffee cup and leaned forward. "Think about those times, Peter—may I call you Peter?" Peter nodded. "This young girl's parents had disappeared, along with many of the family's valuables. Her family's art gallery had been Aryanized. That's what they called it when—"

Peter interrupted. "I know what that means. I do read. In fact, I'm fairly well versed in Second World War history, having acquired an interest in what my father's experiences might have been like, since he never spoke of those times."

"Sorry." He was pricklier than the waiters at Le Bernardin when I asked for tartar sauce. I went on. "After fleeing to the United States and trying to forget the horrors of the war, after building a new life and raising her children, my client has started to look back. And her memories include falling in love with your father. At least, I strongly suspect that your father is that man. He mentioned something about France when I saw him at Friendly Village."

Peter stared at me in the silence that ensued. Amy reached forward to place her cup and saucer on the tea tray, the cup rattling loudly against the saucer. "What is it this client of yours wants?" Peter asked suspiciously.

"Merely to know what happened to Sam. She said she hopes to find that he had a good life."

Suddenly Peter turned to Amy. "I'm sorry, and how do you factor into all of this?" he asked.

Amy gave me a look, then said, "I was your father's psychologist at Friendly Village." She hesitated.

"Amy has kindly volunteered to help me. We thought she might also be able to answer any questions you have about your father's last days."

"Oh," Peter said, his rigid face suddenly slackening. "You know, during this past year, dad was pretty out of it. He was rambling the last time I saw him and not making much sense. Did you see him often?" he asked Amy.

"Weekly. But as you noted, in the past few months, I was treating him for depression, and he would often sit and refuse to say anything. Or insist that I didn't know him. And ask for you. Or someone named Nat. Is that a relative?"

"I don't know anyone by that name," Peter replied, leaning forward in his chair and resting his chin on his hands. "I wish I'd moved dad closer after my mother died, but he was comfortable there and—"

Amy interrupted. "You did what you thought best," she said firmly. "Your father and your mother had many friends at the Village. It was only in the last few months that he changed." I admired the professionalism with which she lifted Peter's guilt from his shoulders.

I didn't see a tassel pulled or button pushed, but a servant came in and switched out the coffee pot.

"The paintings you mentioned on the phone," Peter said, turning his attention to me. "Tell me about them."

The art that hung on the walls of the apartment was obviously from some of the high-end New York galleries. Peter was clearly a collector. "To my client," I explained, "it's an issue of justice. The paintings were stolen from her family and have emotional connotations. But to others they're merely works of art that could fetch millions of dollars from the right collector, someone who wouldn't ask about provenance. So it's possible they're hiding in private collections, museums even."

"Perhaps even here on my walls?" Peter raised an eyebrow.

"Hopefully not!" I laughed, a little uncomfortably, but doing a quick scan of the walls again. All post-1960.

Peter reached over and refilled the coffee cups.

"So, did my father have a good life?" Peter repeated my earlier question. "I'd say he did. After the war—and he did spend time in France, by the way—he came back to the family farm, married a local girl, and had a family—myself, my sister Katherine. My grandmother and my Great Uncle Steve lived with us until their deaths. Dad had a little antique shop for a few years. Both he and my mother enjoyed taking trips and shopping for things at estate sales, junk stores, etc. Eventually they sold that and moved to Friendly Village. He always seemed pretty happy to me."

"Do you have any idea what happened to your father in France, once he left Paris?"

"He wouldn't talk about the war. Just clammed up tight anytime I asked him anything. So, no, I have no idea what went on in France."

"Did your father have any buddies from the war that he kept in touch with? Someone who might be able to shed some light on what happened after he left Paris?"

"No, he didn't. I asked him once why he was never in touch with anyone he'd served with, and he said he didn't want to be reminded of those days. That the minute he came back, he wanted to put the war and everything associated with it behind him, to start afresh."

"Understandable." There was a pause as we each imagined what hell a returning soldier might want to forget. I continued. "Well, do you know what regiment or division he served with? Maybe I could find someone who served with him."

"Hold on a minute, let me go get dad's old dog tags. I've got a box of things he asked me to keep for him after he moved to Friendly Village."

As soon as Peter left the drawing room, Amy stood up and walked over to the fireplace. I followed her. An array of family pictures framed in ornate silver lined the mantel. "Here," she said. "This must be the family back on the farm. And here's Peter as a boy; that must be his sister Katherine being held by her mother. And the man holding Peter's hand, who do you think that is?"

Gliding over the soft carpets behind them, Peter spoke softly. "That's my father."

Amy looked at me, wide-eyed. The young man in the picture looked absolutely nothing like the Iowa farm boy staring out, wide-eyed, from the Green River newspaper.

# 13

## KENNETH

March 1945, Outside of Cologne, Germany

The MFAA (Monuments, Fine Arts and Archives) had been created by an order signed by General Dwight D. Eisenhower himself, at the urging of a group of American and British museum directors concerned for the fate of Europe's cultural treasures. But it didn't take me long to discover that the support just about ends there. We have maybe a dozen MFAA officers in total, each attached to a different army unit and working virtually alone to identify and protect buildings and artifacts. Most army officers consider us nuisances. I've had to pull out a copy of Eisenhower's letter on more than one occasion and quote these sentences.

*Inevitably, in the path of our advance will be found histor-ical monuments and cultural centers which symbolize to the world all that we are fighting to preserve. It is the responsibility of every commander to protect and respect these symbols when-ever possible.*

I get it. These men are fighting for their lives and have seen their friends killed. They're not interested in saving a painting. But we do our best, usually with no guards or vehicles, hitch-hiking from one place to the next. Most are like me, an academic, a museum director, playing soldier in my uniform, with a gun at my hip. But we are like mama bears, who would do anything to protect our cubs.

Yesterday I walked toward a village outside of Cologne, looking for a church that had been built in 1066. According to my information, it housed a pair of exquisite marble cherubim flanking the alter. After some time of torturous walking through rubble, I saw stone walls ahead. As I approached, I could see that one wall and part of the roof had caved in. The inside of the church was deep in the stones that men had once so laboriously lifted to the sky to glorify their god.

Heart sinking, I made my way into the church, wondering how stable the remainder of the roof was. Pews had been shoved up against the doors and spent cartridges littered the floor. Apparently, the church had been occupied at one point by retreating German soldiers. Had the damage come from Allied bombs? Or had the Germans blown it up themselves, in accordance with Hitler's "Nero Decree" that stipulated nothing of value was to be left intact for the enemy? At the east end of the church, behind a huge, fallen roof beam, something gleamed. It was one of the cherubim, nearly covered with gray grit. I blew lightly onto its face, carved into an expression of love so out of sync with this time and place as to make me dizzy; and yet, a twinge of hope speared the dark pit my soul had become. Wasn't this why I was here? So that others might behold such expressions of the human spirit and be given hope? Angling to the left, I searched for the other cherub, beyond more roof beams and a tremendous pile of rubble and dust. Piece by piece, I lifted roofing tiles, chunks of masonry and splintered wood from a pile until I could see the second figure lying amid the wreckage.

One of its tiny, graceful hands had separated from its wrist in a clean break and lay next to its body. It could be saved. I went outside, sat on a pile of stones and lit a cigarette. Several men in priests' robes slowly approached from a half-destroyed structure adjacent to the church. One of the priests said something in German, and I recognized the word help. With my broken German and sign language I communicated what we needed: mattresses, ropes, long boards and strong fabric. And, most importantly, a safe place. Where could the cherubim be stored until I could get a truck and a driver? The priest motioned me toward the building where he and the others had been hiding. Indeed, the basement of the building was cave-like, with rock walls and a roof of heavy wooden beams.

We lifted the fallen statue enough to slide a fabric sling beneath it, two of the men stood at each end and slowly raised the sling by the boards to which they had attached it. I bent low and watched, to ensure that the fabric would not give way under the weight of the sculpture. Then, cradling the tiny, broken hand, I led the way out of the church to the narrow stairway of the adjacent building. Once in the basement, we lowered the sling onto the mattresses that had been set on the floor, then slid the sling out from underneath the cherub. Additional mattresses were placed on top and roped down. Heaving a sigh of relief, I headed back to the church. In like manner, we moved the second statue.

I have no idea how long the cherubim will have to stay buried in that dark basement. The heavy equipment details will need to bulldoze roads through the village before I can get a truck here. For two statues. In one ruined village. At times I despair—the task is so daunting, the progress so slow. But then, I gaze into the face of an angel and know my work is important.

# 14

## NICOLE

Our family had been secular. While we had celebrated some of the Jewish holidays with friends, we did so the way many people celebrate Christmas, with the food and the rituals but none of the religious beliefs. During the war, I felt more connected to other Jews than ever before, because they were the only ones who could understand what I was going through. Later, many survivors were determined to keep alive the culture the Germans had tried so hard to kill. But after moving to New York, marrying a non-Jew and trying to build a new life, I didn't connect with the Jewish community. I wanted to forget. And I was afraid to have my children labeled.

In 1942, when the Nazis issued a command that all Jews wear a yellow star, I had mixed emotions about it. On one hand, to wear it was to acquiesce to the Germans' power, to single myself out for myriad and growing humiliations—taking the back carriage of trains, standing at the end of lines, shopping only between certain hours, keeping out of parks and libraries. On the other hand, not wearing it felt cowardly and a rejection of my identity. There was also the not-inconsequential fact that being caught not wearing it could mean imprisonment and deportation.

The first day, I waited until I was away from the apartment and Madame Vaillaud's prying eyes before putting on the jacket to which I had affixed the star. Suddenly I felt as if a spotlight were following me along the street. Some people looked at me sidelong, then quickly averted their eyes. An older woman and her daughter passed, and the woman sneered "Jew" as I walked by. A middle-aged man came up to me, smiled gently and took my hand. "Courage, mademoiselle. One day we will all have our revenge."

I learned how anyone who's perceived as "different" feels as they walk down the street. It's one of the reasons I later became involved in the issue of civil rights.

Until the order to wear the star, I'd been flying under the radar, more or less. Roland had never asked for my papers. If he suspected I was Jewish, he knew it was in his interest to look the other way. One day, I forgot to take the jacket off before entering the gallery. Roland frowned. "Don't wear that in here. It'll make the customers uncomfortable." He fumbled with some papers on the desk in the office, lowered his eyes and mumbled, "Don't wear it. Ever." I removed my jacket and laid it across a chair so that the star did not show.

On the way home from the gallery, I noticed a small crowd outside an apartment house. A police van stood in the street, blocking the traffic while a family was herded into the van by gendarmes. They wore yellow stars—a mother, a father and a small girl with a tear-streaked face. A woman among the on-lookers said, "Well, they must have done something."

It was about a month ago that I received the envelope bearing a UK postmark. I examined it curiously. I didn't know anyone there, and yet this was hand-addressed. The name above the return address meant nothing to me. But when I read the sender's description of her father, I pictured him instantly, as if I'd seen him just yesterday. I'd never known his name. He was a British parachutist I'd met when he was trapped in occupied Paris. He'd asked his daughter to find me and thank me for helping him.

It all began one day when a lawyer walked into the gallery and asked about Papa. Startled tears diffused my sight, and I bent my head to blink them away, smearing a bill of sale. The lawyer extended a gnarled hand to cover mine.

"There are many of us praying for him, my dear. People you have never met. He is a strong man. He will come back to you. Have faith."

I looked into the washed-out blue of his eyes and saw not only kindness but conviction. The lawyer explained that, because the business took me all over the city, I could help those who had not given up, who were not willing to sit back and wait for an Allied landing. I assented immediately, as if it were an answer to a prayer I had not even formulated. I would have a purpose! Doing something behind the backs of the vipers I worked with every day.

Thereafter, a careful observer of the Galerie Patriotique at lunchtime would have wondered at the nature of our clientele. Persons from all walks of life were likely to enter, casting surreptitious glances backward before pulling on the brass knob. A postman from the twelfth arrondissement; a big-haired blonde waitress who worked at a bistro in the eighth; a rumpled, bespectacled professor from the Sorbonne; and a plumber in his workman's dark-blue shirt and trousers—these were the ones I met most frequently, while Roland was out for one of the many leisurely lunches he could afford to take, now that I kept things running so efficiently.

For the most part, I delivered coded messages. Someone would come in while Roland was out, someone who did not look like an art collector. This person would give me an address and a short sentence that appeared either banal or gibberish. Nothing was written down. I was to memorize the address and the phrase and, as soon as possible, visit the address, ask for "Sebastian" and repeat the phrase. Most times men came to the door, but sometimes "Sebastian" turned out to be a woman. The addresses were all over the city, from the sumptuous apartments on Île Saint-Louis to the ghettos of the Marais and the brothels of Montmartre.

One particularly bright day, I noticed the postman skulking outside the door and signaled to him that I was alone. He rushed in, sweat dripping from his forehead. He kept pushing up the glasses that slid down the oily slope of his nose.

"Something has happened," he hissed. "Can you get away this afternoon?"

I thought for a moment. A new shipment had arrived at the Jeu de Paume and Roland wanted me to go identify the best pieces. I'd tell him I should go this afternoon.

"Oui, I think I can."

The postman told me to meet two men at the corner of Boulevard Saint-Germain and Rue de Buci at 3:00 and keep them busy walking around the city until five o'clock, when I was to meet a contact under the Eiffel Tower and transfer the men to his custody.

"Who are these men?" I asked.

"Downed British pilots. They speak no French, so we can't leave them on their own, but the transportation will not be ready until five. One of our agents has disappeared, which is why we must ask this of you."

My skin prickled. Up until that moment, I hadn't thought much about the danger of my activities. I'd been proud and vengeful. Wandering around Paris asking for "Sebastian" and repeating silly phrases seemed rather tame. But wandering around Paris with British soldiers—now that was definitely grounds for execution. Still, I couldn't refuse. What sort of life did I have anyway, with my parents in prison, perhaps even deported to Germany, my home inhabited by a criminal, and the hearts of everyone around me corroded by fear? For a moment, terror dizzied me, and I wished I'd never become involved with these people. But then, it had been fear that had made me resist leaving France. And where had that gotten me?

"I'll do it. Don't worry," I told the postman, who gave an attempt at a smile and exited as quickly as he had entered.

When Roland returned, I suggested I'd better go tag some of the new paintings at the Jeu de Paume before the other dealers had a chance. The choicest pieces would already have been reserved for Hitler or Göring, but that left plenty of exquisite artworks to be picked over.

"Oui, oui, you should hurry there, absolutely," Roland replied, smiling guilelessly. I threw on my black woolen coat, sans the yellow star. Roland had made it clear I was not to wear it while doing business for the gallery. I grabbed my handbag and walked as nonchalantly as I could out the door. The sky was low and thick with wads of sodden clouds, but although they threatened, they did not break. The streets were dry and the wind had a bite. I cursed my forgotten scarf. My old black stockings warmed my legs. I stopped for a moment to pull my gloves out of my handbag and slip my cold fingers inside them. There were few cars on the street—gasoline was prohibited to ordinary citizens—but the bicycles were thick, steered by a dark and mufflered crowd. German soldiers peppered the avenues, looking smug and well fed.

I went to the Jeu de Paume first, and quickly tagged a number of paintings for Roland, leaving there just before 3:00. I hurried along the narrow, uneven sidewalk, staying close to the stone walls interspersed by shop windows doing their best to display their meager goods. Adrenalin-fueled energy made me want to run, but I couldn't risk drawing attention to myself. So I walked fast, purposefully, with my head down as most others did. Eyes did not meet; casual words were not exchanged. Fear was the unspoken dialogue.

As I turned the corner at Rue de Buci, a break in the clouds illuminated a café, where a few hardy souls sat bundled up outside with their coffees and newspapers. Up past a few more shops to Boulevard Saint-Germain. To the east were Café de Flore and Les Deux Magots, well known just a few short years ago as the stomping grounds of artists and performers, now much quieter and often frequented by German soldiers getting their taste of Paris. As the occupation dragged on, more and more artists fled, either to the South or to London or New York; others stayed close to home and worked quietly, declining to participate in shows. But I knew of others—collaborators, who traveled to Germany to perform—who ate well and had no lack of supplies.

As a girl, I'd often passed by the cafés and pictured myself there, reciting poems to handsome fellow artists over coffee or wine. Jews were no longer allowed. The future I had dreamed of was no more solid than the clouds overhead.

I shifted from foot to foot at the traffic light, unsure which corner was the meeting place. Suddenly, I saw two men across Boulevard Saint-Germain, noticeably taller than average and wearing ill-fitting clothes. One wore a beret pulled low over his forehead, the other had a scarf wrapped up around his neck and covering the lower part of his face. A German soldier was crossing the road toward them from the east. I dodged a couple of bicycles to cross against the light and ran up to the men, laughing loudly.

"Ah, mes amis!" I spoke in French. "I am so sorry to be late! Let us hurry to Claude's apartment. He will be upset with us if we are much later." With that greeting, I threw my arms around the shoulders of the men and hurriedly began walking away from Boulevard Saint-Germain, down Rue du Four. A half-block away, I introduced myself in English as Mademoiselle Vrai, as I had been instructed.

The man with the beret scratched his forehead, exposing his carrot red hair. "Very good to meet you, mademoiselle. Well done. Let's just say our names don't matter." The other man laughed tensely. Their faces were weathered and although young, their eyes were old. One limped slightly.

"Is it painful?" I asked, pointing to his leg.

"No, mademoiselle, all healed up, I'm glad to say. Going to stay this way."

"In that case, I've been instructed to walk you around the city for a couple hours. We don't want to sit in one place too long."

I turned down Rue Mabillon to Place Saint-Sulpice. "Have you been to Paris before?"

"No," said the beret-wearer. The other man shook his head.

"Well, then, I shall be your tour guide."

For the next two hours, I showed the men the sights of my city, staying off the main roads as much as possible. We approached Notre Dame via Pont de l'Archevêché, then crossed to Île Saint-Louis before heading across Pont Louis-Philippe. From Rue de Valois we caught a glimpse of the Louvre, skirting the Jardin des Tuileries along Rue de Rivoli. Then up Rue de Castiglione, passing Place Vendôme, to reach the famous Opéra Garnier. The clouds parted and the gilded statues on the roof, representing Harmony and Poetry, glinted like hope itself—just as they had in 1870 during the Franco-Prussian war.

The men looked exhausted, so I found a busy café where they were unlikely to be noticed. I ordered coffee and baguette sandwiches all around, again using a loud, confident voice. "It's my treat!" I exclaimed as if cutting off their attempts to order. "I insist! We'll all have coffee and jambon et fromage baguettes," I instructed the waiter. Still, we were all nervous, ate and drank quickly, and I threw some francs down on the table as we left.

In the same manner, we saw the Arc de Triomphe and, finally, the Eiffel Tower. On a bench beneath the tower at 5:00, I could feel the sweat begin to chill my body. It had been a long day, and what if this agent, too, did not show up? What in the world would I do with these men? How could I possibly protect them? I was only a girl—I should be studying art, not trying to protect British soldiers, afraid for my life.

"Mademoiselle?" the limping soldier addressed me. "We cannot thank you enough for helping us this afternoon. We know you were not supposed to be the one. But look at us. Without your help we would have been spotted in an instant. We're going back to Britain, and I promise we'll come back to liberate Paris one day."

I relaxed and smiled. These men risked their lives every day in ways I could not imagine. Something—fate, destiny or the mere random waves of history—had brought the three of us together this afternoon and I would never forget them. Each reached out and took my hand in turn, as a slight, balding man in a dark trench coat approached us.

"Mademoiselle Vrai?" he enquired.

"Oui."

"Merci. I will take over from here."

"Merci beaucoup. Au revoir, messieurs."

"Goodbye, mademoiselle."

It was the daughter of the red-haired parachutist who had reached out to thank me so many years later.

---

I was walking past the Alhambra when I felt a huge paw land on my shoulder. I turned to see Maurice, who kissed me on both cheeks and pulled me inside to a table where Roger and Jean sat, deep in conversation.

"Look who I found!" Maurice exclaimed, as the others rose and embraced me. Jean took me by both shoulders and looked searchingly into my eyes. "What do you hear of André?" I shook my head and felt the tears begin to rise. "Don't worry," he said. "André is strong and smart. He will outwit those fools, you'll see." I caught a glimpse of Roger's discouraging grimace before he rearranged his face into a smile and accompanied it with an encouraging nod. They insisted that I join them for a glass of wine.

"Although I really can't afford another drink here," Marcel complained, lifting his empty wine glass to his nose and sniffing morosely. "Good stuff, though."

"Oh, come on. We're celebrating!" Roger said, tugging at his mustache. "At last, the Americans are finally in it. What with that and Hitler's insane decision to attack Russia, the odds have turned in our favor, I'd say."

"Anyway," Jean said, motioning for the waiter. "It's on me. This is the place where all the dirty deals are done, and I need to see who's in town right now. Rumor has it that... well, never mind, you don't need to know. But I need to stay a little longer and I can't be here alone. Big-time art dealer like me!" His laugh was without mirth. He ordered another bottle for the table.

"I went to see the Breker show." Marcel and Jean stared at

Roger after this remark. "Well, I wanted to see what all the fuss was about. Hitler's favorite sculptor and all."

"And?"

"If big were any measure, then you'd have to say he's great! But although the sculptures are executed technically well enough, they're really just monumental figures derived from classicism. But the mere size is imposing. You stand there and feel a sense of awe, just because they're so much bigger than you are. It's effective, albeit rather simplistic."

"Right. The myth of Aryan power and superiority. Breker's one of the best propagandizers they've got." Jean shook his head in disgust.

Marcel leaned forward and lowered his voice. "I heard they melted down some of our own bronzes so he could cast his. While most artists here... I can't even find paint anymore. I'm becoming quite the expert with charcoal."

"When we win, that man will be hanged among all the rest," Jean swore vehemently.

Marcel and Roger were surprised by his sudden outburst.

"But isn't he just an artist doing what artists do? Is it his fault that Hitler likes him? I wish I had a wealthy patron like Hitler to buy paints for me."

Jean reached across the table and grabbed the front of Marcel's shirt, pulling him halfway across the table. "Don't ever say a thing like that again."

People around us were looking. Roger quickly stood and pulled Jean's hand away from Marcel's shirt, staggering a bit as if he were drunk. "Ahh, my friends," he yelled loudly, "stop arguing! No woman is worth it! Right?" He looked over at the German soldiers at the next table, who nodded and laughed and went back to their drinks. "Now kiss and make up! Come on!"

"Quick," he hissed into my ear, "kiss each of them."

I leaned across the table and kissed Jean, then Marcel. They looked at each other belligerently. "Come on, now," Roger insisted. Jean and Marcel kissed cheeks. People at the nearest tables applauded.

Marcel smoothed down the front of his shirt. "Sorry, Jean, you know I didn't mean anything."

"I know. It's just that, well, I'm a little tense today. A couple of our men were captured."

"Oh, no. Have they been...?"

"Not yet. They're being held in Fresnes. But we all know what happens to suspected Résistance members."

"Jean," Roger began awkwardly, "I hate the Germans as much as anyone, but I have to ask you: When the Résistance kills a single German, they retaliate by executing ten, twenty, a hundred innocent civilians. Where is the sense? One German is not going to make a damn bit of difference, and you know there will be horrific retribution."

Jean put down his glass and leaned across the table. "What they are doing is blackmail, it's terrorism; these are war crimes and it's naïve to think that going along, just living like the half of Paris who pretend it's 1938, is any sort of response. People are being killed. Every day. In massive numbers. Those executed in response to a German death are merely more visible."

Jean looked as if he could be discussing an accounting anomaly, unless you looked into the flatness of his gray eyes. One had the sense of suppressed fire behind them. He continued. "I want at least this: that a German walking the streets of Paris does not feel as if he's on vacation in the City of Light. I want a German walking the streets of Paris to be afraid. To know that there are plenty who hate him and what he stands for and will kill him if offered half the chance. You see, that's why people like Breker are not innocent. Maybe a little less guilty than the SS officers or the functionaries who send thousands of Jews to their deaths but not innocent. His work supports the regime. His work helps the Nazis convince the German people that they're better than everyone else and that they have a duty to exterminate the lesser ones. Breker consorts with Hitler. They're friends. Did you know he lives on the Île Saint-Louis in the former home of the American Helena Rubinstein? It was Aryanized and put at the disposal of Breker."

"What happened to her?"

"Oh, I don't know. I think she went back to America."

"I did hear that Breker helped Picasso out with Hitler," said Marcel.

"What do you mean?"

"Oh, just that Picasso was caught in some kind of currency deal—sending money back to Spain, I suppose—and Breker interceded with Hitler to keep him from being arrested."

"Right," Jean said, his eyebrows knitting together. "Amazing how as the war turns against the Germans so many collaborators are finding people to help balance their scales later. We've even had some well-known collaborators approach us wanting to help. And did you know some of our very own POWs and citizens have joined up with the Germans on the eastern front? Apparently, fascists are more loyal to fascism than to their own country." He made a spitting motion to show what he thought of these eleventh-hour converts. "You better believe when the price of collaboration comes due, Breker will make sure everyone knows how he saved Picasso."

Being with Papa's friends made me miss him even more. I wanted to go home with him and further the conversation. What would Papa think about artists continuing to work? If Hitler was fond of their work, did that make them traitors?

Things that had once seemed so simple now seemed a muddy mess.

Roger gazed down into his glass. "I saw them," he said quietly.

"Who?"

"The Jews being put on the buses yesterday." Roger lifted his glass and finished the wine with a grimace. "I saw them."

Marcel and Jean waited.

"Men in suits, women in hats, children clutching teddy bears, all dressed up as if to say, Look, look at us, we're civilized, we're respectful, we're no trouble, you don't need to feed us to your death machine." Roger's voice quavered.

Marcel twisted his fists together, and this time his eyes were not inscrutable but glittered with rage. "Jean, there has to be more we can do. What's the Résistance waiting for? A little bomb here, a dead policeman there. It's not enough! If every Parisian went out and killed one of them right this minute, we'd be free! Surely, after all that's happened, we could find lots of guys like me, ready to fucking kill with my bare hands. How long do we have to sit around waiting?" Marcel asked in a growl.

"You needn't sit around, Marcel. I've always had things for you to do. Come by my apartment tomorrow. You too, Roger, if you're up for it." Jean turned to me with an almost imperceptible wink.

During the time that I worked with Roland, I detested him. I considered that he had stolen our gallery and was a despicable collaborator. After the war, the Allies tried to divide up the collaborators and war criminals into different categories. I suppose Roland would've been what they called a "fellow trav-eler." That is, he did not actually plot or pave the road to hell, but he rode it as long as it served his interest. He was a crook and a manipulator. I don't think he harbored any resentment toward Jews; after all, he let me work there, because I was useful to him. No, Roland saw an opportunity to rise to a level of crime substantially more profitable than the petty thievery he'd been engaged in before the war. And, under German rule, what he did wasn't criminal at all.

Over time, Roland took my presence for granted, so that I was more like a piece of furniture than a human being. That's how it happened that, one day, I overheard him talking about confiscating an art collection.

"Yes, yes, I know!" he was saying. "But we have to get the information before they do. Otherwise, the entire collection will be seized by the Germans and go straight to the Jeu de Paume, with all the best pieces going to those greedy bastards, Göring and Posse."

Here Roland paused while his visitor, a short, stocky man wearing a cloth workman's cap, mumbled a response that I couldn't quite hear. I was in the office, filing paperwork and memorizing transactions to record later in my notebook. Roland and the other man, who worked for a moving company that specialized in fine art, stood in the center of the gallery.

"If your company didn't move the stuff, it must've been the family themselves. But no one knows where they are. I've heard their chauffeur is still around. Go see what you can learn from him. If he doesn't know where the art is, see if he can lead us to the family. If we threaten to expose their whereabouts, they'll tell us where they've hidden it. Make sure he knows it'll be worth his while to cooperate with us."

The family in question were the Steins, who had gone into

hiding as word of the latest round-up of Jews had spread. In hiding as well was their renowned collection of seventeenth- and eighteenth-century northern European art so favored by the Germans. If Roland could determine its whereabouts, he could trade this information for a finder's fee, which could be as much as twenty-five per cent of the value of the collection, or a number of paintings he could sell. I'd learned that it was because of such dealings that Roland had been awarded owner-ship of the Cassin Gallery. He had betrayed a wealthy Jewish family to the Gestapo, who had confiscated their home and their art collection and then imprisoned most of the family.

The man from the moving company spun around and stalked out of the gallery, climbed up into his van and drove off. Roland came back toward the office, his face set in a frown. He didn't even notice me at the filing cabinets as he walked out the back door to the alley and stood there smoking. I wondered how to warn the Steins. My opportunity came at lunch, when the postman appeared in the doorway. Roland was gone and I quickly waved him in. After he whispered my assignment, I told him what I'd overheard earlier. "Merci," he said. "We will do what we can."

Later the same day, representatives from the Folkwang Museum in Germany arrived at the gallery to see the latest collection of paintings, which Roland had been able to purchase at extremely low prices from the ERR at the Jeu de Paume. He had immediately set aside a Holbein, one of Göring's favorites, to offer to the Reichsmarschall at a later time. Roland relied on me to discuss the artistic value of the pieces, having instructed me to say only that the works had become available because their owners had abandoned them when they left the country. My faith in humanity fell even further as I stared at these well-educated and sophisticated museum administrators, so eager to take advantage of a conquered and brutalized people. I made careful mental notes of each piece that the museum purchased, to be listed later in my notebook.

# 15
## ROBERT

In all the years that I'd visited the farm, I'd never brought a lover there. It was where I went to find peace. And peace had always meant solitude to me. It was a shrine to the carefree days of my boyhood, and that sense of boyishness always came back when I was there. Boyishness and selfishness, truth be told. A place where I didn't have to consider anyone else's wishes, or worse, try to show someone a good time. The women I had dated had all been New Yorkers; and, much as country places are romanticized among the urban denizens, I could imagine them after five minutes sitting on the porch looking out over the field, their legs crossed, one foot bouncing up and down, fingers itching for their phone, which would not find a signal. Maybe I hadn't been fair. But I also hadn't been interested enough to take the risk.

Amy was a Midwesterner and seemed less frantic, or maybe I just liked her more, but soon after we'd started seeing each other, I'd begun to picture her at the farm. I'd blurted out the invitation one night, after hours of alternately languorous and impassioned lovemaking. In the cell phone lot at

LaGuardia waiting for her text, I was having second thoughts. Could I make an excuse? Say I wasn't feeling up to it and we should just go to my loft instead? I thought about Jack and his barbs regarding my short-term relationships. If I wanted more out of this, I was going to have to trust her. Within five minutes of getting into the car, Amy asked, "Are you okay?"

Sometimes she was a little too intuitive. I didn't feel like being grilled and I hate that expression. People throw it around as if they really care, yet the only answer they really want to hear is, Yes.

"Just have my mind on the case." I was aware that if I didn't adjust my attitude, the weekend would turn out exactly the way I was afraid it would, and it would be my own fault. I inhaled deeply and exhaled slowly. "How was your week?"

"Well, do you want to hear about the patient who is cheating on his wife with her best friend, or the one who stole a pizza delivery boy's car, believing that God had left it there for him? Technically, I can't tell you about either of them, or I'd have to kill you." Amy laughed.

I'd discovered that Amy picked up all the latest slang and tropes from the young women who worked at Friendly Village. Sometimes her usage of pop culture phrases and jokes really annoyed me. She had even confessed to an addiction to a reality TV show called The Bachelor. I wished she'd try to be more serious.

"I'm sorry, darling," she said. "I can see you're in no mood for banter this morning. Do you have a nice CD we can listen to? Let's just look at the scenery." A sudden yowl erupted from the backseat. "Hello, Felix!" Amy reached back and stroked his ears through the bars of his crate. "No worries, fella, we'll be there soon." She pulled out a selection of Mozart pieces from the glovebox and slid it into the CD player. The music lifted me to another plane. As we drove out of the city in companionable silence, accompanied by the Mozart, I relaxed. What was my problem? The sun threw long shadows over the rolling hills and curvy roads. I glanced at Amy's profile, which was still both familiar and strange to me. She reached out and stroked my cheek, and I smiled.

As we rounded the last bend before turning into the drive that led to the farm, my spirits lightened. I was always euphoric at this point in the journey. I was possessed by this land, and yet nowhere else was I so free. I rolled down the window to inhale the scent of the air, so unmistakably of this place and yet so indescribable.

Amy sniffed, too, as we turned into the narrow, two-track driveway and bumped along the uneven, muddy lane past a fallow pasture on the right and a copse of evergreens on the left. Small patches of icy snow remained here and there. When the farmhouse came into view, she put her hand on my knee.

"Oh my God, it's exactly as I imagined. Classic. I can see why you love it so much. It's wild but not too wild. Homey. Inviting."

"I read about some researchers who were trying to find out what people's favorite type of painting was," I told her. "And it was (no surprise) realism. But rather than the realism of a wild, imposing mountain or a raging sea, people preferred farmsteads. Orchards, vineyards, neat rows of corn. Nature—but nature tamed, controlled. Less intimidating."

I parked in front of the porch and leapt out. Amy followed, catching my enthusiasm. I skipped up the stone steps to the wide porch, lifted a planter flanking the door, picked up a key and opened the door onto a small living room with wide plank floors. A cozy love seat and armchair, both covered with slouchy slipcovers of a silvery blue damask, sat adjacent to a small wood-burning fireplace. A low table strewn with magazines was the only other furniture in the room. Recessed lighting in the plaster ceiling demonstrated some accommodation to modernity.

After running out to retrieve a scolding Felix, I led Amy through the house—small kitchen with an oak table and four chairs, worn Formica counters that were pinkish with gold starbursts. "I couldn't bear to replace that," I said sheepishly. "They truly don't make it anymore—and maybe there's a reason!"

There was a half-bath off one end of the kitchen and a small bedroom off the other, a bedroom and bath upstairs. The upstairs bedroom contained a double bed covered with a yellow-flowered feather bed. "People used to lay on top of these to provide additional cushioning and warmth. I use it as a blanket, though." I could feel my boyishness breaking through the crust of my carefully honed intellectual persona. "Want to play hide and seek?"

"Let's just play find," Amy murmured, slipping her arms around me. I lost myself in her kiss and pressed my body greedily against hers. She raised one leg and wrapped it around me, and we fell back on the feather bed, sinking into its loft and finding each other again, hurriedly peeling off clothes until we were on our sides, pressed tightly together, skin to skin. I drank in her scent of faint perfume and rubbed my chest across her bare breasts. She rolled over onto her back and I stared intently into her black eyes, then gazed down the length of her body to her navel, bending to graze it with my tongue before parting her legs with my knee and lowering myself down. Her arms clasped my shoulders as she raised her hips to meet me.

---

The day after our arrival I rose at the first inkling of light. I'm always like this at the farm. It's like I'm dreaming about being here and then I wake up and I can't believe I really am here. Getting up is the equivalent of pinching myself. I brushed Amy's forehead with my lips and then went down to make coffee. I put two chipped white china cups on the counter before heading out to the barn. I planned to replace some of the rotted planks over the weekend. One rotted plank ignored became enough rotted planks to send the barn leaning sideways. After that, it would just be a matter of time and weather before the loft builders from the city descended like a horde of dung beetles. Although it was used for little but storing some of Grandpa's old implements, I was determined that this barn would remain upright as long as I did. After marking the boards that needed replacing, I headed back in for coffee.

There was only one mug on the counter. I filled it and listened, thinking Amy might have gone back upstairs for a shower. Then I noticed the door to the small bedroom off the kitchen, which I used as my painting room. It was open. I crossed the kitchen quickly. Hadn't I shut that before showing Amy the house? She stood in front of my easel in a thick white robe, cradling her coffee cup in both hands. I reached in front of her and ripped the unfinished painting from the board. "What are you doing in here?"

Startled, Amy whirled to face me. "Why, I was just... I mean, I thought this was the bathroom!"

"Well, it's pretty obvious it's not, right?" I pointed toward the door. "The bathroom is at the other end of the kitchen."

Amy looked puzzled and glanced down at the crumpled painting that hung from my fist.

She put her hand on my arm. "What's wrong? Is that your painting? Because it's truly lovely. You've certainly no need to be embarrassed."

I looked into her eyes. They were innocent and hurt. She hadn't intended to pry. I was acting like an idiot. I really was going to have to stop being so defensive with her. I rumpled her hair.

"My fault," I said brusquely. "I usually keep that door shut. It's just a private little hobby of mine. I'd sort of like to keep it that way, okay?"

"Of course," she replied quietly, turning away.

Standing there with my ruined painting, I felt like an ass. I tried again. "It's not a big deal. Sometimes I paint. And no one knows about it. But now you do, so that's fine. I want you to know me. I do. Let me get my coffee and let's go sit on the porch."

We sat on the metal glider sipping our coffees while I tried to explain something I wasn't sure I even understood myself. "You see, I've loved the Old Masters for so long, I thought that by engaging in the act of painting, choosing colors, putting brush to paper, I'd somehow understand them better. And when I'm in that meditative state of painting, I know that they, too, were in that same space and I sense a connection with them. But I have no desire to be a Sunday painter, exhibiting my hobby at the farmers' market. So I paint, usually finish a piece in one sitting, and then burn it."

Amy looked shocked. "But that painting was exquisite. You'll destroy it?"

"Maybe it's weird, but it's how I pay homage to the Masters. I live for a little time in their space, and then I destroy my work. My day job is all about intellect and analysis and putting a price on things that are truly priceless. Not priceless as in stratospherically expensive but priceless as in they actually should have no price. So I create and then I destroy. Nothing is important but the process, the mindset, the meditation—being in the zone, as you might say—applying emotion to paper, with as little intellectual interruption as possible." I paused, feeling like I was meandering and spouting gibberish.

The morning chill of fog had not quite blown off and steam rose from my coffee. "Have you ever seen Goldsworthy's stuff?"

"Isn't he the guy who makes constructions out of natural materials—rocks, leaves, sticks and stuff?"

"Yeah. And it lasts until the next windy day."

"But people do see it. He photographs them. I've seen books of his work. But," Amy stopped and stared out across the fields. "Never mind. You needn't explain. I, of all people, ought to know that life doesn't always have to make sense. Emotions count, too. This is something you're passionate about and it's private. I totally respect that. Really."

I relaxed, realizing how tense I'd been trying to explain to her—and to myself—something that maybe didn't make much sense. I put an arm around her shoulders and kissed her neck. "Sorry for being a jerk. Forgive me?"

Amy rested her head on my shoulder. "Of course," she murmured. "You know one of my favorite quotes is from *Lady Chatterley's Lover*. It's near the end, when Mellors talks about how the masses have been educated to believe that living and spending are the same thing and how, instead, they should be educated to live. And then he describes a pagan society that sings and dances and makes art. Entirely for its own sake."

I considered this. A whole world of Sunday painters. What would be so bad about that?

That night in bed, Amy's head was turned away when I heard her quiet voice, almost disembodied. "About your paintings..."

"Yes?"

"Would you mind saying how you got into it? I mean, you don't have to if it's private, but I was just curious."

I suddenly felt like a patient on a psychologist's couch. I'd visited one as an adolescent, when my mother briefly worried about the very isolation she and my father had fostered with their absences. The man was a dolt, and I said the things required to earn me the "normal" stamp as quickly as possible. Truth is a gray area, as I see it, and not telling the complete truth does not mean one is lying.

Then I remembered the tinseled Christmas tree in my grandparents' living room, its soft lights the only illumination in the early morning when I pulled on the knitted slippers Grandma had made me and shuffled silently out of my bedroom to wait for my grandparents to rise. My mother would come by for dinner later, but all of my presents were there already, neatly wrapped in the same paper—blue with red Santas printed on it.

"My grandparents gave me a watercolor set when I was eleven or twelve," I began slowly. "Did you ever get a present you'd no idea you wanted? And then, when you opened it? You realized it was the only thing you wanted?"

It was our last day at the farm. We had a picnic lunch in the orchard, then strolled hand-in-hand back toward the house. Amy told me that she'd taken a couple of drawing classes at the local community college after she'd started working as a psychologist.

"I was terrible," she said ruefully, "but I really liked it. I wish I had had your sense that the finished product didn't matter. But I was so disappointed at how little my drawings resembled the objects we were supposed to be drawing that I quit going."

I kissed her hand. "I've got an idea. Let's bring my paints out to the porch and paint some landscapes." I'd never painted outdoors before, but suddenly I liked the idea.

Amy scrunched up her face. "But you're so good! You'll see mine and think I must've flunked out of kindergarten!"

"Now wait a minute. Remember? This is not about judgment, not about product, all about process. It'll be fun. You'll see."

I kind of surprised myself by making this suggestion. It went against everything that painting had been to me up to now. Serious, private. But I looked forward to painting with Amy and just having some fun with it.

I set us up on the porch, a board for each of us with paper taped to it, the paints and jugs of brushes and water between our chairs. I showed Amy the trick of spraying, then dirtying the paper and made up a palette for her from a plastic dinner plate.

"Pretty much everything I learned about painting, I learned from my grandfather. We'd go to museums together and stand in front of a painting while he described what made it great. Pretty soon, he started asking me to describe what I liked about a painting. What made it special."

I remembered standing in front of Copley's Watson and the Shark. "There was a painting of a boat, a man had fallen overboard, and a vicious shark with its mouth open was approaching him—"

Amy chimed in. "Hey, I know that painting! It's in the Detroit Institute of Arts. It always creeped me out."

"You're right. The DIA has a smaller version of the one in Washington. It terrified me but we would stand there as my grandfather prodded me to see beyond the horror—to see what made the horror palpable." I closed my eyes.

*The colors. What about the colors? my grandfather had asked.*

*The colors are kind of a sickly green, all muted and depressing. And the composition is circular, with the wave on the left circling to the right and the shark's fin on the right circling back to the left.*

*Anything else about the composition?*

*Yes, it's unusual that the man in the water and the shark, the most important parts of the painting, are both at the bottom of the picture.*

*And what does that accomplish?*

*It brings them right to you; it makes it more horrible.*

I opened my eyes to see Amy smiling at me. "Okay, let's pick a composition and start painting."

I showed her how to make a square with the thumb and forefinger of each hand and look through it to find a good composition. Then I quickly demonstrated how to mix colors and obtain different effects based on the wetness of the page.

"I'm going in to make some more coffee," I told her. "You just keep painting."

When I returned, Amy barely looked up. She was carefully applying a stripe of green in the middle of the page to represent the distant hills. I kissed the top of her head, then put her coffee on the arm of the chair, sat down next to her and picked up my board.

That evening, Peter Popinski called me. "Peter Popinski," I mouthed to Amy, covering the mouthpiece with my hand as I listened to Peter.

"My great-uncle Steve was like a father to my dad and a grandfather to Kath and I. While sorting through my father's papers, I found a box of Uncle Steve's things, including some letters from my dad. Letters talking about the war, things dad would never discuss after he got back. I dug them out and I think there may be a reference to your client in one of them.

There's something weird about them I'd like to discuss with you. Could we meet again?" Peter didn't sound like the authoritative hedge fund manager I'd met the last time. There was a hesitancy in his voice.

I raised my eyebrows and looked pointedly at Amy. "Yes, of course. When would you like me to come?"

"Could you possibly come tomorrow? I'm leaving for a conference in the Caymans the next day."

"Hold on a minute." I lowered the phone and cued up my calendar. "I can be there at 11:00. Does that work for you? Great. See you then."

"Well, there's been an interesting development in the case," I said, mimicking what I thought a tough detective might sound like and looking over the top of my glasses at Amy. Curled up on the sofa, she beckoned me over with a nod of her head.

"Come sit by me and tell me all about it."

"Peter found some letters his dad had written to his uncle and he thinks Nicole's mentioned in them. He wants to meet at 11:00 tomorrow, back in New York. What time is your flight back to Detroit?"

"12:26, give or take a minute! You can drop me at the airport early. Oh, I wish I could come with you! Promise to call me as soon as you get the skinny!"

Head bent low over the letter Peter had handed me, I silently read the large-penciled scrawl filling the pages.

# THE LOST WOMAN

*September 12, 1944*

*Dear Uncle Steve,*

*You were in the Great War, so I don't have to tell you how it is over here. Pretty bad is all. We claim a bit of ground, then dig in. I swear we just get a good trench dug and do what we can to make it dry and maybe actually get some sleep, and then we're ordered to move somewhere else. I've seen places I never thought I would, under circumstances I couldn't have imagined. I made some friends and I lost some. The hard way. Trying not to like anyone too much. Just keeping to myself, maybe a little talk about the weather or women. I finally get why all the old timers sit kind of off by themselves, don't say much. Don't pay to get close. The Jerries are real crazy fighters. We had them completely surrounded and they just kept fighting. I heard that they have orders not to surrender or they'll be shot by their commanding officers. After we mopped up there, I was assigned to secure a sector in Paris. Man, were those Frenchies happy to see us. And the dames? Running out into the streets and kissing us! You can just imagine how that made us filthy soldiers feel. Almost civilized. There's this one mademoiselle I met in an art gallery that I've been back to see a few times. She speaks real good English, and is very sweet—yet she's got some real moxie. She had to, to survive the occupation. Well, we've got the Krauts on the run now and it looks like my European tour will soon include Germany. I hear the bombing there has been intense. Everyone says it won't be long before they'll have to surrender. I sure hope so. Give my love to everyone.*

*Sam*

When I finished reading, I looked up at Peter where he stood near the fireplace staring at the family portraits. "What are you thinking, Peter? This mention of the girl and an art gallery must refer to my client."

Peter reached slowly into his jacket pocket and brought out an envelope from which he slipped a single, folded sheet. Unfolding it, he walked over to the sofa. "Yes," he agreed, "I think that's probable, but what intrigues me even more is, who wrote the letter?" He handed the sheet to me. "You see, this is a letter in my father's handwriting."

It took only a glance to see that the small, tight black letters written there were nothing like the penciled scrawl from Sam to his Uncle Steve.

"So if this letter was written by Sam Popinski during the war, who the hell was my father?"

I reached into the messenger bag lying next to me on the sofa. "I honestly don't know yet. But these are Sam Popinski's induction papers and the person in your family picture bears no resemblance to this photograph. So I searched around some more and was able to get a copy of Sam's demobilization papers. Here's a copy of the picture on those."

Peter reached for the papers. "Two entirely different people! But my grandmother must've known. And my great uncle, Steve. Why wouldn't they have said something? I am completely baffled."

"What's the date of the last letter from Sam?" I asked.

"October 1944."

"So," I said, thinking aloud, "sometime after October 1944, someone—your father, that is—adopted Sam Popinski's identity. The real Sam was probably killed." I wondered if, in fact, he'd been killed by Peter's father.

"I don't know," Peter said slowly, staring at the pictures. "My dad. I thought I knew him inside out. But now..."

"Did you ever meet any of his friends—maybe buddies from the war—or relatives?"

"You know, years ago, back when dad was about eighty, he told Katherine and I he wanted to go visit some relatives in the old country. We always thought we were Polish, but suddenly here we are, all getting ready for a trip to Russia! Russia, of all places! It was a surprise, but I didn't think much of it then. Never was one to be very interested in genealogy type stuff. So you had a relative who fought in the Civil War or something. So what?"

"What happened? I mean, did you go? To Russia?"

"Yeah, we did, Dad, mom, Kath and I. We went to Saint Petersburg and met one of dad's cousins. She was a poet and spoke excellent English. She and dad spent a lot of time together. Anyway, the rest of us took in the sights and after a week we flew to Paris and did the usual tourist stuff, then came home."

"Did your dad keep in touch with his cousin?"

"I wasn't aware of it at the time, but I found a letter in a chest in my dad's room, only it's in Russian."

"Do you think I could borrow it and have it translated? Maybe it would help us figure out who your dad really was."

"Of course. I mean, who was this man? A Russian who stole Sam's identity? But then why wouldn't the family have called the police when he showed up in Iowa posing as Sam? I just don't get any of it!"

"Me either. But this letter may help us figure it out. I'll have it translated immediately and call you when I have some news."

As I descended in the elevator, I found myself hugging the messenger bag containing the letter. I couldn't wait to tell Amy.

# 16

## NICOLE

Survival brooked no emotional outbursts. I didn't cry. I didn't laugh. I played a role at the gallery all day long, only letting my guard down at Gisèle's. And even there we didn't talk about Papa or Maman or Gisèle's husband. Sharing memories of them would have felt like memorializing the dead. So we spoke of food—where to get it, what to make—and occasionally a few snippets of our workdays; but those were fraught conversations, too, because each of us was doing things that couldn't be safely talked about.

I was just twenty-one in 1943 when Gisèle asked me to take care of her children if anything happened to her. I'd spent an exhausting day at the gallery, the mask of an enthusiastic and cheerful young woman constantly in danger of sliding off. Entering the flat, I dropped the pretense. I'd never realized what a luxury it was to be able to speak freely. Although Gisèle and I were careful not to say too much in front of Lisle, who was only fourteen, after she went to bed we often stayed up talking. Of course, I was hiding things from Gisèle, too. I didn't want to endanger her by telling her of my Résistance activities.

On this particular day, Gisèle was idly frying onions, reaching up to wipe a tear from her smarting eye. Her shoulder-length hair was tied back in a ribbon; a blue-striped apron partially covered her dun-colored skirt and sweater. Lisle was in her room reading.

"You know," Gisèle began, "there are groups. Small groups. Secret groups. Doing things. Resisting, they call it."

I looked up from the table quickly.

"I think," Gisèle continued, "it's a necessary counteraction to the collaborationist groups. But the punishment, if caught, is severe. You've seen the posters, the lists of the executed." Gisèle's voice shook slightly. She hesitated. "I just want to ask... I know it's a lot, but Lisle now thinks of you like a big sister. If anything were to happen to me..."

I leapt up from the table and put my arms around Gisèle's waist and hugged her tightly. "Oh, Gisèle! What are you up to? You know I would always do my best to protect Lisle. But a Jewish girl in Paris? Perhaps I'm not the most reliable choice."

We were both crying now. Softly, to not alarm Lisle.

"Gisèle, you'd better know. I'm helping one of those groups." Eliminating the details, I told Gisèle of my work as a messenger. "You see, they think a young woman running around the city is less noticeable than a man. There are, of course, fewer men since the war began and questions might be asked."

"I'm proud of you, my dear," Gisèle said, sinking into a chair at the table and folding her hands in front of her. "And I, too, am helping in my own small way. There are some of us at the Post Office. We intercept letters of denunciation, letters informing the Gestapo of the whereabouts of Jews, POWs or others at risk of imprisonment. We destroy them."

Although afraid for Gisèle, I was so proud of her, I covered her hands with mine. "Vive la France," I whispered.

"Vive la France," Gisèle replied.

We did as women had done for centuries before us. While men marched through the bloody fields of battle, plotted strategy from seats of power and sealed the fates of millions, we waited. And resisted.

———

Striding along the Champs-Elysées late one afternoon, a bitter wind caroming from one side of the street to the other, I butted forward, head down, arms clutched across my chest to close the hole where a button had been lost from my old black coat. I'd been chanting the message I had for "Sebastian," in this case supposed to be found in a shoe repair shop down an alley. The sound of my name on the wind brought me up short.

"It is you!" A young man touched my shoulder so I'd turn around, and then, before I could take stock, greeted me with a kiss on each cheek, and stepped back again to look at me. I had no idea who he was or how to react. He smiled at my lack of response but otherwise his expression was grim. "You're looking better than I am," he said. "I know, I've lost my boyish good looks!" It was very embarrassing. I couldn't disguise my lack of recognition.

Then it hit me. "François?" I blurted out. "No!" He'd been terrifically handsome at school. Now he was a lot thinner, and serious-looking. His thick chestnut hair flopped from one side of his face to the other in the wind.

Bits of paper skittered along the curb, and some dust churned up by a passing cyclist blew into my eye.

"Merde!" I bent my head and blinked hard while holding my lids apart. When I finally dislodged whatever it was and raised my head, François was slightly blurred, ghostly. I sighed. The flame of romance he had once inspired in me was so dead there wasn't even a spark left. I'd become an automaton whose only emotions were fear and rage.

"What are you up to these days?" François asked tentatively. Asking a question like this of anyone, especially a Jew, was likely to elicit an agonizing recital of terror. I didn't have the heart to go into it and doubted I would ever see him again anyway.

"Just trying to get by. And you? Still at the Sorbonne?"

"No. The exemption for students was eliminated. Now all of us are expected to sign up for the compulsory labor service."

"You'd be sent to Germany!" I was incredulous. Was no one to be spared?

"I know." François grimaced. "My brother is in hiding somewhere outside the city. I don't know what to do. How am I going to get out of the city? And what if I get caught? But if I go work in a factory in Germany, I'll be right in the middle of an Allied bombing target. And how would I get back?" He dropped his head and kicked a pebble, hands shoved deep inside his pockets. "Remember Luc?" I nodded. "He came back on leave from his labor service and said it was horrible. They were treated like slaves and didn't get enough to eat. He's in hiding now, too."

"You can't go," I said bluntly. "You can't trust anything the Germans tell you. You should hide."

"My dad thinks I should go. Says why should I escape hardship while so many Frenchmen are over there as POWs. I think he has some old-fashioned sense that it would make a man out of me!"

"And your mother?"

"As worried as she is about my brother, she tells me to hide. Like you, she thinks anything could happen in Germany."

"What about Albert and Serge? Do you know what's happened to them?"

"Albert went to Germany. Serge was captured by a gang of soldiers who shaved his head and beat him. They've got it in for the Zazous now. He hates the Germans with a passion and went into hiding. I think he might even be with the Résistance up in the hills." He paused. "It's hard to believe only a few years ago we were carefree students. Now we're all wise beyond our years. Painfully wise." He gazed into my eyes. "You be careful, Nicole. Do you have a place to hide if the time comes?"

I nodded, touched by his concern. "I'll be careful. I wish you luck, François. Please, whatever happens, take care of yourself."

François leaned down and kissed me, softly, sweetly, a kiss that spoke of what might have been. "Au revoir, mon amie," he whispered. And he was gone.

It was when I turned to continue on toward the shoe repair shop that I saw her. Or rather, I first noticed the soldier, tall and frightening in his black SS uniform but handsome, too, with thick blond hair visible beneath his cap and strong white teeth behind lips that were parted in a big grin. I instinctively hunched my shoulders, but the soldier had no eyes for anyone but the woman who clung to his arm and looked up at him, her blonde hair blown back from her face in the wind. Marie.

---

The day I was arrested began like so many others. Gloomy. The gallery devoid of customers, the paintings illuminated only by spotlights, the streets gray and deserted. Roland hadn't gone to lunch, so when the lawyer walked slowly by, I shook my head.

Then the long black car drew up, blocking what little light fell through the front door. My throat constricted and I looked at Roland. He quickly turned away and I knew they'd come for me. Two uniformed Germans came in and ordered me out of the office. Roland's head was buried in a filing cabinet. I walked slowly out to meet the soldiers. "May I help you?" I asked in French. Each man seized one of my arms and dragged me to the waiting car. I saw no reason to resist. It would be pointless. They shoved me into the back seat, then sat on either side of me. The driver pulled away.

I thought of Papa; first him, then Maman. This is what had happened to them. I was terrified and yet somehow relieved. The guilt of having been spared while they were imprisoned finally left me, as did the fear of arrest, and I sank back into the seat. My fate had finally caught up with me. I might be tortured, but I would not talk. I bit the inside of my cheek as hard as I could. No, if death were to come, it would come to me only. I vowed I would not bring any of the others down. I watched the buildings go by—shops I had visited with my parents, restaurants where we'd celebrated birthdays, the homes of friends. All lost.

The men had loosened their grips on my arms and were bantering in a jovial, comradely fashion. As if they were not taking a young girl to be tortured. I turned to the one on my right and stared. I caught his eye and he looked away quickly. We pulled up outside Fresnes and my heart lifted a bit. Was it possible I'd see Papa? At least learn what had happened to him?

I was tossed into a dank cell. After two days alone with nothing but a bucket of brackish water in the corner, I was weak from hunger and terrified that I would break. Listening to the intermittent screams from elsewhere in the prison, I pinched myself as hard as I could. What would I be able to withstand? What would they do? My imagination conjured up images too frightful to bear. I thought of killing myself and resolved to look for something to use when they took me out for questioning.

Suddenly, I heard a key in the lock. The door opened and a guard grabbed me by the arm and dragged me down the hall to another room. There was a barred window, through which seeped a glimpse of sky. The guard chained me to a chair behind a desk, then left. I'm not sure how long I sat staring at the concrete floor for signs of others who might have been tortured there. I remember being relieved not to see any blood. The walls were also of concrete and I began to shiver from the cold.

After some time had passed, the door opened and a soldier in the uniform of the SS came in, carrying a blanket. "You're cold," he said in French, as he arranged the blanket around my shoulders, giving me a kindly smile. "Please accept my apologies for your incarceration. It was intended that we would meet sooner, but I was called away. Have you had anything to eat?"

I shook my head. The soldier shouted something toward the window of the door. "They'll bring you something soon," he said reassuringly. "You must be wondering why we have brought you here. But wait, I forget my manners. I am Captain Stoltz, but you may call me Hans." Another soldier came through the door with a bowl of stew and a glass of water. Captain Stoltz said something to him, and, after placing the bowl and glass on the desk in front of me, he unlocked my chains. "We certainly do not need such measures in your case," he said calmly. "Please, eat, while I tell you why you are here."

Although I was extremely hungry, fear made it hard to eat. I took small spoonfuls of the stew, the most delicious thing I'd tasted in months. I wished I could take some home for Gisèle and Lisle. I chewed the beef slowly, all the while examining Stoltz. He was of medium height and stocky, probably the age of Papa. Gray streaked the temples of his ash-blond hair. He had smile lines around his mouth and eyes like spring cornflowers. The collar of his uniform was unbuttoned, giving him a relaxed air. He certainly did not look like a torturer.

"Now," he began. "Let's just put all our cards on the table here. We know who you are, Nicole Cassin." He put particular emphasis on Cassin. "And we believe that you can be useful to us. The fact that you are a Jew and that you have a long association with the art gallery where you now work puts you in a prime position to gather information for us."

I lowered my spoon and listened carefully. They knew who I was, but he'd said nothing about the Résistance. I took a deep breath and waited.

"As you are no doubt aware, our Führer is amassing a collection of art for what will be the finest museum in the world. The Jews who are abandoning the country no longer own the rights to their collections, and so we set aside the best pieces for the museum. In truth, isn't it better that such masterpieces are available for everyone to see, not just a wealthy few?"

I sat quietly, waiting for what was coming.

"Unfortunately, many of these Jews do not see it this way and have taken pains to hide their collections, in the vain hope that the Allies will prevail and that they will someday retrieve these artworks. We believe that you are in a position to help us find these hidden collections." Captain Stoltz paused and opened the desk drawer. He took out a pack of cigarettes. "Excuse me, do you mind if I smoke?"

I shook my head slightly.

Stoltz tapped the pack against his fist, drew out a cigarette and lit it. As he inhaled, his cheeks sank and his eyes narrowed. His appearance changed briefly from that of a kindly uncle to that of a wolf. Just as quickly, he became the kindly uncle again.

"I know you must be concerned about your parents, yes?" He reached into the desk drawer again and pulled out a file.

I sat forward, unable to squelch the look of hope that lit up my face. "Do you know where they are?" My voice had come out in a bleat.

Stoltz opened the file, holding it up in front of him and flipping through some papers. The cigarette dangled from his lips. It was all I could do to stop myself from leaping across the desk and grabbing the file. Slowly Stoltz extracted two pages from the file and laid them face down on the desk.

"I have a proposition for you. Consider it a business proposition. Or even a favor in exchange for a favor."

He turned over one of the pages. The top half contained a photo of Maman. She was lying on a mat on the floor. Her hair was tied back in a scarf and dark shadows lay beneath her eyes and cheekbones.

"It says here," Stoltz said, pointing to the paragraph printed in German beneath the photograph, "that Frida Cassin is scheduled to be transferred from Lévitan to Drancy on... let's see... March 2. Why, that's next week, isn't it?" He smiled and relit the pipe. So Maman was in Lévitan! That was so close. But Drancy...

Stoltz continued. "You know where prisoners in Drancy go next, don't you? 'Deportation,' we call it. But let's move on. There may be a way to prevent that." He turned over the second page. It contained a picture of Papa at the top. "André Cassin. Tsk, tsk. He has not been very cooperative. Even though the soldiers at Drancy, where he is now, can be a little rough at times." Papa's face showed numerous abrasions. His shirt hung loosely about him and his left arm was twisted at an odd angle.

I gasped involuntarily. I was hot with anger and wanted nothing more than to gouge this smug man's eyes out.

Stoltz put the pictures back in the file and returned it to the drawer. "As I said, perhaps we can do each other a favor."

"What do you want?" I asked, anger conquering my fear.

"For every art collection that you find for us, we will return the favor. One art collection, one parent freed. Two art collections, two parents freed. After that, we'll talk about other possibilities. Perhaps passage to America."

I remained silent, quickly running through the ramifications of what I'd just heard. I was not being asked to betray Résistance members or fellow Jews. Only to trade art for lives. My parents' lives. Stoltz told me to think about his proposal. He had business in Germany but would return in a few days to meet with me again. I was returned to a different cell, one with a cot and clean blankets, a pillow, and a commode behind a partition. There I passed two days, with warm, full meals delivered regularly. I couldn't erase the pictures of my parents from my mind. If I did not agree to help, Papa would be deported in a few days. Rumor was the trains from Drancy were sent to Auschwitz, a Nazi-run camp in Poland with a very low survival rate. Some even said that prisoners sent there were executed immediately. And if Maman was sent to Drancy, the same fate would befall her. Stoltz had said nothing about what would happen to me, but clearly my refusal to cooperate would mean that I, too, would be imprisoned. I sat at the head of my bed, scrunched against the wall, a blanket clutched tightly around my shoulders.

What if I did agree to help? Was it even possible? I knew about the Steins' collection but not where it was hidden. Still, it was possible that I could find out about others, with my contacts and some subterfuge. Chances are the Germans would get hold of everything eventually anyway. And would anyone really fault me if I sacrificed some paintings to save the lives of my parents?

When Stoltz called me back into the office, I was ready. "I don't know if I can, but I'll try. But it will take a little time. And you said my parents' transfers were imminent."

Stoltz held up a hand. "I know, I know. Now that you've agreed to my proposal, I'll put a hold on the transfers. You'll be freed today and someone will stop by every few days to receive a report. If you get any news that needs to be acted on immediately, call this number." He handed me a card. "Oh, and don't say anything to Roland LaPierre. He is untrustworthy."

Ironically, it would be Roland who delivered the information that I sought.

When I returned to the gallery, Roland looked me up and down but said nothing. At lunch that day, the postman came in and questioned me. My arrest had been noted. He, too, looked at me carefully. "They didn't torture you?" he asked. "They didn't ask for names of fellow Résistance members?"

"No," I insisted. "They don't know of my work with the Résistance," I told him. "They want my help in assessing some of the artwork at the Jeu de Paume." The postman looked at me quizzically, and I knew he mistrusted my story. Those who returned from imprisonment had either given up names of others or agreed to cooperate in some way. I had no further lunchtime visitors after that.

The week after my release I overheard Roland talking on the phone. "The Mandels' maid says that they were good friends with the Bocuses. The Bocuses have a lake house outside the city. She thinks they're storing the art collection there. Write this down." He read an address off a slip of paper. "Can you get there tonight? Tomorrow, then. Don't delay."

I was on pins and needles until Roland left for lunch. The Bocuses and the Mandels were clients of the gallery. We saw them socially on occasion, and Madame Mandel and Maman had become good friends. I sometimes babysat for the Mandel children. The lawyer who worked for the Résistance had told me both families had gone to relatives in the South. I was sure the Mandels wouldn't object to trading their art for my parents' lives. I dialed the number Captain Stoltz had given me. He himself came to the phone and I gave him the address that Roland had spoken into the phone. "Very good, very good."

"What about your end of the deal?" I interjected as Stoltz began to wrap up the call.

"If the information proves fruitful, we'll be in touch."

The following week, a car pulled up alongside me as I walked along the Rue de Seine. The door opened and a soldier beckoned to me. They took me back to Fresnes and up to Stoltz's office. He was waiting there with a file on his desk.

"Please, sit down, Mademoiselle Cassin."

Today his uniform was buttoned up and he wore a cap. An overcoat hung from a hook next to the door. He was all business. "Your information proved to be useful. We were able to acquire many paintings for the museum." He opened the file and placed the pages with photos of André and Frida in front of me. "Now, which one do you wish to save?"

I blinked. What was this? I was silent.

"Come on," Stoltz goaded me. "We agreed that for each collection, you could free one of them. Now which one do you want in trade for the information you gave us? Or do you just want me to pick? Flip a coin?" His smile was mocking. "If you find another collection, it won't matter will it? So why make a big deal of this?" He pushed the pictures closer to me.

Yes, I thought. This was the way to ensure I'd find another collection. These bastards would use anything.

"Haven't got all day," Stoltz said, drumming his fingers on the desk. "In fact, maybe there's an expiration date for this offer. Maybe in thirty seconds." He looked at his watch and began counting down. "Twenty-nine, twenty-eight, twenty-seven..."

I thought fast. Papa looked bad. He was already in Drancy. Maman was in Lévitan. People said conditions were better there. I'd find another collection somehow and save Maman, too.

I reached out a finger and silently tapped Papa's photo.

# 17
## ROBERT

I've always thought of love as something for reality TV fans or Hallmark movie addicts. Needy people without the spine to face themselves, alone. Love at first sight? Romeo and Juliet were deluded. We prefer the reality of lust to be cloaked in the myth of love. I do believe in love but not as salvation—and not at first sight. As the outcome of admiration, friendship and, yes, lust. "Falling in love" seems more like losing one's senses.

It was most shocking to me to see Jack in the early throes of his affair with Ellen. A perfectly sensible man, he turned into a jittering mass of nerves every time she was around. He stuttered, dropped things, his face turned red, he couldn't keep up his end of a conversation. I remember one night in a pub, shortly after Ellen and I had broken up. We were still friends, and she met Jack and I there. He became so ridiculous I had to leave. I'm more of a Professor Henry Higgins, I suppose. I'm often accused of being an Anglophile, and I must admit to being a fan of Evelyn Waugh. I could've lived in one of those British country houses, worn tweeds, smoked a pipe. There's something about that "stiff upper lip" approach to life that makes a lot of sense to me. Too smart for love's illusion, practical, pragmatic, above the fray and looking down bemusedly—that's me. And that's why I think I've gone barmy.

It was after Amy's phone call. "An old friend has come to visit for a couple of days," Amy had said. "Someone I used to work with—Jim." A "friend?" A former lover? A current lover? My stomach began to churn, bile rose in my throat, a sense of violation, threat, anger, fear. All vied for dominance as I pictured Amy with this "friend," Jim. So that was it. The green monster. Jealousy.

<hr>

Amy had left me four messages over the last five days. I just didn't want to talk to her while that other guy was hanging around in the background. I hated that I let it bother me so much, so I immersed myself in my work to an even greater extent than usual. I convinced myself that I was too busy to talk to her. But I missed her and knew that if I didn't call soon, I would lose her. I was undoubtedly already looking like an ass. "Buy the ticket, take the ride," Jack was fond of saying. At this rate, I had a pretty big down payment on a ride to eternal bachelorhood. I picked up the phone.

She answered with a cheerful "Hi!" and then, with concern, "Is everything okay?"

"Oh, all right," I replied, in the weariest tone I could muster. But I was irritated, too, feeling put on the defensive. Did something have to be not okay for me just to not call her for a few days?

"You sound really tired. And we haven't talked in a while. You're not mad at me for something, are you?"

I sucked in my breath, then paused. "You know, Amy,

everything's not always about you. I've been really busy with work." Even I could hear how callous that sounded.

There was silence on the other end. Then a drawn out "Okay" and more silence.

This wasn't going the way I'd intended. "Look, I've just been locked into libraries and staring at computer screens and sometimes when I get involved in a project, I lose track of time. I should've called you back."

"No, Robert, there's no 'should' here. I thought you enjoyed talking to me every day, the way I enjoy talking to you. So when days went by without a word, I got concerned. Besides, I was hoping for a project update." She hesitated, and I could hear her sudden intake of breath. "But really, if you need more space, I understand that. Just be up front about it."

Oh Christ, really? "More space?" More pop lingo. "You've probably noticed by now," I told her, "I'm an introvert. I would've made a good hermit. And you're a psychologist. You want to probe, not only hear what's going on but listen for all the possible secondary meanings. It was Freud who said sometimes a cigar is just a cigar, you know."

She gave a small laugh. "True enough. Things between us developed pretty quickly, so we don't really know what to expect from one another at this point—or, for that matter, what we even want from one another. But I'm just sitting here getting a glimmer that there might be a sizable disparity between what you want from a relationship and what I want."

I wanted to avoid the "relationship talk" at all costs. "Oh, come on, let's not have this conversation right now. I think you know more about me than anyone ever has. I'm tired and you're irritated that I didn't call. Let's not make it out to be bigger than that."

"Okay, fine. Truly, I am glad you called. Why don't we just talk tomorrow?"

"Good idea." I was relieved. She was letting me off the hook. "Sleep well."

"You, too."

I hung up and went over to the sofa, lifted Felix off the cushion and replaced him on my lap. Felix eyed me skeptically. "Yeah, yeah, I know buddy. What I do know is that I don't know what I want."

It could have been any hotel conference room, with its rows of long tables striping the cavernous space. Pencils and notepads imprinted with the hotel logo were arranged like place settings in front of each chair. Dry, overly sweet pastries and coffee urns sat on a table in the back of the room, the air itself generic and stale. I was sprinkling powdered "cream" into my bitter coffee, wishing I hadn't agreed to do this. Inspired by the Cassin case, I was presenting a paper titled "Finding and Authenticating Lost Art: World War II." It was considered an honor to be invited to give the keynote speech at the annual meeting of the International Center for Art Authentication and, much as I hated the limelight, the recognition was good for business. Among the art history crowd, I had what passed for fame, and speaking at such events put an extra layer of gloss on my reputation.

Getting into the room early helped alleviate my nervousness. I introduced myself to a few attendees and greeted some others I'd met before, which made me feel a little less like a trained monkey about to ride a bicycle on a tightrope. People drifted in and settled into their seats, while Betsy, the conference organizer, went to the podium and adjusted the mike. She was wearing a sleeveless green dress that matched the green of her eyes. Her hair was shorter than I remembered and she moved about the front of the room with a brisk efficiency. I couldn't help remembering her smooth white skin, marbled with pale blue veins, and her red hair resting in waves across my pillow during last year's conference. I noted that she still wore a wedding ring. That made it all very convenient. No strings. She'd made it clear to me last year that she had no intention of leaving her husband and two girls. I recalled her soft round breasts spilling out of a black lace brassiere. Better think about something else. Besides, what exactly was my own relationship status these days? And how did I feel about cheating? I didn't seem to have any compunction about sleeping with married women. But that was their moral choice, not mine, I concluded conveniently.

Betsy was beckoning me to my seat at the front table. Another art scholar, a professor at Princeton, would introduce me. I walked to the front of the room, greeting a few people seated on the aisles. The professor introduced me via a long list of educational achievements and other honors that both embarrassed me and, to be honest, made me proud. Then came a brief anecdote about one of my more famous exposures of a forgery. Squirming a bit, I clutched my notes in sweaty palms, ready to stand when the applause began.

---

Suddenly, I was exhausted. I called room service to come and pick up the food cart, then lounged against the pillows and picked up the remote, scanning the channels for a news station. The travel, the nervous anticipation of giving my speech, sex with Betsy. I closed my eyes. Betsy was definitely a Rubens. Round and smooth, her white skin tinged with shades of rose and blue, that red hair. I could picture her in a blue robe holding an infant. I smiled to myself. Not quite that saintly.

Now, Amy... Amy was a Goya. Those eyes of jet and black hair with untamable curls. Serious. Almost intimidating.

I had a sudden, uncomfortable thought. I'd always maintained a distance in my relationships with women. If things got complicated, I got out. Jack often teased me about it. "There's more to sex than sex," he'd said once, "there's love. And once you have sex with love there's no going back." I'd laughed and thought, Yeah, that's what all married men want you to believe. But was I just taking women for their beauty, comparing them to paintings, acquiring them the way the Nazis acquired art— with no emotional connection? Grandpa had taught me not just to look but to think, to feel. What was below the surface of the painting? What messages from the artist were buried in there? Why did I have such a hard time looking below the surface of the women I got involved with?

More specifically, why was I resisting Amy? Because she was a challenge? And yet, I loved the way she could surprise me—with insight, a witty remark. She made me think and she made me laugh. And she was sexy as hell. I had an overwhelming urge to talk to her. But I couldn't call her now, not with Betsy's vanilla scent still on my pillow. Why had I slept with Betsy? Amy would probably say it was because I was afraid of getting more deeply involved with her and had subconsciously been trying to sabotage the relationship. I could hear her in my head, the way she analyzed other people she knew. And maybe she'd be right. The image of her in bed with another man suddenly came to mind, causing a pang in my gut like nothing I'd ever experienced before. I needed to talk to her —but not tonight.

"I have to go out of town again," I announced after Jack's assistant put him on the phone.

"I hate to ask you, but my cat sitter's on vacation. Can you look in on Felix? I'll be gone next Wednesday through Sunday, so if you could, just swing by on Friday, make sure he's okay, plenty of food and water left, whisper sweet nothings in his ear."

"Oh, yeah. That is one invisible cat you've got there. I never see hide nor hair—literally—of him when you're not around. Panics me. Think he got out somehow, my fault, you're gonna kill me. But no, you open the door and there he is, waltzing out of whatever secret hidey-hole he uses to avoid me."

"Don't take it personally, Jack. He's like that with everyone. Lately, he's been a little friendlier to Amy."

"Oh, really? Don't tell me you're actually going to keep a girlfriend longer than six months this time."

"Maybe."

"Hey, how's that case going, the one involving the missing paintings?"

"Well, we have a new development, which is what takes me out of town. My client has remembered something. Something she saw in a dream."

Jack let out a horsey laugh.

"Yeah, I know, but I think there's something to it. She says the dream sparked a memory of a time her father took her to a cave outside of Paris. Now she's thinking maybe her father hid a painting in it. I'm going to France to take a look."

"Sounds positively Nancy Drew-ish. The Dream of the Cave Painting."

"What would you know about Nancy Drew?"

"Hey, you may recall that I have a nine-year-old precocious daughter. She's into it. You should see her room—all of them lined up on a shelf, little yellow spines, Gothic covers. Apparently dipped into one and couldn't stop. So how are you going to find this mystery cave?"

"Nicole told me everything she can remember about the time she went there. I've got topographical maps and am just going to have to use some old-fashioned orienteering skills. It's in a park and she sort of remembers where they parked and which way they started walking. Worst case? A nice trip to Paris."

"Not the worst outcome by any means. Taking Miss Marple with you?"

"Not sure. We're sort of 'on hold' right now."

"On hold? What's that mean, exactly?"

"Oh, I guess she's probably upset because I haven't been calling her as much as I was."

"Why not?"

"I was busy getting ready for the conference and said I couldn't come to see her. Then she wanted to come here, but like I told her, that would've been distracting."

"You're an idiot. Call her."

"Yeah, yeah, I will."

"Sure you will."

"No, really, I will."

"I'm just going to say one thing. I couldn't be happier that your need for 'freedom'"—Jack made quotation marks with his fingers—"left Ellen available for my won't-take-no-for-an-answer courtship style. There are so many benefits to a long-term relationship with someone you love that I can't begin to enumerate them. Just take my word for it. And the children? They're so fucking magical. You're gonna miss it if you don't change soon." I bristled, as Jack shook his head. "I've had my say."

When I saw the envelope from the translator in my mailbox, I couldn't wait to go upstairs. I stood in the lobby with my briefcase shoved under one arm and ripped it open with my forefinger. My eyes sprinted down the page once, then returned to the start and read it again, more slowly, reading not just to know, but to understand. As soon as I was in my loft, I called Amy and read the letter to her.

*Dearest Alexei,*

*I'm so, so happy we were able to meet again. If only I had been able to track you down earlier, but so many soldiers never returned. We believed you had died. And now, knowing about your name change, I never would have found you. But I have my "baby" brother back and it brings me great joy. I am working on a poem about our reuniting after such time and distance. And, though we have both changed in many ways, we were still able to feel that connection. I wish our parents could have... Well, what's done is done. Please write often and visit again when possible. My health will not permit me to travel such a great distance. Your children are miraculous! Hugs and kisses from your big sister,*

*Natasha*

I lowered the letter and listened to Amy's breathing on the other end of the phone.

"Oh... my... God!," she exhaled. "Sam was a Russian!" We were both silent for a moment. "If only we could've been there when they went on the trip to Russia. I'm sure Alexei must've told Natasha the whole story at that point—how he came to be Sam Popinski and, probably, what happened to the real Sam." I could hear a pencil or pen being tapped nervously against a table as Amy talked.

"Too bad Peter thought they were just a couple of boring eighty-year-olds," I said.

Amy scoffed. "If there's anything working at Friendly Village has taught me, it's that old people are not boring."

"It seems likely that the real Sam was killed in the war and Alexei somehow got his dog tags and posed as an American. The Russians weren't too kind to returning soldiers. Their attitude was, if you weren't dead, you didn't fight hard enough for Mother Russia. So he probably figured going home was out of the question." I paused.

"When he kept saying, 'You don't know me,'" Amy interjected, "he meant it literally: he really wasn't Sam Popinski."

"I've got to get this info to Peter. He may want to do more research on Alexei, as his family history has been an utter lie."

"That's almost like finding out you were adopted. Alexei really was his father, but he has no idea who Alexei was!"

We were silent again.

"I think I'll give Peter a call right now and tell him I'm mailing these translations tomorrow."

"Don't forget to make copies first," Amy suggested.

"Naturally," I replied. "Oh, and one more thing I wanted to tell you."

"Yes?"

I paused briefly. "I'm sorry. Sorry I was an ass about us getting together and then not calling you. I really miss you."

"Good," Amy said emphatically. "I miss you, too."

---

I woke with the sense that I had been doing something important in my dream, something I had willed myself to remember, but now it was gone, as inaccessible to my conscious mind as if one of those roll-down metal security doors had been slammed shut. Damn it! What was it? I turned over, pulling the flannel sheets closer. Shutting my eyes again, I tried to relax, to recapture the dream. My stomach growled. The image that surfaced was of the almond croissant I had picked up at the French bakery yesterday. On Sundays I allowed myself to splurge on calories, relax, even sit in front of the television and watch sports. I cursed my brain and wriggled free of the entangling sheets, careful not to disturb Felix, who lay in a ball behind my knees. Coffee—that's what I needed. And a hot shower.

I'd been up until 4:00, immersed in a world of criminals, victims and soldiers. It had never been so real to me. My quest for Nicole's missing paintings had begun as a hunt for a fairy-tale treasure. But after looking through the archives, I found myself in a story grimmer than any tale told by the Brothers Grimm. The death lists were carefully notated, with a bureaucratic distance that implied the prisoners were nothing more than widgets past their sell-by dates.

I put on the coffee, then grabbed my thick white terry robe and headed for the bathroom. The hot water splashing on the top of my head and running down the back of my neck was the next best thing to a massage. Craning in front of the computer screen for hours had really put a crick in my neck. I breathed in the steam. Wait a minute! The dream. Not exactly a dream. It had been an idea of what to do next that I'd wanted to remember. It had to do with the property cards. That was it. I needed to go through the property cards to see if any of Nicole's paintings had been returned to the military collecting points. It was possible that one or more of them had been sent to another country or museum. Based on what I'd been reading, I hoped they weren't in Austria or Switzerland, neither of which had been very cooperative in returning stolen art. Now I just wanted to get the shower over with and return to the computer.

Coffee, however, was a must. I dressed in my Sunday uniform—sweatpants and Syracuse hoodie. My damp hair combed back, I caught my image in the mirror and saw my father. I ruffled my hair up, grabbed my coffee and returned to my desk, hoping the property cards were in some sort of order. Else, I'd be at the computer all day, looking at thousands of cards.

I'd try the Munich Collection Point records first. If the paintings had been part of Göring's collection, it was likely they'd have been on one of his trains to Germany. Felix batted my leg. "Hey buddy, you want up?" I reached down and lifted him onto my lap. After a few turns, Felix settled into what I thought of as his nautilus shell imitation. Thankfully, I found a search function on the database. I entered Rembrandt and came up with only one record, a painting that was described as a copy of a Rembrandt. After another dozen attempted searches, I had no confidence that, if Nicole's paintings were on a card, I'd find them this way. Clearly, the search function of this database still needed some work. I would have to look at every card. I groaned. Better have that croissant first.

Dislodging Felix, I headed back toward the kitchen. The rumpled bed beckoned invitingly. Now that I knew the task would be gruelingly tedious, my enthusiasm waned. It was possible I would find nothing. Likely, in fact. But then, that would prove I needed to turn my attention to the dealers. I put my croissant on a plate and went back to the computer. Ah! Music would make this better. I turned back to the stereo sitting on a low shelving unit in the living area. Something a little rousing but not too attention-grabbing. I selected a compilation Amy had given me, Romantic Classical Pieces from the Ages. She knew nothing about classical music, but this hadn't been a bad choice. As the graceful strains of violins filled the air, I glided back to my chair, resettled Felix and bit into the croissant.

It was only after I began the task that I realized how absolutely daunting it would be. The Munich records were divided into three separate databases. Each of these listed 100 different property card ranges, and each of these contained approximately 600 individual property cards. That was 180,000 cards for the Munich records alone! At least the Marburg Central Collecting Point records were divided by medium. But the paintings alone totaled 2500. The Wiesbaden collection had 363 paintings. The volume was astounding. Could there really have been so many artworks stolen? I searched the internet, finding an article that claimed five million cultural artifacts had been located and returned by the Monuments, Fine Arts, and Archives unit alone. I dropped my head into my hands. Maybe I should watch a football game.

I went back to the screen, checking the time. I'd do 100 and see how long it took. After ten minutes, I had viewed fifty-one cards and they had all been metal and sculpture. I scrolled down and found that the entire lot was metal and sculpture. More scrolling around and I discovered that, although they were not labeled in categories, the cards were actually sorted into categories, and paintings represented less than a quarter of the works in the file. I calculated a worst-case scenario of 150 hours total. I figured I'd get faster as I went on. At this point, I still couldn't stop myself from pausing at a card, seeing the typewritten "Confiscated by Hitler" and imagining that particular story. And multiplying it by hundreds of thousands—no, millions. Sixty million dead during that war, mostly civilians. And here I was, in a beautiful, warm loft, coffee and croissant in front of me, cat on lap, the latest in technology at my fingertips, a woman who loved me. Lucky.

After several hours, even Felix had tired and gone off to sleep on one of the heat registers. I had viewed close to a thousand property cards, describing all manner of paintings.

I was working through a set of cards in the Berchtesgaden collection. Berchtesgaden was the town Göring's train of treasures had been headed for when it was parked under a bridge at Unterstein to protect it from Allied bombing. There, it was partially looted by the townspeople. These cards indicated "Possessor" as Göring and "History and Ownership" as Hofer. I sensed I was getting close.

Then I found the first one: the Corot, described as Children Playing in Field and "Presumed Owner: France." Under identifying marks were listed a G and a C. "Arrival Date" was listed as June 6, 1945, and "Exit" as August 10, 1949, to Paris. I leaned back and sighed. So the painting had been confiscated from the Cassin collection and appropriated by Göring. In his last-ditch attempt to save his treasures, he'd crammed them into the train headed for Berchtesgaden. Thankfully, the locals hadn't managed to snag this Corot. It had been sent to Paris.

Suddenly, my torpor lifted. Maybe all of the paintings had been appropriated by Göring and put on that train. It wasn't long before I found another, the La Tour, returned to Paris on the same date. Only a few cards later, I found the Cranach. Exhilarated, I plunged ahead. At this rate, I'd at least establish that the paintings had been recovered after the war and sent back to Paris. But then what?

Two hours later, I stood and stretched my back. Tall and thin people like you ought to do yoga, my doctor was always saying. He was probably right. After fixing myself a tuna sandwich and, of course, tossing a few flakes Felix's way, I phoned Amy and told her about my discovery. Her excitement over the phone made me wish she was with me. I wanted to take her back to my rumpled bed and nestle in to savor my victory before continuing the search. Barring that immediate gratification, I told her I'd probably need to go to Paris to follow up on the paintings that had been returned there. When I asked her if she'd like to go along, there was a moment of silence. I'd thought she'd jump at the chance.

"No shit?" she suddenly screeched.

"No shit," I replied. We hung up laughing.

After another hour, I finished going through the Berchtesgaden files. There had been no more of the Cassins' paintings. Slump-shouldered, I moved to the sofa. My eyes were too tired to read. An episode of Foyle's War seemed fitting.

That evening, I ordered in—sushi from the Japanese place two blocks away. I paid the bicycle delivery boy—actually, I guessed I should think of him as a man, since he had a braided goatee about six inches long—then went back to the computer. The paintings I had not found were the Picasso, the Cézanne and the Rembrandt. The Picasso and the Cézanne would have been considered degenerate by Nazi standards, so those would not likely be found in the collection of any of the Nazi hierarchy, such as Göring. They had most likely been confiscated, held at Jeu de Paume, then bought by one of the dealers to sell to a private collector, who would be happy to get a masterpiece on the cheap. Hopefully, a French collector, although Wendland often supplied the Swiss. The Rembrandt, however, would've been prized by the Nazis. In fact, it might've been something Hitler would've wanted for the Führermuseum. So I'd look for a dataset that indicated Hitler as the possessor.

I got lucky. The next set of cards I looked at, labeled "Aussee," showed Hitler as possessor, and the works had been marked for Linz—his birthplace and the site of his planned museum. The first painting was by Fritz von Uhde, the subject

Mary and Joseph on the Road. The presumed owner was listed as Brauntal. Underneath Brauntal was typed the word "Jewish." On the back was stamped "No claim or documentation available." Again, I felt myself sinking into a whirlpool of despondency. Who was Brauntal? Had he been killed?

At this rate, I would never finish. I clicked onto the next record and stopped again, my eyes snagged by the writing on the back of the card. Under the heading "Condition and Repair Record" was a handwritten note that indicated the painting had been cleaned and re-secured to its frame. But it was the signature that had caught my attention. "K. Ames." My grandfather.

# 18

## KENNETH



I was expecting to spend the day sorting my field notes, examining my list of monuments and searching out the corresponding locations on a large map spread out on a desk when the call came in from Lieutenant Carlson. "You gotta get out here and see this," he yelled. "As soon as possible. I've got no idea what to do about it. So get your ass out here. Bernterode mine." And, with that, the lieutenant rang off. I grabbed my knapsack and helmet and started walking north. Although Carlson was skeptical of the MFAA's goals, he'd begrudgingly helped me in the past. I waved down a Jeep and hitched a ride to Bernterode. Twenty miles on bombed-out roads lined with crumbled buildings and broken-down trucks took us to the outskirts of the town, where the Jeep driver dropped me off.

As I neared the mine, I saw Carlson standing in a circle with several other soldiers looking at something on the ground. The men stepped back as I approached. There, on a grubby green blanket, outside a salt mine in the middle of a forest, lay a jewel-encrusted scepter and orb. "What is it, sir?" one of the soldiers asked.

"Well, it looks to me like you may have found the coronation regalia of Frederick the Great." I gently lifted the scepter, turning it so that the diamonds glittered in the weak sun that filtered through the trees. The King of Prussia had held this very object in his hand upon his accession to the throne in the 1700s. The gems were flawless and huge. What could it mean to these men to view this sort of treasure in a quiet forest after battling for your lives? Something most of them would never have seen, or certainly only in a museum. The men were curious and began to ask him questions about Frederick the Great. "Come on!" Lieutenant Carlson said with a serious expression. "We'd better get going. There's more where that came from."

We descended more than a quarter of a mile underground. "No smoking," Carlson yelled over the sound of the metal wheels on the trolley. "We're surrounded by approximately 400,000 tons of munitions." At the end of the descent, we reached an open area lit by lamps on stands. From here, tunnels led in several directions. Across from one side-branching tunnel was a block wall, its mortar freshly white. And in the center of the wall was a hole the soldiers had smashed through it. Stepping through the hole, I found a large room, brightly lit and stuffed with paintings, tapestries, decorative items and, most eerily, several large ornate caskets. According to the inscriptions, here were the remains of Frederick William I, Frederick the Great, Feldmarschall von Hindenburg and Hindenburg's wife.

It took several days of packing before most of the paintings and other objects had been evacuated from the mine. Finally, all that remained were the coffins. The casket of Frederick the Great was massive, crafted of steel and estimated to weigh more than a thousand pounds. This was saved for last, in case the old mine elevator was not up to it. I thought I might be hallucinating when I heard a staticky rendition of "The Star-Spangled Banner" in the distance. As we neared the opening to the mine, I heard "God Save the King." It was no hallucination. The day was May 7, 1945, and Germany's unconditional surrender had just been announced on the radio.

# 19
## NICOLE

Why did I survive? Gisèle Lefebvre, for one. If she hadn't offered me refuge, I don't know where I would've gone. And the fact that I had inherited enough of my Swedish grandmother's traits that I could pass for Aryan. And there was my usefulness. Roland needed me. And the money that I made kept me fed. And I'd always been a stubborn girl. The religious faith I lacked was supplanted by the faith I had that I would somehow find my parents. But, truly, in the end, so much boiled down to sheer chance. Escaping when the Nazis came to possess the gallery. Not being stopped and arrested for not wearing the star. Captain Stoltz believing that I could provide useful information to him. Paris not being blown up.

But, more accurately, that answers the question, how did I survive? I've asked myself why many times since. For what purpose was I saved when so many others, more deserving, were not? I cannot answer that. I no longer believe in logic or fairness. I tried to shelter my children from my existentialism. What good does knowing the randomness of life do? Knowing evil can claim your life at any moment doesn't make it any easier when it comes. There is bliss in naïvety. Who knows? Maybe my children's lives will run along some more or less predictable courses.

One consequence of putting the past behind me was that I lost touch with Gisèle. For that I am sorry. We exchanged a couple of postcards at first. I let her know where I was and that I was all right. But soon I stopped answering hers and she stopped sending them. But she had taken good care of me, just like a second mother, letting me live there until the time that my temper got the best of me once again and rendered that refuge unsafe.

I'd been careful to avoid confrontation with Gisèle's concierge, Madame Vaillaud. But one day my nerves were more than usually frayed. There had been dozens of clients in the gallery, all pawing over the latest batch of looted paintings. Roland, whom I'd discovered was completely ignorant of art and almost everything else as well, was smart enough to stand aside and let me discuss the works with the clients, fellow looters as far as I was concerned.

There had been no time for a lunch break. On the way home I'd stopped outside a grocer and joined a long line of women. I'd asked what was available. "Potatoes," the women replied. I stood there for two hours, until the shop owner shuttered the place and went inside. Empty-handed and exasperated, I returned to the apartment. Madame Vaillaud stood on the landing outside her door. Her dress of silk crêpe, shiny with wear, hung on her angular body as if on a wire hanger.

"Bonsoir," she said in an oily voice. "You must be Madame Lefebvre's niece. I've forgotten your name?"

"Nicole," I said shortly.

"You know, you should persuade your aunt to join our group. We find that a little cooperation with the Germans has benefited us. Who knows how long they will be here? We may as well get along and make the best of it. Besides, they are ridding us of the Jewish problem."

My ire was like a sleeping rattlesnake that had just been poked with a stick. "The Jewish problem? And just what problem is that?" I barked.

"Well, of course, you're awfully young, but they really had too much control of our businesses, denying the true Frenchmen opportunities."

"Excuse me, but I think a Jewish citizen of France is as French as anyone else," I snapped, turning my back on Madame Vaillaud.

"Be careful, my dear. One could be reported for comments such as that."

"Yes, and after the war, one could be reported for collaborating with the Germans!" I retorted, stumbling into the apartment.

I took off my hat and threw my handbag on the table before sinking into a chair and burying my face in my hands. What had I done now?

---

As much as we longed for an Allied invasion, its rumored imminence heightened tensions in the city to an almost unbearable level. Deferential as houseguests when they first arrived, over time the Germans had become the ruthless bullies everyone had expected. Now, incredulous at their sudden vulnerability, they doubled down on their show of power and developed an unquenchable thirst for revenge. Executions of suspected Résistance members increased. Jews and other prisoners were sent to perish in German camps at accelerated rates. And the air was rife with denunciations.

I sat at the table with Gisèle one day, as she reached

beneath her dress and extracted a letter addressed to Gestapo Headquarters. She slid her finger beneath the flap, ripped it open, then angrily pulled the stationery free. She unfolded it and, as her eyes scanned the spidery handwriting, she froze, seeing the letters of her own name: "Gisèle Lefebvre." She glanced quickly over its contents, then handed it to me. The letter-writer asserted that Gisèle Lefebvre was harboring a Jew, a young woman posing as her niece. The letter was unsigned, as most of them were, but we both knew who had sent it. That witch, Madame Vaillaud!

That evening, we sat at the table nursing weak tea and discussing the situation, while Lisle was in her room doing homework.

"The letter is gone, but who knows what that woman might do? What if she grabs some random soldier on the street and brings him up here?"

"She just might. She hasn't spoken a word to me since I accused her of being a traitor."

We looked at each other, neither one wanting to be the first to say what had to be said.

"I have to move out." I said it first. "I'm not the only one in danger. You and Lisle could also be arrested."

"But where would you go?" Gisèle's expression was changing as quickly as cloud shadows sweeping over the sea. "Perhaps one of the other women at the Post Office who intercepts letters would be willing to take you. Maybe someone has an attic or hiding place. It won't be for too long. Everyone's saying the city will be liberated soon."

"I think I could hide at the gallery," I replied. "Behind the office, where we store extra paintings, spare frames, that sort of thing."

"But what about Roland?"

"I'm almost always there to close up. He hardly ever stays

upstairs; he's usually with some woman in the Fifth. And I'm always the first one there in the morning. I have a key, so even if he stayed later, I could leave and come back and let myself in."

"Oh, I don't know. What about me asking one of the women at the Post Office?"

"I'd rather not involve anyone else at this point. Even if Roland suspected I was living there, I don't think he'd do anything. I'm his golden goose. I'll take a few things over there at lunch tomorrow, then I'll just stay there after work. Madame Vaillaud will not see me again! Let her think her letter did some good and I've been arrested!"

"Oh Nicole, I'm going to miss you so much. Will I be able to see you?"

"Don't worry. Just come at lunch someday. Roland's almost always out."

As the Allies got closer, the percussion of bombs and gunfire was audible from within the city. In preparation for their retreat, the Germans had created fires in the streets, piling on files and valuables they wished to prevent the Allies from capturing. Parisians retreated to their shops and apartments, waiting for the next set of soldiers to march into their city.

Roland was packing a large duffle with cash and some personal items from his desk, as well as a few small, valuable paintings. He reached into a drawer and pulled out a pistol. "Here," he said, offering it to me. "In times like this, anything could happen. You might need it. You've been a real help to me, and I... I wouldn't want anything bad to happen to you. You know... soldiers. And you need to get out of Paris. It's going to be destroyed. Tonight."

I stared at him. "What are you talking about?"

"Hitler's orders. Revenge, I suppose, for Hamburg, Berlin." He shrugged. "They're going to blow up everything and everyone in Paris. Brutal assholes when it comes right down to it. Anyway, get out of the city."

He stepped closer to me and placed the gun in my outstretched palm. I closed my hand around the grip, felt the cold metal and stepped backward, pointing it at him.

"You get out. Get out of my family's gallery. Now."

Roland's face twisted into a grimace of shock, then anger. "I saved your life, you know." He opened his mouth, as if to say more, then grabbed his bag, whirled on his heels and stalked out of the gallery.

My hands trembled. I put the gun down on the counter, then locked and bolted the door and, out of habit, placed the Closed sign in the window. I dragged a chair and a bureau in front of the door for good measure, then ran into the back storage area where I had been sleeping on folded blankets that had been used for transporting paintings. Bunching my coat into a pillow, I curled into a ball and sobbed. As much as I wanted to go to Gisèle's, I dared not leave the gallery right now. Would the Germans really blow up Paris? How could I leave? Where would I go? And if my parents were still alive, this is where they would come to find me. I pulled my coat over my head and curled up even more tightly.

After a fitful night, I went to the door and peered out the window. In the early dawn light nothing moved. There were no cars parked on the street. A few bicycles stood propped against the buildings opposite me. The stone edifices took on a reddish glow, as if a great conflagration was casting its light from afar. But it was the sunrise. Suddenly, I noticed something else. The silence. No guns. No Germans visible either. A yellow striped cat trotted across the road. I made a cup of tea with the rare tea that Roland had managed to acquire. As I sipped it slowly, the light brightened, and a few sounds began to filter through the silence. Occasional gunfire and another, more consistent sound. A motor—or motors.

---

Keeping partly hidden, I watched tanks roll past. American tanks. Soldiers walked alongside and slowly people came out of the buildings, blinking like hibernating animals greeting the first day of spring after an unnaturally prolonged winter. Bit by bit their exuberance grew, and they began to wave French flags and American flags and children laughed, not knowing why everyone was so happy, and women kissed the soldiers. And the soldiers smiled too, sick with relief that this was the greeting— flags and women's kisses, not the German snipers they had been told to expect. The city had not been blown up. But I did not go out. I still didn't feel safe.

The soldiers were checking the buildings. I could see them banging on doors and then entering by twos. And so it was that, on this day of liberation, fate brought Sam Popinski to the door of the gallery, on which he banged loudly with the butt of his rifle, while shouting, "Ouvrez vous!" in his terrible French accent.

I moved the chair and bureau that blocked the door. The two soldiers waited impatiently, watching through the door. Sam's buddy O'Rourke lit a cigarette. I heard him scoff, "Like some old furniture is going to protect her." Finally, I unlocked and unbolted the door and opened it slowly inward.

"Merci, messieurs, merci beaucoup," I said, my breath coming in gasps. "You are very welcome here," I continued in English.

"Whaddya know?" O'Rourke smiled. "A pretty one who speaks English. Any Germans around?"

"No."

"Sure about that?"

"Of course. You are free to search, if you please."

O'Rourke started up the stairs and called over his shoulder to Sam. "You check the back and any basement if there is one."

Sam smiled at me. "I'm sorry for any trouble, miss. It's just we have to make sure. Snipers, you know."

I smiled back, noticing large brown eyes under prominent brows. His thick hair was ashen with dust and a scruffy beard covered the lower part of his face. When he smiled at me, something inside cracked. The vessel into which I had buried all my emotions those last four years—fear, hope, faith, love, hate—cracked under the gaze of this tired, dirty soldier who could still look at me and smile. Suddenly, unwillingly, I burst into tears.

Sam's smile was replaced by a look of concern. "What is it? Are you all right? Are you sure there aren't any Germans here? Were there?" He stepped toward me and awkwardly put a hand on my shoulder.

"No, no, no, it's okay," I said, as I tried to stifle my sobs, looking up into his kind face. "It's just that after all these years... I can't believe you're here. You see, I'm Jewish." And here I thought of Maman and Papa and broke into inconsolable weeping. Sam slung his rifle over his shoulder and steered me toward a chair, lowering me into it.

"What's up with her?" O'Rourke asked, bounding down the stairs two at a time.

"Just pretty shook up by the whole thing, I think," Sam replied, as my shaking subsided and I looked up.

"This was my father's gallery," I tried to explain. "It was— what did they call it—Aryanized? Given to a Frenchman who was really a German at heart. I don't know where my parents are. Arrested three years ago..." My voice caught and I put my fist up against my mouth, embarrassed by this show of weakness.

"O'Rourke, check the back room and basement, eh?" Sam nodded toward the back and O'Rourke stumbled quickly in and out of the office.

"Is there a basement?" he asked.

"Just a cellar," I replied, sniffing. "Only accessible from the alley."

"Okay, we'll check it on our way out. C'mon Sam, we'd better get a move on."

"You gonna be okay?" Sam asked, wiping a tear from my cheek with his thumb.

"Oui, I mean, yes, thank you." Overcome with emotion and having watched the young women on the street kissing the soldiers, it seemed most natural that I should stand and kiss Sam's cheek. "France thanks you," I whispered.

The end of the war brought joy, yes. You see the pictures in the history books, the documentaries, women kissing soldiers, streamers and flowers filtering through the air. In the long story of history, it's a moment, a turning point, like a light switch suddenly turned on, illuminating all that was dark. But such moments are never, in reality, so definitive. There's a toggling between the before and after, until eventually the balance settles on the after and that's how people remember it.

From enemy-imposed order—curfews, rationing, censorship—to chaos in a matter of days—this is what we citizens of Paris experienced when finally liberated. One might even say that anarchy reigned, at least temporarily, as there was no official French government and only slowly did the American military governor grasp control of the situation. For days after the liberation, gunfire was still heard, but instead of coming from the Gestapo headquarters, it was indiscriminate. A random German sniper, determined to extract his revenge on the now insolent populace; the Résistance fighters and their back-alley executions of suspected collaborators; the Allied forces routing the last of the Germans and attempting to restore order: all wielded their weapons with a righteous, last-ditch fervor.

Those concerned that their fellow citizens might recall them as being just a little too friendly with the Germans were the first to denounce, castigate and jeer at the poor women whose heads had been shaved as punishment for "horizontal collaboration." I watched a half dozen women being paraded through the streets, heads bald and blue, eyes downcast, nude. Some had swastikas painted on their backs or chests. I hoped I would not see Marie. Then I recognized a "Sebastian" from the brothel.

"No, no, no!" I shouted, shoving my way through the jeering onlookers. I rushed up to one of the men brandishing a stick at the women and tugged at his sleeve. "Listen! You must listen! She's in the Résistance!"

The man was young and yet had a well-fed look about him, lacking the gauntness of a soldier or prisoner. He shrugged me off. "Your friends, are they? Maybe you, too, are guilty of fucking the Germans." He reached an unusually clean hand out and lifted a section of my curls. "Maybe you're needing a haircut!" He yanked and twisted his hand until I cried out and pulled away. "Sebastian" caught my eye and shook her head. I pushed past the man to catch up to her. She walked proudly, with her head up, staring at the onlookers until they looked away uncomfortably.

"No, let them have their fun. They won't listen to reason now and you'll only put yourself in danger. We'll be okay. Now, hurry, run away." She gave me a shove back toward the crowd. I stumbled, then looked up to see Madame Vaillaud loudly calling out, "Whores! Traitors!" When she saw me, she quickly turned and melted into the sea of angry people.

I walked away, cringing at the cacophony. Finding food had become even harder as the unknowns piled up, like one of those mazes I had loved to solve as a child. Trace a route from the bunny to the carrot. Only, these days I really couldn't see a way out; nothing but dead ends. A street blocked by piles of chairs, sofas, bicycles and junk that had been set up by the Résistance to battle the Germans as the Allies advanced. A shop, previously reliable, with its windows broken and shelves empty. A line, blocks long. Should I wait? Keep moving and try another shop? I took my place at the back of the line. "What do you think they have?" I asked the old, gray-haired woman in front of me. The woman turned and I saw that she was not old at all. Her face was unlined, but her eyes were dead and the skin below them chapped and dark.

"It's said potatoes, and maybe a bit of cheese," the woman responded wearily, shifting to her other foot. I nodded and my shoulders sagged.

Added to all my other worries was the fear of no news—or the worst news—about my parents. I knew Papa had been in Fresnes and Drancy and had heard that he'd been deported either to Auschwitz or to Buchenwald. After the meeting I'd had with Captain Stoltz, in which he promised to free Papa, I never heard from him again. The number he'd given me had been disconnected. The last I knew of Maman was that she'd been at Lévitan. And so I entered a sort of self-imposed limbo, a numbness that acknowledged I could do nothing but focus on staying alive.

Rumors were rife about when the POWs and deportees might return. But with those rumors came appalling news of the camps that had been liberated by the Allies. The knowledge of what had gone on there, the condition of the prisoners —it could not be set aside. How I wished for just a moment of oblivion. But even my sleep was fitful and fear-ridden.

---

Marcel, the wild-haired painter, stopped into the gallery to ask about Papa. I told him I had no news yet but was trying to get the business in some sort of shape so that we could reopen when he and Maman returned. I'm sure I looked done in, and Marcel suggested I take a break and come up to his studio. We went to Montmartre and I was looking at some of Marcel's charcoals when the door opened and Jean nearly fell inside, panting. "That hill is murder," he gasped. "Why is it you artists all have to live up here?"

"Closer to God?" Marcel quipped. "Cheap rents. Nobody else is willing to climb up here. Keeps the real riff-raff away from us."

"Let's hope the Métro gets back on some sort of predictable schedule soon," Jean said.

Marcel poured a generous glass of wine into a tumbler and handed it to Jean. The center of the room was dominated by an easel containing a large blank canvas and surrounded by tables laden with dirty jars, squashed paint tubes and piles of brushes and rags. Half-completed paintings leaned against the walls. A multitude of colors spattered the old wooden floor.

"It's bloody chaos out there, Jean. Your guys are taking justice into their own hands. Executing people as collaborators with nothing but someone's accusation to go on. Did you hear they strung up a Vietnamese laundress thinking she was a Japanese spy?"

"Don't call them 'my guys,'" Jean retorted sharply. "I think most of these vigilantes are collaborators accusing others, just to look innocent themselves. It's chaos all right, but don't blame us."

I thought of Madame Vaillaud.

Marcel sighed deeply and lifted the half-empty bottle of wine. "I suppose we should save some for Roger, but who knows when he'll get here."

Jean froze. "You mean you don't know?"

"Know what?" Marcel waited. "What are you saying?"

"Roger."

"What about Roger? Spit it out!"

Jean rubbed the back of his neck and looked down. "He's dead. Executed a week ago."

I gasped and tightened my grip on the rickety chair.

Marcel stared frozen for a moment. "How? Why?"

"Remember that day he said he saw the round-up, all the women and children?"

We nodded.

"He separated a couple of children from the edge of the crowd and took them home. He'd been hiding them ever since."

"Merde! And he never said. He didn't trust us?"

Jean shook his head. "I'm sure it wasn't that. There just wasn't any reason to tell us and we were better off not knowing."

"So all that time—and just last week?" Marcel's voice broke. "Why?"

"Someone probably informed on him, because the Germans stormed through his place, went straight to the hiding place, marched them out and executed all of them in the middle of the street."

Marcel and I were silent, each picturing what had happened to Roger.

"Bastards! Poor Roger, I can't believe it!"

"Nor I," murmured Jean. "The assholes were more brutal

on their way out of town than ever. If only he'd been able to last a few more days."

"We have to find out who the informant was. I'll kill him with my bare hands," Marcel shouted angrily.

Jean stared at him. "You see how it is."

---

My memory of the apartment above the gallery that was my home for so long has the quality of a double exposure. Or of that drawing I've seen—look at it one way and you see a young woman; adjust your sight and you see an old woman. Sometimes I remember it filled with flowers and paintings and people. Sometimes I remember how it looked the first time I went up there after Roland left.

Most of our possessions had been taken as part of Operation Furniture. The living room was empty, save for a sagging armchair and a lamp, some magazines scattered about the floor and an ashtray overflowing with burned pipe tobacco on a table. Above the fireplace was a hole in the plaster where Maman's portrait once hung. There was nothing in the dining room. Cheese rinds and a hard baguette lay on the kitchen counter next to a knife. Roland never cooked and ate either at a restaurant or at his mistress's apartment, where he generally slept. My parents' bedroom contained a dingy-looking single bed, the bedclothes half on the floor, and a dirty wine glass on a windowsill. A few items of men's clothing were strewn about. It smelled stale.

My own room was stripped bare, except for the built-in bookshelves containing a sole book, a dog-eared copy of the course catalog for the Sorbonne. A dead dream. I picked it up and threw it against the wall, then heard knocking downstairs. I crept down far enough to look through the door at the far end of the gallery. It was the soldier. The nice one with brown eyes. Sam. I hurried to the door and opened it. His smile faded when he noticed my tears. "Are you all right?" he asked.

I wiped my face with the heel of my hand. "Yes, yes, I'm fine. Must seem like I'm always crying, but, really, I'm not. It is nice to see you. Do you need to search again?"

"No, I just wanted to come by and see how you were doing."

"Oh, thank you. Please come in and have some tea." We sat down in the office and drank Roland's tea.

"Probably didn't introduce myself properly last time," Sam said, "and I apologize for that. It's just when you're lookin' for snipers, you've gotta be quick about it. Tryin' to keep them from shooting any more people."

"Je comprends—I mean, I understand. It's fine."

"Well, my name is Sam Popinski, and may I ask what yours is?"

"Nicole Cassin."

"I am sure pleased to meet you, Mademoiselle Cassin."

"Please. Do call me Nicole."

"Okay then, and you'll call me Sam?"

"Yes, Sam. I am pleased to make your acquaintance also."

Sam had brought bread with him and some tinned meat. I opened the cupboard where Roland kept his wine and pulled out the last bottle of burgundy. Over this simple meal, I learned where Sam was from and told him about my life as a Parisian schoolgirl before the war. I spoke little of what had happened since the occupation. I was even then trying to forget. Although Sam had been young and naïve before the war, his experiences as a soldier had caused him to question many of his prior assumptions about life. He retained a boyish innocence, even as he talked about watching his comrades die and wondering about God and the meaning of life.

After a couple of hours, Sam stood. "I have to get back now. It looks like I'll be stationed here for a while, so if it's okay with you, I'd like to come back and visit again."

"I would like that," I said, walking him to the door.

Sam paused. "Do you think it'd be okay if you gave me another..." He blushed and pointed to his cheek. I stood on my toes and kissed his cheek, undoubtedly blushing myself.

"Well, okay then," Sam said. "Or revor."

"Au revoir."

Over the next few weeks, I gradually restored my former home to a rudimentary living area. Gisèle relayed my story to her friends at the Post Office, one of whom donated a small sofa, another a single mattress. With the help of Sam, who became a daily visitor, we moved the furniture to the upstairs flat and dumped Roland's bed out on the street. One day Sam brought a ladder. I stood and watched as he pulled down the sign, Galerie Patriotique, letter by letter. My fists, closed tight with rage, gradually loosened, as the shape of the letters for Galerie Cassin emerged. Sam was barely off the ladder before I threw my arms around his neck and buried my head in his chest. "Merci, merci, merci!" He tipped up my chin and kissed me. A few soldiers walking by made kissing noises and whistled. Sam saluted and laughed.

Food was still scarce and money scarcer still, as I now had no income. The buyers who had been so eager to plunk down cash to snag valuable paintings at deep discounts were gone. Besides, I was determined to return any looted artwork to the original owners and would only sell what I could prove the gallery legitimately possessed. And that wasn't much. A few former clients drifted back in, and I was able to sell enough small decorative items to get by while I waited for my parents to return.

There was no information to be had yet. No bureaucracy

for tracing the missing. The Germans were still fighting and in control of areas to the north. Only when the Germans surrendered and the camps were liberated did most officials expect there to be any reports for those families in such dire need of news.

The dark imaginings that had filled my brain during the occupation—scenes from my visit to Fresnes, Papa's wounded face, Maman's disappearance—had been made more bearable by Sam—his sweet smile, his rough chin against my cheek, his long arms holding me close. Just as I had been unable to banish the nightmarish thoughts, I was now unable to suppress my happiness, even as I told myself I was being disloyal to my parents to feel any spark of joy while they were imprisoned, perhaps even dead. Further, the war was not over, and Sam was a soldier. Weren't these joyous feelings just a cruel joke, relics from a world that no longer existed? Wasn't I just setting myself up for even more heartache, a blow that, when it came, piled on top of all that had gone before, would finally kill what little spirit I had left? But try as I might to be the practical, driven Nicole that I'd been during the occupation—obsessed with nothing but getting food and successfully carrying out my Résistance activities—I was inescapably a young woman in love.

The strength and power of love cracked my hard shell of grief the way a plant will crack asphalt to reach the sun. I found myself humming all the old French love songs my parents had once listened to. Every flower, every butterfly, every ray of sun that lit up the faded shutters across the street —all were new and miraculous. And when the bell downstairs jangled, it tugged something inside of me. Sam, Sam, Sam. Sam framed by the door, silhouetted by the outside light, tall, lanky Sam, with the soft lips, piercing eyes and deep voice. Whenever he could get away from his duties,

Sam made his way through the streets of Paris back to the gallery.

---

Amid such tumultuous times, nothing was more desirable than routine. Predictable days, terror at bay. For most of us, dreams had been parsed to a good meal, enough coal to warm the night and physical safety. The fighting in Paris was over, the Americans had established order and a surreal calm had descended. Sam's role had become more that of a policeman than of a soldier, and he was assigned a day shift that allowed him to arrive at the gallery every evening in time for dinner. I continued to scrounge for food as best I could and used my imagination to put together a meal reminiscent of better days. But for both of us, food was the least of it. Of course, I'd been right to question the wisdom of a love affair in wartime. But when has love ever been wise?

The last time I saw Sam, he approached the gallery with leaden steps, expression grim. I ran out to meet him, linked my arm through his and looked up questioningly. "What is it?" I asked reflexively, although I knew. We'd both known this was coming. Tomorrow he would leave Paris with his unit. Destination as yet unknown, but most of the guys thought they'd be heading north to continue chasing the Germans out of France.

We walked arm-in-arm up the stairs like always. Always being not quite six weeks. An eternity in light of the world's uncertainty. Sam crushed me to him more tightly than ever, rocking me from side to side as he buried his face in my hair. I cried and tried out some wild ideas. Couldn't he just desert and hide out in the gallery until the war was over? Couldn't we both slip away to Marseilles and from there get a boat to South America? Sam let me go on until I wore myself out and sat silent. He made two cups of weak tea and sat by my side. Suddenly, I jumped up.

"Well, if that's the way it is, we are not going to ruin our last night with sorrow. We have this evening, and it's more than many people get. Who knows? Perhaps the Germans will surrender tomorrow and the war will be over. We mustn't think about it. Let's make dinner."

Like actors in a staged romance, we spent the evening together, each of us playing the role of a lifetime for the other's benefit.

# 20

## ROBERT

Amy and I left our hotel in the center of Paris. We then drove for about fifteen minutes before seeing the sign for Bois de Vincennes one kilometer ahead.

"But it's so congested here! I can't believe we're that close to a park," Amy observed. "What do you think it was like here in the Forties?"

"I don't know. Now it's like Central Park, completely surrounded by the city, yet way-back-when, of course, it served as a hunting ground for the royals."

As we approached the park, I glanced at Amy, who was like a thoroughbred, straining for the jockey to let loose the reins. "Now don't go getting too excited," I cautioned. "You know this is in all likelihood a wild goose chase."

"Hey, this is givin' me life, bae!" she mimicked, grinning widely. "You, on the other hand, probably never believed in Santa Claus!"

"Well, now that you mention it..."

"See? I knew it! Anyway, I once found a message in a bottle, so perhaps I will bring us luck. And anyway, you look like Indiana Jones in that silly hat. I hope there are no snakes in the cave."

I wasn't sure what she was talking about, but I was wearing my L.L.Bean canvas hiking hat. I found myself grinning and had to admit that underneath my placid exterior was a ten-year-old boy who had a secret fort in the woods. To dream of finding a priceless painting in a cave wasn't completely beyond me.

Amy was looking down at her travel guide. "So I can see the lake here and paths all around it. Give me that map Nicole drew for you."

I reached into my vest pocket, pulled out a folded piece of paper and tossed it into Amy's lap. She unfolded it and peered back and forth between the paper containing Nicole's sketch and the map in the guidebook that lay open in her lap. "I still think you should've talked her into coming with us!" she muttered. "Hey, she's got the lake on here and in the direction she shows to go there are only two paths, so it's gotta be one of those!"

"I sure hope so, or I'm going to have some serious work to do to get you over your disappointment."

"You got that right."

"Luckily, this isn't my main reason to be here. I expect a lot more out of my visit with Edouard at the Louvre." I'd crossed paths with Edouard at various symposia and we'd developed a friendly acquaintance. When I'd briefed him on the nature of my visit over the telephone, he had asked me to send him Nicole's list of paintings and he'd see what he could find out prior to our meeting.

Amy clutched my arm. "Hey, listen to this. During the occupation, Germans used the moat surrounding the Château de Vincennes to execute Résistance members. Fuck. I wonder if Nicole knows that. I wonder if they'll have a memorial of some sort there. After we find the painting, can we tour the château?"

She was chattering like a child. I reached over and tugged a piece of her hair. "You're crazy, you know that?"

"What? I like old stuff." She slumped down in the seat and put her feet up on the dash, continuing to pore over the map.

The day was hot, even for June, and, as we pulled into the park, we saw only a few people—just some joggers and cyclists and an old couple sitting on a bench, feeding the pigeons. Trees veiled the place from the busy cadence of the city. The slam of our car doors intruded upon the silence. I pulled my pack from the trunk, then lowered the lid slowly, leaning hard on it to fasten it quietly. I slung the pack over one shoulder, then pulled my hat down lower over my forehead. Amy donned a baseball cap and, holding her guidebook and Nicole's sketch, led the way along a paved path toward the lake.

Bird song was all that broke the silence. The warm stretch of weather had shriveled the landscape and it smelled faintly of hay and decomposed wood. I walked behind Amy, willing myself to remove my eyes from her slim form in closely fitting jeans. She turned back toward me. "Come on, come on!" she called, waving me on and jogging in place.

The lake captured the motionless reflections of the trees along the shore, like facets striating an emerald. In the center, a slow rowboat broke the reflections into abstract prisms. I thought of Matisse's paper cut-outs. Sweat began to break out under the rim of my hat. I took it off and fanned myself.

"So it could be either the first or second trail leading off from this lake trail. From the looks of the topographical map, both of them approach an escarpment of sorts that could be the hill Nicole was talking about. The first one should come up pretty quickly."

A cyclist came up behind us and rang her bell. "Hey, I had

one of those when I was a girl!" Amy exclaimed. "That exact same sound. How cool. I should get one."

"I'll remember that on your birthday. Probably cheaper than roses." I took Amy's hand. The first trail leading off to the right was surfaced with wood chips and much narrower than the one around the lake.

I looked at my watch. "Okay, Nicole says they were picnicking within sight of the lake and she thinks she and her father had only walked ten minutes or so before he found the cave." After another ten minutes the land began to rise slightly. I stopped. "Well, that was ten minutes and there's certainly no hill that would contain a cave here. Let's continue for another five, okay?"

"Sure. She was really just a kid back then. Probably excited to be on a hike with her dad and time just flew by."

Amy dragged a damp piece of hair back behind her ear. I noticed it was getting even curlier. I thought I detected a note of nostalgia in her voice. "Did you do things like that with your dad?"

"My dad was so busy with his car repair shop that he had little time for anything else. So the few times I do remember doing something with him really stand out in my memory. Mostly handing him tools while he was fixing cars. In the freezing cold. That's when they usually broke down, of course!"

We continued in silence, occasionally stumbling over a root or having to duck under a low-hanging branch. My shirt stuck to my back. After another five minutes, I stopped. "Yeah, I don't think this is it. The escarpment must be off to our left, but far enough that it wouldn't have been accessible from this path. Let's go back and try the other trail."

We walked briskly back along the path to where it intersected with the lake trail. Amy pointed to a large, flat-topped boulder facing the lake. "Maybe we should have our picnic now."

"I thought you were eager to find the cave."

"I am, but I'm also eager for a sandwich." She paused. "And maybe I want to put off the moment we find out this really is a wild goose chase. I'm enjoying the anticipation."

Amy bent forward to stretch her back. I walked over to the rock, sat down and pulled out the baguette sandwiches we had bought from the bakery near our hotel.

"Did you bring the wine?" Amy asked with a smirk.

"I wish! You'll have to wait till we get back to the hotel."

"Well, no matter what happens, I have to say I'm enjoying this trip so far," Amy murmured before sinking her teeth into the crunchy crust of the baguette.

"Me, too. A picnic with a beautiful woman in the French countryside. Doesn't get much better."

After finishing our sandwiches, I stood and extended my hand to Amy. She grasped it and allowed me to pull her up from the rock, pretending to lose her balance and falling forward against me. After a long kiss, we reluctantly separated, and I pictured the cozy hotel room waiting for us.

Across the lake, banks of flowers created an abstract palette of magenta, pink and purple. Green shrubs framed the composition. I memorized the view for a future watercolor. The sun peeked under my hat and beamed a prickly but not unpleasant ray of heat onto the lower part of my face. I lifted my chin and closed my eyes for a second. When was the last time I had just relaxed in the sun? Anywhere? I brought Amy's hand to my lips. "We should go on a vacation together. Someplace like this. Warm and sunny and perfect." She bumped her shoulder against mine, looked up and smiled.

A pleasant stroll along the lake brought us to the second of the trails, veering off to the right. It, too, was narrow and wood-chipped. I checked my watch. "Okay, let's go!" I walked purposely ahead, with Amy close behind. A squirrel skittered across the path, startling me.

"Oh, so it's squirrels you're scared of!" Amy poked me in the back.

The path began to curve left. A crow cawed from the top of a dead tree. The wood chips petered out, so that we were now treading hard-packed soil strewn with last year's leaves. Insects rustled and whirred. I waved a mosquito away from my face. Then another. Why did they always seek that space between my hat and forehead? I took my hat off and dried my forehead with my sleeve.

Amy poked me again. "Look, the land is definitely starting to rise on our left."

"It's been eight minutes. We probably should start walking along the rise, parallel to the path." I plunged into the deep weeds and began to walk between the path and what was slowly climbing to become a high hill. I held back a branch of a spindly tree as Amy pushed her way through the knotty brush.

"This is unbelievable," she cried. "I mean, we might really find it! But, Robert, do you think any painting could have survived so many years in a cave? What if all we find is a soggy pile of canvas? After all this time..."

"Nicole said if anyone would know how to protect a painting, her father would. And if you notice the terrain here, it's dry and rocky. Hopefully, this cave is just as dry and rocky." I tripped over a tree root and stumbled onto one knee. "I think we better just concentrate on looking for the cave." I pulled my phone from my pocket. "I'm gonna take a GPS reading here. We're veering further from the path and, painting or no painting, I don't want to get lost!"

The trees became taller and created an understory that was a bit easier to traverse. I told myself this was impossible, I was not going to find a priceless painting in a cave, this was going to turn out to be a nice walk with a woman I loved, and I should not be disappointed. Still, I was as edgy as a game show contestant waiting for the door I'd picked to open. I fought the urge to run; I needed to take it slow, be aware of every signal the landscape was willing to surrender. Nicole had said to look for an outcropping of rock behind some shrubs and search for the entrance. Every so often I stopped to examine jutting boulders.

Images from *The Treasure of the Sierra Madre* surfaced in my mind—Humphrey Bogart, dirty and grizzled, traipsing through the stony landscape looking for gold. Didn't turn out so well for him. Treasure had a way of being elusive. And cursed. Think of the things that would have caused a painting to be hidden here so many years ago. Maybe it was cursed. If the hairs on the back of my neck had not been plastered down by sweat, they would have stood up. Then I spotted an especially large outcropping.

"Amy!" I was about twenty feet ahead of her, near a pile of large boulders that interrupted the plane at the base of the hill. "I think we've found it!" She half-ran, half-stumbled up to where I held back the branches of a pine sapling. A narrow passage appeared to lead straight into the hill. I pulled off my backpack and rummaged in it for my flashlight. "Follow me. Watch your footing."

I shone the small cone of light forward, directing it back toward Amy every few seconds, so she could see where she was walking. In a few moments I could see the passageway open up into a small cave. It was dry and stony. I grabbed Amy's hand. We moved along the perimeter of the cave while I shone the light slowly over the floor and walls. It was empty. Another passage led further south, but when we reached it, we saw it was a dead end. "Well," I sighed, already accepting the disappointment, "we both knew it was unlikely."

Amy took my hand. "But just think. André played here as a boy. Nicole was here with him, in this exact spot. We should take a moment to reflect on those happy times for them." Amy shut her eyes. I stood silently, my arm around her, conjuring a dream of Nicole, a happy girl on a picnic with her parents. When I opened my eyes, I idly played the flashlight's beam around the cave.

"Wait!" Amy called. "What's that?" She took the flashlight and moved it back across one wall of the cave near the ceiling. On a small ledge sat an old metal box, barely distinguishable from the dirt and rocks surrounding it. "Not big enough for the painting, but..." Amy whispered. I stepped toward the box and brushed away a net of cobwebs, then lifted the box from its ledge and set it on the floor. We knelt in front of it. The clasp was rusted and had to be jiggled free. I opened the lid. Inside, the bodies of a dozen tin soldiers stared up at us. I met Amy's eyes and saw tears there.

"It's okay," I said, reaching an arm around her shoulders and drawing her close. "We didn't find any paintings today, but we will."

"No," she protested, "it's not that. I'm just thinking of the small boy who once played here, a boy who thought life was trips to the country and soldiers were toys."

Walking through the Tuileries, I marveled anew at these magnificent gardens, graced with classical statuary and ponds. Banks of flowers were set off by sweeps of green lawn and gravel paths. The grandeur of the palace rose in the background against an overcast but bright sky. I couldn't name many of the flower varieties, but I recognized the irises and lupines my grandmother had grown. Although it was only 9:00, the fine weather had brought people out. They dragged the green metal chairs scattered throughout the park to favorite viewing spots, some along the rim of a pond, some looking straight down the central alley. As I neared the Louvre, the clouds thickened and darkened. The glass pyramid in the courtyard looked like a volcano that had spewed dark plumes. I hoped it wasn't a bad omen.

At the Louvre's Paintings Department, a young woman in a black skirt and white blouse ushered me into a softly lit conference room. The far corner radiated color. I stared at the painting resting on the easel there, unable to look away from the glorious summer scene that evinced the smell of hay amid thick daubs of pure light. My vision tunneled and for a moment I was the painter with brush in hand, standing in a peaceful field, hearing the laughter of children, smelling the linseed oil and capturing the joy of that day for others to know. Stirred from my reverie by a rustling behind me, I turned to see Edouard, smiling with an outstretched hand.

"Bonjour, Robert! And welcome to Paris."

"Merci, Edouard. It's good to see you. I've been admiring this masterful painting. Is it, by any chance...?"

"You're—how you say—jumping the gun?" Edouard laughed and indicated the table and chairs. "Please, have a seat."

As I sat and stowed my briefcase beneath the table, Edouard lifted the Corot from the easel and brought it to the table, which was covered with a soft cloth. Carefully, he turned the painting over. He pulled a small pointer from his breast pocket and indicated the stamp on the back of the painting. It was a swastika.

"You see," Edouard explained, "every canvas that came into the hands of the Germans was stamped with the swastika. But look more closely." I leaned in as Edouard lowered the arm of a lamp that was clamped to the table. "See the letter C underneath in a faint red? That was the mark of the Cassin Gallery."

Edouard gently set the painting back on the easel and returned to his chair. We were silent for a moment as we gazed at the masterpiece. I found my throat tightening. At first, I'd found this case fascinating, in an objective, rational way. But now, looking at this painting, which had belonged to a man whose life had been brutally taken, I viscerally understood Nicole's need to recover the paintings. In fact, I even found myself a little irritated with her for waiting so long. It was about justice. And paying homage to the lives of André and Frida. And Nicole. And all the other victims.

I pulled my gaze from the painting and cleared my throat. Edouard had been typing on the laptop in front of him and now turned the screen toward me. "Look here. This is the museum's digital index card of this work. Artist, name of the painting, year acquired—1949—and this code, R347P." I pushed up my glasses and peered at the digital image of the painting and the accompanying notations Edouard had pointed out.

"And the code means?"

"The R stands for 'Recuperation.' Meaning this painting was one of the thousands of works recovered from repositories all over Europe after the war. That explains the fact that there is no provenance associated with it, no donor listed. The 347 means it was the 347th artwork to be entrusted to the Louvre. And the P merely designates that it is a painting."

"But didn't anyone ever try to find out what the C stood for? Who the real owner might be? In all these years?"

Edouard slowly shook his head. "Not at first. Imagine the chaos. More than 60,000 works of art had been found and returned to France. And 45,000 or so were successfully returned to their owners. That left about 15,000 unclaimed works. Of these, the most important 2,000 were put under the protection of the museums, while the remaining 13,000 were sold at auction. Of course, it was thought that the owners would eventually come looking—if they were still alive, that is. You must understand, in the aftermath of the war many other concerns were paramount." He paused, perhaps to let me imagine the brutalized people, the ruined cities.

"But since the recent publication of several books on the subject, there's been renewed interest in finding the rightful owners. That's our goal. Some have accused the museum of just wanting to keep the paintings. I don't believe that. I think that, as the years slipped by, people just forgot. But much work has been done recently. We now have a website that can be searched, and it contains a lot of data on these paintings." Raking a hand through a fall of silky, shoulder-length hair, Edouard asked, "As a matter of curiosity, may I ask you why your client never sought these paintings before?"

"Once she emigrated to the United States she began a new life and wanted nothing more than to forget everything associated with the old one."

"Ah, understandably so." Edouard pressed his lips together. "It was an era of unbelievable horror. Of course, we're also finding owners who perished in the war and whose heirs were not even aware of their ownership of specific paintings. Does your client have any papers—any receipts, photos, gallery records—that show her to be the rightful owner? Because even with the C on the back, it's possible the Cassin gallery had sold it to someone else. Of course, if the sale was coerced or at an unfair value, as many were in those times, Cassin would still be considered the rightful owner."

"I'm working on that," I replied. "Apparently, some of the gallery's old records were archived after the gallery was closed. And I'm researching exhibition catalogs."

Edouard pulled the laptop back toward him and typed in a

few keystrokes. "Now, here's some more good news." He pushed the laptop across the table. I stared at the screen.

"Good God! Nicole's La Tour and Cranach?"

"Indeed, I think so. The same C is underneath the swastika."

I leaned back in the leather chair. Three down, three to go —including the Picasso. "Can we have another look at the back of that Corot?"

"Of course!" Edouard retrieved the painting.

"This—this mark here." I indicated a scrawled notation alongside the swastika. "What does that say?"

Edouard leaned in for a closer look. The handwriting was a spidery, old-fashioned European script. "Ah, yes, that. That says 'Göring.' This must have been claimed by Göring, probably for Carinhall."

"Can you look at the other two paintings to see if there are any additional marks on them? Perhaps we can piece together a trail from these paintings that will suggest where the others may have gone. It's a long shot, I know."

"I'd be happy to. I can do this tomorrow and call you. What hotel?"

"The Crillon."

"But of course."

"How difficult will it be to prove Nicole's ownership?" Amy asked. She had met me in the Tuileries after my meeting with Edouard, and I'd filled her in on my confirmation that three of Nicole's paintings were in the Louvre.

"Well, given what happened, it's unlikely that written records of sale will be found. But maybe. Maybe if the family bought them from a gallery that's still operating or whose records were archived. Also, Nicole kept records for her father when she worked at the gallery and later, too, when Roland ran it. When she closed the gallery after the war, she archived its records somewhere. I haven't talked to her about that yet.

"Other evidence would include any photos that might exist of their apartment, with the paintings on the walls. Or the paintings might be found in a catalog of an exhibition, listing the Cassins as current owners. Lacking any other documentation of the work until it shows up after the war, one could presume it still belonged to them when it was confiscated by the Nazis. The records of the Nazis themselves might prove the most useful. But lacking anything else, Edouard thought the C on the back of the paintings and a sworn statement by Nicole might be enough."

Amy leaned over and turned my chin toward the scene in front of us. "Look! It's a painting! Whose?"

I cast my gaze over the wide pool surrounded by children pushing small boats and splashes of colorful flowers. "Well, Pissarro perhaps, as he painted many versions of the gardens. Monet did as well—in particular, a beautiful depiction from a high vantage point. And, of course, many would say Seurat, thinking of *A Sunday on La Grande Jatte*, but that wasn't really painted in the Tuileries. One that is less known, but which I like a lot, is by Joseph Caraud, generally known for interiors. But his *Feeding the Birds*, with its depiction of a small child and her maid in the foreground, is really charming." I stopped suddenly and looked at Amy. "Uh oh, I think your eyes are glazing over," I observed, pulling her up and toward one of the sandwich kiosks.

The next day Edouard phoned me and reported that the La Tour and Cranach paintings also had the designation for Göring and the Cassin gallery on them. Amy shot me a puzzled look. "Why do you think these three pieces showed up at the Louvre, while the others are still missing?"

"That's what we have to figure out. Starting with Göring's primary dealers: Hofer, Lohse and Wendland. And that fellow Nicole said took over the gallery—Roland something. I have it written in my notes. I think we should see what we can find out about their activities at the end of the war and afterwards."

# 21

## NICOLE

I'm known as a forceful woman who can get things done. Unbeknownst to my admirers, it's because I abhor waiting. By the end of 1945 I had experienced the torture of waiting in line at the prison wondering if I would see Papa or be imprisoned myself. I knew the tedium of queuing day after day for a morsel of food. I had suppressed hope while waiting for a broadcast that would announce an Allied attack. I waited for each day to end and then waited for the sleep that was elusive. But there is no waiting like the waiting for a lover's reassurance of his love. If asked, I would've said it was not the most profound thing in my life, but that would've been a lie.

After the chaos of the liberation, some semblance of order was established by the American and Free French forces occupying Paris. The Germans were gone. But we weren't yet free. And the shortages remained. As did the fear. Some citizens had forgotten what it meant to be civilized and mimicked the very actions of our barbaric conquerors. The city's people experienced a dissonant symphony of conflicting emotions—celebration, grief, fear, joy, anxiety, hate, nostalgia, hope, confusion, love, greed—all dialed up to maximum volume. Acceptance and forgiveness were like the tiny beseeching notes of a precious violin, unheard in the din. Meanwhile, freedom to speak openly meant freedom to gossip; and speculation was rampant regarding what would happen next.

After Sam's departure, I moved back in with Gisèle. The gallery was haunted by too many pasts. My girlhood, Roland's occupation, my interlude with Sam. I reclaimed my old, practical self; and this Nicole went to the shops and stood in line for food, dodged the leers of soldiers, helped Lisle with her lessons. But inside, another Nicole observed it all as if from a great distance.

Sam's friend O'Rourke was assigned to security duties in Paris. He had agreed to receive Sam's letters and deliver them to me, as mail delivery had the reliability of a drunk's promises. Waiting elasticizes time. When waiting for something pleasant, time passes slowly, the way a late summer creek trickles along. When waiting for something unpleasant, time rushes forward like a riverful of spring rain. Every day that O'Rourke didn't come, I set an internal clock ahead twenty-four hours, during which my fears multiplied.

The greatest terror was reserved not for the thought of Sam's being killed. No, what carved the biggest chasm in my heart was the fear that he might stop loving me. Had I been just as silly and naïve as other girls the gossips gorged on? Had I fallen too easily for an American soldier's charms? Had he said things he didn't mean? Was he even now bragging of his conquest to his friends? Had there been other women, too? What about those nights he'd been assigned to guard duty? What if he'd gotten me pregnant? No, I wouldn't allow such a possibility. Anyway, should that disaster occur, I vowed I'd never tell him. Because the worst thing I could imagine was his pity. I reminded myself over and over: I was tough, I was a survivor. I must focus on practical issues, find a bit of milk for Lisle, who'd become as thin as a sapling.

Every day when O'Rourke brought a letter, I noted my trembling hands and rushing pulse and thought to myself, Look at the naïve girl, so excited over a goodbye letter. But my finger slid quickly through the blue tissue that contained my name in Sam's large and loopy scrawl. Sam's salutations were breezy and affectionate and sometimes silly: "My Dearest Darling," "Ma Chérie," "Sweetest Girl in the World," "My Little Kitten." In this way, I'd know immediately that he was not writing to say goodbye. Tight as a shrunken garment, my body loosened upon reading his endearments. There was no news of war in Sam's letters. Rather, they were classic love letters, full of praise for me, recollections of special moments together and projections of a long future. The tattered and smudged envelope was the only indication that this missive had come not from some idyll, where the lover sat in a bower of flowers imagining his love, but from a war zone.

And then, the next twenty-four hours slowly passed.

---

Every day I went to Gare d'Orsay where it was said that most of the returning prisoners would arrive. The men staggered from the railroad cars into the light, some in tattered uniforms, others in rags of unknowable origin. Beyond the barricades, people shouted. Where are you coming from? Anyone from Belsen? Have you seen my husband? My boy, Denis? Denis Beaumont? Please? Names were shouted and the men looked up, dazed, uncertain. One answered Auschwitz, and the crowd became louder, more insistent. Names rang out desperately, over and over. The men shook their heads and were herded into waiting trucks to transport them to processing centers and hospitals.

I, too, shouted. "André Cassin! Frida Cassin! Anyone seen them? Alfred Lefebvre? Lefebvre?" Gisèle went to Gare de l'Est and called out for her husband and my parents. In the evenings, we reunited at the apartment, exchanging glum looks that required no explanation.

Everyone in Paris was looking for someone, most turning away in disappointment. Once in a while, there was an answer. Yes, he's alive! I saw your husband two days ago at Belsen. The crowd would turn toward the woman who hugged herself, crying. Stirred by this small bit of good news, everyone would stare at its recipient with envy so palpable that she'd look around, embarrassed, and leave hurriedly. But sometimes a man would approach the questioner, shaking his head sadly and grasping her hands. Then the crowd averted its gaze.

Lists of arrivals were posted outside the processing centers. Either Gisèle or I checked them daily. As time passed and the flow of returnees dwindled, I began to hope for no news because what could the news be now? Then came the day a returning deportee lifted his head as he heard my call. "Cassin?" he repeated.

I shoved my way to the front of the barricade. "André, Frida Cassin, my parents. Have you seen them?" I leaned heavily on the barricade, fearing the news would rob me of what little strength I had left. The man approached, dragging one foot. He was thinner than anyone I'd ever seen and had a long gray beard. A few stray hairs straggled from the top of his head.

"Nicole?" Suddenly I recognized his smile. Luc DuPont, one of Papa's friends. I grasped his hands, kissed the backs of them, tears clogging my vision. I remember wanting to prolong the moment, this moment in which I still didn't know, this moment in which my parents could still be alive. I waited.

"They're alive," Luc said. "I talked to someone on the train who was at Auschwitz a few weeks ago. He met them."

"They're alive. They're together." My words drifted off. I was stunned and knew that I had been expecting the worst. I almost didn't know how to react. Then my heart broke through, with all its irrepressible hope. "Thank you," I cried, clutching Luc's hands, pressing my cheek to them. "Thank you, thank you, thank you."

One of the soldiers overseeing the prisoners' return came over and gently took Luc's elbow. "Come now, you can catch up later." He nodded at me as I pulled my sweater down over my hands and used it to wipe my eyes.

***

These days I allow myself the luxury of a slow rising to consciousness, fighting to stay in the dream state, to blur the sharp edges of what passes for reality. There is a grief that's deeper than tears and, well, once you've been there, tears seem frivolous. I didn't cry when my husband died. Everyone thought I should—that it would somehow ease the grief. But those tears would've been for show. To prove to others that I loved Walt. Real grief is quiet, relentless, a steady current. An eruption of tears signifies nothing.

I remember many things now, painful things I had tried so hard to forget, and yet, with that forgetting, I lost precious memories as well. Lounging with my parents over café au lait and newspapers on the terrace of our flat. Maman's gentle hands combing my hair. Papa's gruff voice when he tried to be angry, quickly dissolving into a chuckle and a mild admonition. Sam. The way he looked that first day, ducking his head in through the door, shyly asking if they could search the gallery. Brown-eyed, chestnut-haired, rough-whiskered, lanky Sam.

Even now, after all these years, I can feel the craving I felt then, and the curiosity—of what was this creature made? I remember our first kiss, the first time we undressed and held each other close, the warmth of his skin against mine from lips to toes.

Why hadn't I tried harder to find him? Oh, what good are recriminations? I'd been so young. I'd lost everything else, so it was easy to believe that he, too, had abandoned me. But somehow, those days of my youth in Paris are becoming more real to me now than the decades with Walt, going through the motions of being a wife and mother and small-scale philanthropist. I walked through those years in a fog of unacknowledged grief and a determination to forget. The Nazis had almost killed Nicole; I finished the job.

I pull my hair back tightly until it hurts, then twist it up into a clip, feeling a migraine coming on. The light pains me. Fingers pressing my temples, I walk across the plush oriental rug and draw the drapes closed, then lay on the sofa, clutching a pillow to my chest. No, no more. Forget the paintings, forget the war, forget. I press the pillow to my face until I can't breathe. Extinguish. Escape. Exterminate.

*October 1945. One of those fall days that brings hope against all odds. Yes, the days are getting shorter, the weather cooler. Yes, the winter cold and rains are coming. But this day is redolent of summer: sun-soaked, dry, the rustle of papery leaves like the pages of a new book being written. The scent in the air is clean, like cedar chests opened up, blankets drying on a line. Food is more plentiful; prisoners and POWs are returning; visions of a life after war are taking shape.*

*I am buoyed by Luc DuPont's report of seeing my parents alive and together. I had received a letter from Sam, full of loving promises. I am at the gallery, typing up my notes on the acquisitions and sales of artworks during the occupation, confi-dent these will be useful eventually. People are returning from all parts of the country and city, like birds blown off course in a hurricane and finding their way home again.*

I turn over onto my stomach and press the pillow to the back of my head. The apartment is eerily quiet. No humming from the furnace or refrigerator. No creak of elevator. No footsteps from the upstairs neighbors. Just the memories, insistent, banging away inside, like desperate prisoners. No, please, not this one.

*The bell jingles and I look up. "Madame Bocuse!" I exclaim, rising to greet her. We graze each other's cheeks and I see lines where few had existed before. I know that I, too, look different. I invite Madame Bocuse back for tea and put the office kettle on. Madame Bocuse sits in Papa's chair.*

*"My dear girl, what do you hear of your parents?" she asks, as I sink into the chair opposite her. I fill her in on Luc DuPont's report and ask about Madame Bocuse's family. "Well, we suffered like many, with not enough to eat and bowing down to the German pigs," she said. "But not being Jewish, of course we did not face the atrocities that you had to deal with."*

*I retrieve the kettle and pour hot water into a small teapot, watching the water slowly turn the dregs a pale rust color.*

*"But my dear, did you hear about the Mandels?" Madame Bocuse speaks in a low tone.*

*"No. What?" I pause, the teapot poised above an old mug.*

My head is on fire. I will be in pain for days. I must get to my bedroom, which I can make completely dark. I stand and am seized with a dizziness that brings me to my knees. No, no more.

*"They were hiding at our lake house. The Germans came looking for their art collection, then shot every one of them, right there and then." Her voice breaks. "Even little Ricard... He was two." Madame Bocuse begins to cry.*

*I picture them. Astride, Pierre, their twin daughters, Ricard.
"The girls..." My voice wanders.*

*"All of them."*

Maybe the Mandels would have been killed anyway. So many were. But the instant I have that thought, I am so ashamed of myself. There is no excuse. Then I think, did those I saved working for the Résistance balance out what I did to the Mandels? Again, no excuse. And as odious as I found collaborators, wasn't that what I'd done, by giving Captain Stoltz what he wanted? I thought of it then as a negotiation—a negotiation for my parents' lives, against which some paintings counted for nothing. But it didn't turn out that way, did it? Papa was never freed and the Mandels were killed. That was the problem with collaboration. The Germans had the upper hand and there was no such thing as negotiation. I was so young, my conscience pleads. Old enough to see what the Germans were capable of, though. I didn't know the Mandels were there; I thought I was only giving up the paintings. I should never have trusted a German soldier. But I couldn't have forgiven myself if I'd passed up a chance to free my parents and then they'd died. I can't forgive myself for the death of the Mandels. But maybe I can find a way to live with myself.

<h1 style="text-align:center">22</h1>

<h2 style="text-align:center">ROBERT</h2>

I gripped the arms of the chair, unsure how to deliver my news. Since taking on Nicole's assignment, I'd found myself stopping in at her apartment fairly regularly, to deliver progress reports or, as more often was the case, lack of progress reports. She had not asked for such regular updates and seemed surprised and grateful for them. It wasn't some sort of super customer service ethic on my part. No, my motive was much more selfish. I'd become hooked on Nicole's story and wanted to hear more and more. In the process, I'd discovered her fine intelligence and knowledge of art. And a wry sense of humor that seemed to startle even her. She took on a sheepish look after delivering a perfectly apt snide remark.

I had the feeling that these were remarks she once would have censored. There were always fresh flowers in front of the window. Yellow roses today, fluttering as if beckoning me to begin. "I've unearthed some information of interest," I stammered, recognizing how unemotional a prelude those words were to the news I was about to impart. Nicole's eyes were fixed upon me. I cleared my throat. "Sam Popinski died shortly after I first met you."

Nicole's hand went up to her throat and she gave a small gasp. Her eyes blinked rapidly.

I hurried to add, "But, you see, I also discovered later that this Sam Popinski was not your Sam Popinski." Nicole slowly lowered her hand and gazed at me expectantly. "As best as I can reconstruct this, a Russian soldier appropriated the real Sam's identity near the end of the war; and after coming to the US, lived out the rest of his life under Sam's name and with Sam's family. I can only conclude that Sam was killed during the war, and this man took on his identity to save his own life." I had spoken rapidly and now paused to let this sink in. "I'm sorry to bring you this sad news." God, I sounded like a moron. I am sorry for your loss, etc. The standard words of consolation that never console.

The silence was thick, absorbing all sounds, even that of our breathing. Then Nicole spoke. "Sad and yet a part of me is relieved. Because now I can believe that if he'd lived, he would've found me. I can mourn him without bitterness, without recrimination, and only with regret that I didn't trust his love." She paused, gazing at something in the middle distance. Perhaps it was the past. "I might've been different."

Nicole's eyes returned to me as she asked, "What about the paintings?"

Relieved that I'd delivered my news about Sam and we could move on to less emotional territory, I glanced down at my notebook. "Well, there the news is remarkably positive. Three of them have been stored in the Louvre all these years—the Corot, the La Tour and the Cranach."

Nicole nearly jumped out of her chair and paced the length of the living room, hands clasped in front of her. "Incredible! Really?" Her face was alight and she looked years younger.

I briefed her on my research, the trip to Paris, my meeting with Edouard. I think she looked forward to my research reports as much as I enjoyed her stories of her youth.

"If you have the time today, we can start the process to have them returned to you."

She swallowed hard. "Thank you. I don't know what it will be like to see them again, but I want to very much. And the others?"

"The Rembrandt was something Hitler probably would've wanted for the Führermuseum, so I think I may find it in one of the German or Austrian museums. The Picasso and the Cézanne would've been considered degenerate by the Nazis, so I suspect they were sold to private collectors. I'm in the process of tracking down some of the dealers and their business activities after the war."

Nicole made a noise that almost sounded like a growl. "Yes, Hofer. Hofer and Wendland." She practically spit their names out. "They were around the most often. Vultures picking over the carcasses of dead Jews. Looking for the highest bidders. And then getting off with fines and going about their business again. I couldn't stand it. Once I saw there was no justice, I went into denial. Isn't that the popular diagnosis today? Denial? Well, they denied their crimes and I denied my former existence."

Nicole raised her hands and pulled the clip from her hair, then dragged her fingers through her curls. "I traded Nicole's soul for the veneer of happiness, to become Nicky, to forget. Now Nicole has come back—and Nicky? It's as if she's been erased. I don't know who Nicky was. Perhaps only who Walt believed she was. Maybe that's why I waited so long to come back. I couldn't while Walt was still alive." She stood. "Excuse an old woman's ramblings. I'm sure you had no idea what you were getting into when you signed up for this project." Her laugh was tinged with bitterness. "Let me get us some tea," she said, walking briskly from the room.

I thought about what she'd said. About Nicky having been a veneer. Something about it hit a little too close to home. Was I, too, living a facsimile of my life, a sort of seventeenth-century Persian miniature of myself, painted with a brush of two or three hairs from a white cat on carefully prepared paper, elaborately framed, but only truly appreciated through a magnifying glass? Had I allowed others to paint me into this tiny frame? Or had I willingly chosen to sit still and be captured thus, bound by constraints that I, like Nicole, might someday regret?

Finding the Rembrandt was ridiculously easy. It wasn't hidden; it was just that no one had ever looked for it. On a sudden whim, I plugged in "Rembrandt paintings" and found a site that catalogued known Rembrandt works and locations. Although Rembrandt painted numerous self-portraits, it took only minutes for me to find Nicole's Self-Portrait, in the Rijksmuseum, Amsterdam. According to the website, in 1942 the painting had been bought by Walter Andreas Hofer from Hans Wendland. It was briefly in the private collection of Adolf Hitler. How it ended up in the Rijksmuseum, I could only conjecture. I hadn't found an index card for it, but then again, I hadn't looked through every single one. Maybe it hadn't gone through the recovery process but had found its way to Amsterdam by some other route. After all, Rembrandt was Dutch, so it would be easy to see how someone could surmise it'd been stolen during the Nazi occupation of Holland. Once I put together documentation of the Cassins' ownership, I didn't expect to have any trouble retrieving it from the museum. That left two paintings unaccounted for—the Cézanne and the Picasso.

Back at the computer, I picked through the Office of Strategic Services Art Looting Investigation Unit reports. They included a transcription of an interview with Walter Andreas Hofer. As Göring's chief agent in Paris, and one who, according to Nicole, frequented the Cassin Gallery and the Jeu de Paume, he had to be the key to finding the missing Cézanne and Picasso. Thankfully, the reports were also digitized and online. The blurry type and gray pages were hard to read, but after two hours of going through them, I had yet to find any mention of Nicole's pictures, even though there were detailed descriptions of various paintings and murky transactions.

# 23
## NICOLE

For most of my life people have commented on how strong I am. Even when I learned that my parents had died at Auschwitz, I didn't cry. But now, I wonder. Did my armor ward off as much joy as grief? Are the truly strong those who are strong enough to be vulnerable? Feel the pain and be open to the joy? It's rather late for such questions. I remember the faces of my children when they were small. I did love them. But that love was tempered by caution. I feared for them. And I feared for me. I could not stand more loss.

I'll never stop wondering what would've happened if I had disobeyed Maman and stayed with her at the gallery that day. It wouldn't have been the first time I rebelled. I was a willful, somewhat spoiled girl. I see that now. Why did I listen to her that day? Was it cowardice? But I had faced up to the Nazis before, when they came into the gallery before the war. Still, that was before Papa's arrest, before I'd seen him bruised and beaten at Fresnes, before lists of the executed began appearing on the sides of buildings. Did I really believe Maman when she said she'd meet me later? I remember the icy feeling of inevitability when she disappeared. I must have been in shock from everything that had happened. Today we have a name for this: post-traumatic stress disorder. Of what use is it for me to try to dissect my behavior from such a distance? Because I can't forgive myself for not staying with her. In my heart of hearts, I believe I could've saved them.

They were alive at the liberation of Auschwitz. But the spark of life they had left could not outlast the bureaucracy and delay of the Allies in getting the prisoners relocated and treated. Had I been with them, couldn't I have managed to take care of them, find them a little more food, shelter them, insist that our liberators hospitalize them? I would not have let them die.

# 24

## ROBERT

Amy's Pleasant Ridge neighborhood resembled a Norman Rockwell painting. Mature plantings of dogwoods, crabapples and lilacs bloomed in front of brick homes graced by an occasional turret. I parked my rental car in front of her Arts and Crafts bungalow, with its wide, welcoming front porch, and felt oddly expansive as I bounded up the steps, as if I weren't contained by my own skin. I knocked briefly, then pushed the door open. Amy stood in the center of the room, her dark hair held back beneath a hairband. She wore jeans, faded and ripped at the knee and an old University of Michigan tee shirt. "You're early!" she shrieked, as she threw her arms around my neck. "I look a fright!"

I pulled off her hairband and tousled her curls. "I got to the airport early and went standby on an earlier flight. Thought I'd surprise you."

"Mmmm," she murmured between kisses. "Good surprise."

Inside, the floors were a warm golden oak and at one end of the living room stood a fireplace tiled in Pewabic pottery. The fireplace was flanked by built-in cabinets with leaded glass

222

doors. Amy's collection of American pottery cast colorful pinks and greens through the doors, echoing the shades of the drapes and pillows she had made. She looked me up and down. "You're out of uniform," she observed.

I grinned. I was wearing a denim shirt and khakis, no sport coat. "Trying to loosen up. Don't worry, my uniform is in the car, in case I get too insecure." We sat in the small, diner-like booth at the end of the kitchen that faced the narrow back yard. The sun emerged from behind one of the clouds clotting the sky and I noted the green tinge of leaves beginning to unfurl at the tip of each twig on a dogwood tree. Amy served sandwiches from her favorite Jewish deli in nearby Oak Park.

"So what have you learned?" she asked.

I held up a finger, avidly chewing pastrami and Swiss on marbled rye. I swallowed, then gulped down some coffee. "Well, Karl Haberstock went through 'denazification' after the war so he could recover his gallery and artworks."

Amy put her sandwich down and straightened in her seat. "Wait a minute. You're not kidding are you? 'Denazification?' Really? Please tell me at the very least it involved shock treatment."

"Sorry, no. Actually, it was the Allies who first came up with the term. The idea was to remove Nazis from positions of power in Germany. They came up with categories, from 'Major Offenders' down to 'Exonerated,' and intended to investigate and assign people to each one, with corresponding punishments. But there were millions of Germans who had been members of the Nazi party. The task was overwhelming. And as usual, idealism was trampled by practical needs. Some aspects of society required the skills of former Nazis in order to prevent collapse, or so it was believed. Nuclear scientists, regardless of their war crimes, were whisked off to the US. Americans clamored for their soldiers to come home. So the process was turned over to the Germans. They, too, struggled with the caseload, the shortage of certain types of skills and the unpopularity of the whole thing with the German people."

Amy shook her head. "So Haberstock got off."

"Not exactly. First, he was judged to be a 'Fellow Traveler' and fined. 'Fellow Traveler' was the designation given to those judged to have just gone along with, but not actively initiated, war crimes. After an appeal, he was completely exonerated. He and his wife moved to Munich and he resumed his business as an art dealer. His past seemed to be forgotten in proportion to the number of artworks he donated or loaned to various institutions. There's even a bust of him in the Schaezlerpalais museum in Augsburg." I paused to resume my attack on the pastrami, while Amy stared at me.

"I'm losing my appetite. I'm not sure I want to know any more."

I looked up and continued relentlessly. "Hofer had become Göring's chief dealer. While Haberstock's actions were highly questionable, Hofer's were utterly heinous. He helped confiscate art owned by Jews that was stored in bank vaults, and he regularly visited the Jeu de Paume with Göring to select pieces of looted art. He had no compunction about using his position to trade visas for valuable artworks. Many people were literally trading art for their lives, to escape Germany or France. That is, if the deals they made were honored. Hofer was slick enough that, after the war, his wealth could not be found."

"Surely he went to prison!" Amy exclaimed.

"Wrong again. He was sentenced to ten years by a French court, but he was long gone—settled in Munich just down the street from Haberstock and continued to deal in art. Wendland was let off by the Swiss in return for one painting."

"So even after the war, paintings were being used to buy lives." Amy clutched her fork and banged it angrily on the table. "I can't believe it! Thieves, murderers, grave robbers. And all was forgotten?"

"It gets worse. At least from my perspective. A lot of museum directors and art historians were involved in the looting, and most of them were 'rehabilitated,' too, and went on to prestigious careers. Kai Mühlmann, an Austrian art historian, actually put together commando squads for the express purpose of looting art in Poland. Churches, museums, monasteries, private residences—nothing was spared. Mühlmann was in a camp for SS men for a couple of years, but incredibly he concocted some story about being in the Résistance! Can you believe it? He was still being questioned when he escaped in '48 from detention in Munich. Although he lived the rest of his life as a fugitive, apparently no one tried very hard to find him, and he had plenty of money, since he could continue to sell artworks in his possession through a network of shady dealers."

"What about that man who took over the Cassin Gallery? Roland something or other."

"LaPierre. It looks like he hightailed it to Germany and threw in with a small-time dealer there for a few years. His name surfaces in France again in the '60s, where he continued to ply his criminal trade by getting involved in gun smuggling. He was imprisoned in '68 and died in '72."

"What does all this mean for Nicole's paintings?"

I tossed my napkin on the table and looked up over my glasses. "They could be anywhere," I said slowly. "On the walls of a private owner, most likely. Possibly still in the possession of one of the dealers or their heirs. Most of them used secondary dealers to assist them in hiding the provenance of stolen pieces. We need to track some of those guys down. My FBI buddy Jack's helping me."

"I'm thinking there might be an upside to this," Amy said slowly, her eyes narrowed.

"What could that possibly be?"

"Well, if these guys got off mostly scot-free and, in fact, continued to ply their trade, for one thing, they'll be easier to find. And for another, they'll think of themselves as innocent. People don't like to think of themselves as criminals and the further the past gets behind them, the more these guys will believe their own myths. Community leaders, prominent citizens, art dealers. They might let their guard down enough that they'll talk more freely than they should."

"Good point. You can coach me on how to approach a conversation with them. The data point to Munich. One, the Cassin paintings in the Louvre have Göring's stamp on them. Two, most of his dealers were German. Three, many German dealers relocated to Munich after the war. So, you up for a trip to Germany?"

A map of Munich was spread out on the floor in front of my sofa. I marked a number on it corresponding to an address that Amy read to me from a list provided by Jack. It contained the location of a gallery that had once been associated with Hofer and also the addresses of the currently living relatives of Hofer and Haberstock. Wendland had returned to Switzerland after the war. "There's probably a way to plot these electronically," I surmised, "but it would take me longer to figure it out than it will for us to do it this way. Besides, I love maps."

"Of course you do," Amy teased me. "Actually, I do, too. Maps somehow make us believe the world is all sorted out. The i's are dotted, the t's are crossed, the physical world is all plotted. Nothing that can't be controlled."

"Enough with the analysis. Give me the next address Fräulein Wexford."

Amy smoothed down the map folds. "Both Haberstock and Hofer ended up living in Munich, on the same street, the Königinstrasse. Their families still live in the area." She read off the addresses.

"So," Amy leaned back on her heels. "How exactly are we going to go about this? Any ideas?"

"Two thoughts. One approach for the dealers' heirs and one for the galleries. For the dealers' heirs, I think I'll use my real identity and suggest that, as an art historian, I want to write an article about the dealers. I can make it clear that I think the whole story about the wartime transactions was one-sided and the dealers were treated unfairly, when they were only plying their trade. After all, they weren't the ones who stole the art works."

"I think you're going to have to work on that line. Maybe don't touch on the past but say you're doing an article on prominent Munich dealers. Don't forget, these guys convinced themselves that they were pillars of their community. I'm sure their heirs came to believe that as well."

"Right. Good point. Then, as far as visiting galleries goes, how about we pose as a wealthy American couple and put it out that we're looking to round out our collection. Cézanne and Picasso. Maybe throw in a couple of others so we're not too obvious."

"That should work. No one's going to suspect us. After all, the dealers we're talking about are dead. More than likely their successors are only vaguely aware of the sketchy provenances of some of the works they trade."

"Right again. Besides which, there's a long history of secret deals among private art collectors. Ownership of just the right painting is as much a competition and statement of position as it ever was, sad to say. More than likely, the paintings we're looking for are already in some private collection, but you never know when an owner might be interested in selling. Especially if we indicate we're really hoping to find something specific—a Picasso cubist portrait, for example. A dealer could contact the owner, if he knows of it, and see if they'd be interested in selling. Since none of Nicole's paintings have ever been sought or even registered on the Lost Art Database, no alarm bells would go off."

"So how do I look wealthy?" Amy asked. "Are you going to drape me with diamonds?"

"Maybe," I answered, crawling toward her, "but first I'm going to drape you with me."

The Munich gallery owner wore a severely cut black suit, white silk blouse and very high heels. I took Amy's hand as we walked toward the center of the gallery. The woman greeted us in German, tossing a fan of jet-black hair out of her eyes. I'd never seen lips so red. She reminded me of someone from a cartoon, maybe a pretty version of Cruella de Vil. I returned her greeting in German, which caused her to switch to English. "Ah, my accent's that bad, is it?" I grinned.

"No, no," she protested smoothly, "I just like to practice my English whenever possible."

I introduced myself as Mr. Wexford and Amy as my wife. The woman in black was named Helga. How appropriate. She asked how she might help us. "Oh, we're just looking around mostly. But we do have some areas of our collection that are thin and could be interested in a Picasso, or Cézanne, maybe Matisse."

Helga nodded. "We have some Impressionists." The room we had first entered had been bright and very spare, with a polished stone floor, modern sculpture on plinths and huge abstract canvases on the walls. We followed her into another room that was more dimly lit, with warm hues of ochre on the walls and smaller, colorful canvases in ornate gilt frames.

I smiled and nodded approvingly. "A nice selection."

Amy immediately walked over to a still life. "Oh, Robert, you know how I just love Matisse. Look at this!"

I joined her in front of the painting. "Lovely. But we already have one. I thought you wanted something figurative." I turned to Helga. "Do you have any Picassos with figures in them? Perhaps a Cubist portrait?"

"Not in our current inventory," she replied. "But I'd be happy to make inquiries for you, if you'd like."

"Perhaps," I replied, trying to sound casual. "We'll just look around a bit for now, if you don't mind."

"Certainly," Helga said, tipping her swag of hair sideways. "Let me know if I can answer any questions." With that, she clicked over to the arched entryway and stood there more or less unobtrusively.

Amy and I circled the room, admiring the paintings. I made sure to comment in a way that showed my knowledge of art, thus establishing myself as a serious collector. As we approached the archway again, I addressed Helga. "Do you have any Cézanne landscapes? We have the perfect spot for one, preferably one of the smaller ones."

Helga nodded. "Yes, I, too, love Cézanne. While we don't have anything at this moment, it is something I can research for you. But did you see the small Pissarro snow scene over there? I think it is quite exquisite."

"But I really want those Cézanne blues and greens," Amy interjected like a decorator choosing art to match a sofa. She smiled at Helga conspiratorially. "You know how it is when you get your mind set on something."

Helga smiled tightly. "Of course. If I can get your contact

information, I can make some inquiries among other galleries and private collectors for you."

"That'd be great, wouldn't it, honey? Save us some time and we can go to that shopping area I read about in the guidebook," Amy said with what she hoped was an appropriate jot of venality.

Helga took our names, phone number and hotel—the most expensive in Munich—and shook our hands. "Very nice to meet you. How long will you be in town?"

"Only a few more days," I replied, "so if you can find out anything for us, we'd really appreciate it. We'd love to have some new pieces to add to our collection when we go back to the States."

"I'll do my best," Helga replied. We shook hands, then I put my arm around Amy's waist and we walked through the gallery and back out onto the street.

"I think we nailed it," Amy whispered. "How about you?"

I laughed. "I think dollar signs blocked any possible scrutiny Cruella de Vil might've employed."

"She did look like Cruella. I can see her with a large Dalmatian on a leash. No puppies though."

"No, no puppies. But seriously, I don't think it'll be long before the entire art community of Munich knows there's a collector—and his typical American wife—in town with some big bucks to spend."

# 25
## ROBERT

Thomas Engel was one of the secondary dealers who had worked with Hofer. I'd wrangled a meeting with his son Erik, at his home in Munich, under the pretense of writing a book about prominent dealers. Amy had been right. The man guilelessly droned on about his own experiences and readily answered questions about his father. But I wasn't learning anything that I hadn't already discovered through my own research.

Engel crossed one thin leg over another, exposing a bit of calf above his sock and loafer. "My father and his colleagues did much for the city. Our museum's collection would not be the same without their contributions. We also have a rather large group of dedicated collectors here, who lend important pieces for exhibitions. I think you will find the 'art scene,' as you call it, thriving."

"So I believe. But I've been distracted by the painting above the fireplace. Is it a Beckmann?" I tilted my head up toward the painting. Engel uncrossed his leg, then walked over to the fireplace. He was a tall man, who moved with aristocratic grace.

"Yes, yes, I can see you have a good eye," he said, turning and standing in front of it, blocking my view. "A very good copy, very good indeed. My father knew a painter who would copy the Old Masters and sell them. Not as forgeries, mind you, just as a way for those who loved the paintings to look at them every day."

I looked at Amy and nodded. That was our signal for her to ask to use the bathroom and see what other paintings might be displayed in the bedrooms. Engel's lie about the Beckman, which I'd bet my career was genuine, confirmed my suspicions that he was a key figure in dealing looted art.

Amy excused herself to use the bathroom and had been gone a while when Engel interrupted my line of questioning with one of his own. "Is your wife all right?"

"Amy!" I called. "Are you okay, dear?"

"Sorry," Amy said with a rueful smile as she rejoined us. "Something I ate, perhaps? I'm not quite used to the German cuisine." Engel's bushy white eyebrows rose above his faded blue eyes. His shock of hair was white, thick and slicked back, except for a forelock. "What a shame. May I get you a soda?"

"No, no, I feel better now," Amy moved back to the sofa and gave me a tight smile and a meaningful nod I didn't know how to interpret.

"We've just been discussing art. Herr Engel may be interested in helping me with my article on the art scene in Munich."

Engel suddenly away from the fireplace toward the door. "I must apologize. I am not a well man and am very tired. I think we must resume this at another time please."

We followed him to the door. "Of course," I said, extending my hand. "Thank you so much for your time. I'll call you soon to set up another meeting."

"Yes, my pleasure," Engel shook my hand and then held Amy's fingers briefly. "Wiedersehen," he said, as he closed the door behind us.

---

Amy gripped my hand tightly as we walked down the stone steps of the apartment building. Glancing back at the second-floor window, I caught sight of Engel behind the blinds. The blinds closed quickly.

"Oh my God, oh my God, oh my God, Robert, there was a room full, absolutely crammed, bursting with paintings! I mean stacks lining the walls, with barely enough room to turn around in, and shelves, too, stacks up to the ceiling, wooden frames, all carved and old looking."

I yanked her into the first café we came to. "What?" I was stunned. Why would Engel store so many paintings in his home? I stared at Amy. "Now, slow down. Think. Picture that room exactly as you saw it. Did you see any specific paintings?" My heartbeat was racing and I put my two hands over hers, pressing them into the table, as if to steady us both.

"Well, yes, but only a couple because I'd sneaked into the room next to the bathroom and I was so nervous my hands were shaking but I bent to look at the nearest stack of paintings and then I started to flip through them but then you called me and I had to come back, so I only really saw two." Having said all that in one breath, Amy inhaled loudly.

I gazed at her intently and spoke slowly. "Now, I want you to take another deep breath—yes, that's it, in and out. And I want you to sketch the paintings you saw and tell me everything you remember about them."

I pulled out a notebook from my briefcase and ripped out a sheet of paper. "You sketch and I'll take notes."

"Okay, so the one in front, I thought that was a Monet. It was one of those country scenes with haystacks in it."

"Shut your eyes. Picture it. Now open your eyes and sketch it as quickly as possible."

Amy took the pen I handed her and made a rectangle on the page, then blocked in a large haystack in the foreground, at the right edge of the painting, and another one further back and to the left. Behind this one, she sketched a row of tall trees.

"Shut your eyes again and pay attention to the colors. Keep your eyes shut and describe the color of each object or area of the painting."

Amy began to describe the colors, as I took notes. "The haystack was a sort of reddish gold with a shadow on it," she said slowly, as if in a trance. "The other haystack was bright gold and the trees were dark green. The sky was pale, sort of whitewashed, and the field was kind of yellow, like fall."

In this way, Amy described the first painting completely. The second was more difficult.

"It was dark in the room and the scene in the painting was dark. Here." She began to sketch. "I remember there was a table, and it had stuff on it, like writing materials and a globe, and in front of it sat a person, a man, I think, in one of those old-fashioned Dutch shirts." She made a few quick lines to show the composition. "But everything had that dark brown and gold quality, no particular color stands out."

"Do you think if you saw a reproduction of that painting, you would recognize it?" I asked.

"I think so."

I picked up the sheet of paper and stared at it. "This is good; this is really good." I couldn't believe my eyes. "If we haven't found Nicole's paintings, I think we have at least found some others that have been missing for a very long time. If we can establish that either of the two paintings you saw are pieces that have been missing since the war—or that Beckmann, for that matter, 'cause I'd bet my career it was not a reproduction—we can get the police involved."

Amy leaned back and plowed into the apple pancake she'd ordered. "So where do we go next?"

"To the internet, of course!"

Any first-year art student knew that Monet painted haystacks. I went back to the Holocaust Files database and found: "List of Dealers from whom Engel made Purchases." Within minutes I had found this: "From HOFER, WALTER ANDREAS." The fifth painting on the list was Monet, Haystacks in Giverny.

I leaned back in my chair and took a deep breath. This was it. Documentation that would support my accusation against Engel.

I had no such luck looking for the other painting that Amy had described. But the Beckmann over the mantel in Engel's living room was another story. I had gotten a really good look at it and found what I thought could well be it on the list of Engel's purchases from Hofer. I was ready to contact the German authorities.

"It won't be long before Nicole gets her paintings back from the Louvre."

"What about the ones in Erik Engel's apartment?" Amy asked, stretching out on my sofa. "How can we find out if any of them were Nicole's?" Amy had been spending a lot of weekends here lately. I explained that it would take Germany a while to sort out all the ownership issues associated with the

Engel paintings. Engel himself had disappeared, although a lawyer purporting to represent him had surfaced to lay claim to the paintings. His argument was that his client's father had just been a businessman during the war, an art dealer, and that he had purchased or traded each of the paintings in legitimate business transactions. The argument wouldn't hold water, but it would take time to work its way through the courts.

I picked up my laptop and joined Amy on the sofa. "Move over!" Amy swung her legs round and sat up. I lifted the computer lid and directed the screen toward her.

"An internet catalog of the Engel paintings has just been put up by the German government."

"Is it Nicole's Cézanne?" Amy asked.

"Yes. I do believe we've located Nicole's Cézanne. And in no small part because of your bit of spycraft at Erik Engel's. We'll have to verify it once we get access to it and can examine the back to check for the C that identified the Cassin gallery."

Amy's eyes filled.

"What's wrong?"

She shook her head. "I don't know. Nothing, really. It just makes me sad. All of it. What happened. Nicole. Her parents." Her voice trailed off.

I put my arm around her and she rested her head on my shoulder. "I hope it makes Nicole happy," she whispered.

"Me, too. But it's got to be bittersweet at best."

"Still no sign of the Picasso?"

"Nope. Probably on some collector's wall somewhere, not to be seen until a money-hungry heir decides to sell. Even then, these are often private sales that are never found out. Just one collector to another. The Swiss have taken the position that after five years of ownership, the art belongs to the possessor. And if Wendland was party to the transaction, it's very likely it's in Switzerland—maybe even Russia. The Russians are having a hard time imagining they're not entitled to whatever they looted by virtue of the horrendous loss of life on their part during the war. They see the loot as reparations. Ownership isn't as black-and-white as we might wish. Even before the war began, the Germans had a list of everything taken from them in prior wars, going back hundreds of years, that they thought was rightfully theirs."

"It's, like, where do you draw the line? Maybe there could be an international art museum organization, sort of a UN of art museums, and all the art that belongs to all the museums goes into one big computer file and there are rotating exhibitions, and stuff travels from one place to another every few years."

"Yeah, I'd like to see you make that happen. In a world where terrorists are blowing up ancient masterpieces because, well, I can't even really explain why."

"The Bamiyan Buddhas? When I saw the picture of them before they were blown up, well, I cried."

We were quiet for a minute. Amy's heart was so big and tender, sometimes I wondered how she could survive in this world. I kissed the top of her head.

"By the way, Nicole has asked me to come to see the paintings from the Louvre. I'd like you to come, too. After all, I don't want you to suffer from FOMO."

A slow smile spread across Amy's face as she looked up at me. "I'd love to!"

# 26

## KENNETH



Neuschwanstein castle's spires rose from the top of the mountain, like narrow fingers scratching the sky. The morning mist erased the base of the castle so that it looked as if it were floating. I had long wanted to see this nineteenth-century fairytale castle, built by King Ludwig II of Bavaria in homage to Wagner and combining elements of Romanesque, Gothic and Byzantine architecture. Savoring the view, I stopped and lit a cigarette, knowing that what I would actually find at the end of this particular quest was not the royal family, but soldiers, tanks and Jeeps. We'd been racing for weeks against the Germans' threat to blow up everything in their wake during their retreat.

My friend, Ronald Balfour, had been killed by shrapnel. And another MFAA colleague, Walter Huchthausen, had been hit by gunfire and killed when he and his assistant got lost. These deaths brought home the danger of working so close to the front, and yet every delay brought the possibility of another cultural treasure looted, blown up or bulldozed. The Germans were on the run, moving through towns so quickly that in some cases the damage was minimal. It was odd to some that we were just as concerned with saving the monuments in Germany as those in the countries so brutally occupied by the enemy. But we took a longer view of history than most. These works of art were touchstones, reminders that the current era, too, would pass.

According to Rose Valland, the former curator of the Jeu de Paume, Neuschwanstein was a major repository of stolen French art. The soldiers standing guard at the entrance aggressively questioned my credentials. Valland had been right. The castle contained thousands of paintings and other treasures, many stamped with the codes the ERR had used to indicate Parisian origins. My satisfaction with the discovery was tempered by my next thought. How the hell would we get all this stuff down the treacherous mountain road? And then what? How on earth would we figure out who owned what? This last concern was alleviated when I walked into a room to discover meticulous ERR records of more than 200 private collections taken from France. I mouthed a silent prayer of thanks for Nazi record-keeping and the German captain who, at the last minute, had prohibited the planned destruction of Neuschwanstein. My service is nearly over, and I look forward to slipping back into my life as a museum director, husband, father, and weekend farmer.

# 27
## ROBERT

I was on the train, indulging in a spy novel. Just as the hero was either going to kill or be killed for the umpteenth time, my phone buzzed. I moved my bookmark to the open page, closed the book and answered the phone. "Robert Ames."

"Robert, it's Peter Popinski."

"Peter! How are you?"

"I'm well. I just called to thank you for all your help in unraveling the mystery of my family."

I slid the book onto the seat next to me and sat forward. "I was afraid you'd hate me for it. I mean, here you are, just going about your business, a normal American family, and I throw a bomb into your lap."

Peter laughed. "Yeah, well, I kind of resented it at first. But the more I thought about it, the more it explained a lot of things about my family. And I've discovered an ethnicity I never knew I had. Now I'll have to learn to like vodka!"

We both laughed, then Peter went on.

"But seriously, I'm a guy who loves facts and, I don't know, in some weird way, this truth about my father solidifies my own identity. I can't explain it any more than that, really." He paused. "The weirdest thing to me was how my dad could've gone to Iowa and posed as Sam, when they were nothing alike."

"That's been something I couldn't figure out either."

"My Aunt Susan cleared that up. She's in her eighties now but still has a mind like a steel trap. She was fifteen when Alexei arrived. She knew Alexei wasn't her brother Sam, but Uncle Steve had told her that it would be best for all of them to let him be Sam. Aunt Susan had seen what grief had done to her mother, and it just seemed like a good idea to go along. She said Alexei had been a wonderful young man, so grateful to be there and so affectionate and playful with her that soon she truly accepted him as a brother. The war had shaken up people's lives, so when Uncle Steve started putting out the word that the family had a new 'Sam,' the community just went along."

Robert let out a low whistle. "That's quite a family history."

Peter laughed. "Sure is. The best part is, I have a Russian aunt still living. Katherine and I are going to visit her and learn everything we can about the family we never knew we had. So again, I just wanted to fill you in and thank you."

"You're welcome, Peter, and bon voyage."

Three easels were arranged about ten feet from the windows. The backs of the canvases faced the center of the room. "Go ahead," Nicole said. "Go see my masterpieces."

I took Amy's hand and we walked around to the front of the paintings—the Corot, the La Tour and the Cranach. The muted light from the overcast sky softly illuminated them. My breath caught as I looked at each in turn. Magnificent. Transporting. I looked at Amy. Her eyes were wet.

As we settled in on the sofa in front of the tea set the servant had brought in, I cleared my throat. "I have even more good news," I began. Nicole looked up expectantly.

"I believe your Cézanne was part of the Engel stash we discovered in Munich." I pulled up a photograph of the painting on my phone and handed it to her.

Nicole stared at it for a moment, then sighed, "Yes."

"This one may take a while to recover, as the German government must first go through its legal process to seize the paintings and verify ownership claims. But I've already sent them a formal letter claiming your painting." I hesitated. "I am sorry to say that we still haven't found your favorite, the Picasso portrait." Amy jabbed me with her elbow. I picked up a flat package wrapped in brown paper and string and handed it to Nicole. "This is for you."

Nicole held the package in her graceful hands. "Thank you." She pulled the string from the package and folded back the paper. "Oh!" she exclaimed. "It's the Picasso—but a water-color copy." She looked up. "It's incredible! It's like my mother, seen through the mist of memory. Beautiful. Who's the artist?"

I looked down, embarrassed. Amy piped up, "It's Robert's own work, although he is shy about calling himself an artist."

"Oh, my dear, it's wonderful. Thank you so very much!" Nicole held the painting up and gazed into it.

"I found a picture of it in an old exhibition catalog and copied it. Of course, it can't replace in any way what you have lost, but it's my way of expressing my admiration for you and what it has meant to me to get to know you. You are an inspiration."

"No," Nicole protested. "Save your admiration for those who died bravely. Or those who lived bravely. Facing the past and still finding a way to believe in a future. They are the heroes."

"I have more news," I announced as I finished arranging the wood in the fireplace and held a match to the newspaper at the bottom of the pyramid. Amy sat on the small sofa, her feet in checked woolen socks curled beneath her, her hair still damp at the edges where it had trailed from beneath her hat as we walked through heavy snow from the car to the farmhouse. I laughed at her suddenly serious expression. "Don't look so worried! It's good news!" Sitting beside her, I leaned into her and pulled one of her tendrils straight, watching it bounce back up. "I've decided to shut down my business. And I've had an offer from Princeton to teach art history."

Amy was quiet for a few seconds as she processed this information. "Princeton—wow. How exciting!" she replied. "Professor Ames. I love the sound of it! Tell me all the details."

"Well, you know that I've always been uncomfortable about the way art is used as an investment. And I hate how little we as a culture value the process of creating art—just for art's sake. At the same time, here I am, literally putting price tags on the products via authentication, provenance research and so forth. But Nicole's case, learning how art was used to buy and sell lives—well, it put the commodification issues into a context that was just completely unacceptable. I enjoy lecturing at conferences, and I've built up a pretty good reputation, so when I put it out there that I might want to teach, well, I got some offers."

"Princeton! I'll say. La de da!"

"Well, I had some other offers as well, and the one I'm taking is from Lakeville Community College."

Amy's eyes widened as she tilted her head inquiringly. "Where's that?"

"It's just a bit north of here. In the next village up the road."

Amy looked a little puzzled.

"Here's the thing," I continued. "I could work for a prestigious university like Princeton, further polishing my reputation, teaching wealthy kids whose parents probably have been taking them to museums here and in Europe for years, kids who already know something about art and appreciate it."

"Or?"

"Or I could try—and you know how I hate these trite phrases, but it fits—I could try to make a difference to kids who can barely afford any school, are working part- or full-time, think of college as the key to a decent job, may never have been to a museum or taken an art class. My challenge will be to make the class interesting enough that they want to take it, that they tell their friends about it, because it won't be on anyone's list of requirements."

"You've been thinking a lot about this, haven't you?" Amy asked, lightly touching my cheek.

"Yeah, I guess I have."

"Princeton's gonna be shit outta luck, I'd say," Amy laughed.

"So you don't think I'm crazy? I won't make as much money, but I can still work the lecture circuit and take cases like Nicole's."

"Not crazy. Just you. The real you."

Amy's kiss quickly erased any fears I'd had that she would disapprove of this sudden change in my life. I could foresee lots of time spent together here and, who knows, maybe the college could use a psychology professor.

# 28

## NICOLE

The paintings stood on the mantel above the fireplace. I lifted a glass of champagne to them. I had no photographs of my parents and for years had been unable to picture them clearly. The paintings were like keys that released the memories. The night Papa brought the Corot upstairs from the gallery, declaring, "I give up! I have been staring at that painting for three days and cannot possibly sell it to someone else. We must have it!" Sometimes Maman would protest that they used up all their profits on artwork, but she was just as guilty as Papa. I saw the look of satisfaction on Maman's face when the Corot was in its rightful place.

How many nights had I looked at the La Tour as I entered my bedroom at night, followed by Maman and Papa, who bent down in turn to kiss me goodnight? And the Cranach. Looking down over our dining room table, witness to so many spirited debates and so much laughter. "To you, Maman and Papa, with love." I placed the champagne glass on the glass-topped end table nearby and picked up a silver-framed photo of the Kincaid family—Walt, me, our children Eleanor and Jeff—

taken about five years earlier. It was fall, Central Park, and we were all rosy-cheeked and smiling. I thought back on all the family holidays, the milestones of graduations and weddings and grandchildren. My two families could live side-by-side. There was no need to choose. I was part of both. It was high time I acknowledged it. I was grateful for my life. Even in the darkest days of the war, there had been moments of incredible human kindness, compassion and self-sacrifice. And, as for Walt, I hadn't fallen in love with him the way I had with Sam. But I had loved him. And he had loved me.

It was time to get the children together. To introduce them to Nicole, the girl who once lived above an art gallery in Paris.

# SELECTED BIBLIOGRAPHY


Aksyonov, Vassily. *Generations of Winter*. Vintage International, New York, 1995.

Alford, Kenneth D. *The Spoils of War: The American Military's Role in the Stealing of Europe's Treasures*. Carol Publishing Group, 1994.

Berr, Helene. *The Journal of Helene Berr*. Weinstein Books, 2008.

Carter Hett, Benjamin. *The Death of Democracy: Hitler's Rise to Power and the Downfall of the Weimar Republic*. Henry Holt and Company, 2018.

Diamond, Hanna. *Women and the Second World War in France 1939–1948: Choices and Constraints*. Pearson Education, 1999.

Dreyfus, Jean-Marc and Sarah Gensburger. *Nazi Labour Camps in Paris*. Berghahn Books, 2011.

Duras, Marguerite. *The War: A Memoir*. Pantheon Books, 1986.

Edsel, Robert M., with Bret Witter. *The Monuments Men*. Center Street, Hachette Book Group, 2009.

Edsel, Robert M., *Saving Italy: The Race to Rescue a Nation's Treasures from the Nazis*. W.W. Norton & Company, 2013.

Feliciano, Hector. *The Lost Museum: The Nazi Conspiracy to Steal the World's Greatest Works of Art*. Basic Books, 1997.

Gantter, Raymond. *Roll Me Over: An Infantryman's World War II*. Ballantine Books, 2007.

Gilbert, Martin. *The Second World War: A Complete History*. Revised Edition. Henry Holt and Company, 1989.

Haas, Aaron. *The Aftermath: Living with the Holocaust*, Cambridge University Press, 1995.

Hastings, Max. *Inferno: The World at War, 1939–1945*. Alfred A. Knopf, 2011.

Jackson, Julian. *France: The Dark Years 1940–1944*. Oxford University Press, 2001.

Kershaw, Alex. *Avenue of Spies*. Broadway Books, 2015.

Manvell, Roger and Heinrich Fraenkel. *Goering: The Rise and Fall of the Notorious Nazi Leader*. Skyhorse Publishing, 2011.

Nicholas, Lynn H. *The Rape of Europa: The Fate of Europe's Treasures in the Third Reich and the Second World War*. Vintage Books, 1995.

Petropoulos, Jonathan. *Art as Politics in the Third Reich*. The University of North Carolina Press, 1996.

SELECTED BIBLIOGRAPHY

Petropoulos, Jonathan. *The Faustian Bargain: The Art World in Nazi Germany*. Oxford University Press, 2000.

Poznanski, Renée. *Jews in France during World War II*. Brandeis University Press, 2001.

Riding, Alan. *And the Show Went On: Cultural Life in Nazi-Occupied Paris*. Alfred A. Knopf, 2011.

Rorimer, James J., in collaboration with Gilbert Rabin. *Survival: The Salvage and Protection of Art in War*. Abelard Press, 1950.

Rosbottom, Ronald C. *When Paris Went Dark: The City of Light under German Occupation, 1940–1944*. Little, Brown & Co., 2014.

Sinclair, Anne. *My Grandfather's Gallery: A Family Memoir of Art and War*. Farrah, Straus and Giroux, 2014.

Spotts, Frederic. *The Shameful Peace: How French Artists and Intellectuals Survived the Nazi Occupation*. Yale University Press, 2008.

Strik-Strikfeldt, Wilfried. *Against Stalin and Hitler: Memoir of the Russian Liberation Movement, 1945–1945*. The John Day Company, 1973.

Vinen, Richard. *The Unfree French: Life under the Occupation*. Yale University Press, 2006.

# ACKNOWLEDGMENTS

Many thanks to the members of my writing group for their encouragement, suggestions and, most of all, friendship. To my early readers—my sisters and many dear friends—thank you for your insights. Much appreciation to Stephen Games of EnvelopeBooks, who published an earlier version of this book. To my partner, Dan Malski, thank you for believing in me.

While many history books helped me frame this story, of special note are Lynn H. Nicholas's *The Rape of Europa* and Robert M. Edsel's *The Monuments Men*. These and other resources are listed in the bibliography.

# ABOUT THE AUTHOR

Karen Mulvahill has a BPh and an MFA in Creative Writing. Her poetry, nonfiction and short fiction have appeared in a variety of publications. She lives with her partner and two orange tabbies in Michigan.

www.ingramcontent.com/pod-product-compliance
Lightning Source LLC
Chambersburg PA
CBHW030431160726
47991CB00005B/1688